Quest for the Scroll…

By R. L. Rinne

ISBN: 978-1-962168-64-9

Dedicated to Dot

Contents

Preface

Are the world's challenges real or imagined? The greatest gift in this world may be the ability to look beyond the discordant issues that frame the limits of earthly life and see the reality of situations through a spiritual perspective. Bible passages are utilized in this manuscript to illustrate the character's thinking in the time period following the death and ascension of Jesus. The ancient world was in turmoil. Life spans were usually short and wretched. Christianity was spreading throughout Europe even as it faced seemingly insurmountable challenges. Most people adopted brutal and harsh methods of life and survival, while others tried to cherish and nurture the fading concepts of the Apostles.

Try to approach this book with an open mind. When Pontius Pilate asked what he had done and if he was "King of the Jews," Jesus answered, **"My kingdom is not of this world:"**1 Is this world real? Mankind continues searching in matter for answers on health and happiness rather than to God. Material science continues to prove matter to be separated collections of smaller particles. Which is real, the seeming solidity of matter, or the ethereal concepts of Spirit?

I wanted to write a story that illustrated the zeal of early Christians who understood the infinite reality of Spirit and its possibilities, before the Council of Nicaea in A.D. 325 injected mankind's limited concepts into a temporal institution. God's laws are unchanged, but individuals are continually blinded by material images throughout their lives.

Some of the included healings are historically credited to Saint Martin of Tours, along with others personally experienced by the author. They present options to the limits thrust on humans in everyday life and tread upon cherished theories and sanctimonious knowledge of this world. This book is about breaking barriers and perceiving an unseen reality. It was written to provide a view of life from a primitive Christian perspective. Our protagonist struggles against a myriad of human trials, relentlessly seeking solutions and safety in a world filled with danger and treachery. Seeds of transcendent thought are scattered throughout this text. With that said, it is not overtly religious but a rousing adventure with didactic threads...

Settings and Background

Saint Martin of Tours earthly ministry in Gaul (present-day France) ended, by most accounts, in 397 A.D. His life and reported healings, more than three centuries after Jesus, were a major part of the inspiration for this book.

The adventure begins in Dumnonii (presently Cornwall in Southwestern Britain) at the end of the summer season in 407 A.D. a few weeks before the feast of Mabon, the second Celtic celebration of harvest. Mabon was similar to our present-day Thanksgiving but also included efforts to joyfully remember those souls who had passed on before.

Celtic holidays:

Yule – This was a celebration of the shortest day of the year. The idea of giving presents came from hanging gifts on the Yule tree for Gods and Goddesses. - December 22

Imbolc – Celebrates the Goddess of healing, and metalworking, along with the beginning of the spring quarter as daylight gets noticeably longer. - February 2

Ostara – Celebrates the arrival of spring. Celts saw a rabbit in the full moon (Easter). - March 21

Beltaine – The beginning of summer included dancing and singing. It eventually became May Day. - May 1

Midsummer – Summer solstice is when the sun is at its highest point in the sky and thought to be a time of magic. - June 21

Lughnasadh – The first day of Celtic Autumn as the harvest season begins. Activities consisted of political and legal discussions, games, and feasts. - August 1

Autumn Equinox (Mabon) – The second Celtic harvest celebration included expressions of thanksgiving. - September 21

Samhain - The Celtic New Year and the beginning of winter, it began the traditions of Halloween including communication between the living and the dead. Druids believed in energies coming from open portals to another world. - October 31

Prologue

The Scroll – 397 AD Gaul (Northern France)

"I'm going to be a soldier." announced Jaral as he thrust a stubby finger toward Magnus's ribs.

Laughing, Magnus parried the blow with his hand. "I'm going to be a healer like Father Martin."

"That's boring. Even he used to be a soldier," Jaral added. "I want to be a man of action when I grow…" he immediately stopped talking and hurried toward the rough bench, with Magnus close behind.

"Good morning, students." Bishop Martin of Tours said with a wide smile as he entered the classroom and walked to the lectern wearing a plain brown habit.

"Good morning, sir." came the reply from ten small faces.

"Be seated. I have some important duties to attend to, so we will only be able to have class today for about an hour." He paused as a joyful murmur filled the room. "I know you are all sorry to hear that. I think we will discuss what God is and how he touches our lives. I want you all to take out your tablets and write a list of what you think God is."

Magnus dug into his bag and pulled out a bees wax tablet and a stylus. Then he started to scribble. "Powerful, Strong, Kind, Loving, Compassionate…"

After a number of minutes, Bishop Martin said, "Now, stop and set your tablets on the shelf." The students milled around the front of the room until they had all placed their wax tablets and returned to sit on the heavy wooden benches.

The man paced back and forth as he perused their words while stroking his white beard. "Jonathan, what do you mean when you say God is vengeful?"

"Sir, it states in Romans 12:19, **'Dearly beloved, avenge not yourselves, but rather give place unto wrath: for it is written, Vengeance is mine; I will repay, saith the Lord.'**2

"I notice that most of you have written words like vengeance, punishment, mighty, powerful, and so on in these descriptions. The same descriptions could be made of mankind's Kings and Emperors. Does God punish and manipulate men with the same methods this world's leaders use?"

The group was silent until one hand rose slowly.

"Yes, Magnus, what do you think?"

"It can look like God avenges and hurts people when your perception is only of the material world. There are storms, earthquakes, and disease… but they aren't limited to punishing only bad people or pagans. All the world seems to suffer."

Bishop Martin raised a finger. "Ah yes, they all seem susceptible to suffer the same experiences, but what can change a man's fate?

There was another long silence in the room, and Bishop Martin broke it by asking, "Magnus, why do you say God is powerful?

Magnus thought for a moment. "Well, as it says in 2nd Corinthians 10:4, **'For the weapons of our warfare are not carnal, but mighty through God to the pulling down of strongholds;'**3 Like when King Hezekiah and Jerusalem were saved from King Sennacherib of Assyria."

"I agree. The power of prayer is stronger than any material force you will meet in this world, but to have the power of the Almighty on your side, what do you need?"

The silence was pervasive again as children averted their eyes and wiggled uncomfortably on the benches.

"I will tell you. You need humility, love, patience, and

most of all an understanding of the world Jesus our Master could see. A world beyond our complete comprehension, perhaps. A world beyond mortal limitations of time, space, and physical barriers." The old man's eyes glistened as he spoke, and Magnus knew that he must be seeing spiritual images as the kids struggled to remember his words.

Bishop Martin looked out the window as a red bird hopped on the sill and took flight again. "It is a beautiful day today, and I think you need to reflect on these ideas and make them your own. That will be today's lesson. Tomorrow, you will all let me know what and where the heaven is that our Lord Jesus saw. You are all dismissed, except for Master Magnus, please remain seated. I wish to speak to you."

Magnus squirmed atop the rough wood plank, trying to find a more comfortable position as his classmates quickly exited the room. His friend Jaral winked and stuck his tongue out at him as he picked up his tablet and hurried out. What could Bishop Martin want with him? He nervously wrung his hands as he waited.

The man closed the massive oak door behind Jaral and walked over, sitting down heavily next to Magnus.

"Magnus, my boy, I have a favor to ask of you. You have a certain spiritual outlook on life that I have not seen in the rest of this class. I am consistently surprised and gratified by your answers to my questions."

"Thank you, sir," the boy sheepishly uttered.

"No, I thank you. It warms my heart to see one so young striving for the knowledge of God. For that reason, I want to bequeath this to you." He reached deep within his tunic and drew out a worn leather cylinder.

"What is that?" Magnus wondered aloud with wide eyes.

"This contains a scroll with concepts of how I have been blessed to heal others, including you. Remember?" he asked with a wink.

Magnus nodded his head eagerly, recalling several of his healings.

"It also contains my thoughts on how mankind can grow

and experience harmony in this world. I am leaving copies of it with people I trust to protect and share its ideas. Guard it, young man. I pray it will bless you and others in your life. For now though, keep it a secret just between us!" he admonished.

"Yes, sir!" As Magnus grasped it with sweaty hands.

"We are in a battle with the darkness that strives to obscure true Christianity," the old man continued as he tapped the cylinder with a gnarled finger. "It is a battle we must win for the world, however long it takes. That is why this knowledge must be kept safe from any who would destroy it."

"Yyyes, sir." Magnus stammered as he felt flushed, and a tear rolled down his cheek.

The man's eyes glistened again as he looked down approvingly and patted Magnus's shoulder. "A tender heart is the best protection, my son."

Chapter 1

407AD Dumnonia Region, Briton

The Inn

Cynde wiped the perspiration from her forehead as she finished cleaning the day's crumbs and ale stains from the tops of rough-hewn tables, one of her many duties as the innkeeper's daughter. Daily, she watched travelers come and go while she repeated the same tasks over and over. Lost in her thoughts, she suddenly tensed when she heard heavy footsteps approaching the inn, followed by a weak knock. She lurched toward a broom and held it as a defensive weapon, staring at the door. It was well past the hour that most honest patrons arrived. "Away with thee. We be closed till the morn," she yelled in the deepest voice she could muster.

"Please, good lady, I ask only a drink and some morsel of food. I will pay well. Please." a hoarse sound, heavy with a strange accent, replied.

Cynde did not trust any night traveler, especially a foreigner. Still, her heart could not ignore the earnest pleading in the voice. "You may enter, but if I scream, our warriors will come running and slay you!"

The heavy oak door slowly swung open, and she stared at the young man who stepped unsteadily into the room. His face was sunburned, leaves and twigs were entwined in his long dark hair, and his clothes were shredded in places and filthy. He was nothing but a penniless beggar without a coin to his name.

He reached deep into a leather pouch as if he could read her mind. "I have money." His eyes suddenly focused intently on hers. She took another step backward. Cynde couldn't escape the effect of his intense stare. "Are you sure you can pay?" she murmured, wiping a long wisp of blonde hair from her face. His eyes immediately betrayed the hurt her comment caused. "I'm sorry. It's late, and I'm being rude. Sit, and I'll bring you something to eat and drink," As she motioned to a table with the end of the broom.

"Here." He dropped his gaze and showed her a handful of strange gold coins. "You are quite right, of course. I do look horrible," he rasped with a slight smile as he reached up in a feeble effort to smooth his wild curls.

Cynde couldn't suppress a grin. Despite his ragged appearance, he expressed a gentle kindness that she seldom noticed in strangers or her own family during these dark times. "I didn't mean to be impolite, but we are extra careful around outsiders now that the Romans are beginning to withdraw their legions. Folks say that barbarians from the North are raiding nearby settlements now."

"Why are they leaving?" He stumbled toward the closest table and sat down.

She watched as he inadvertently rubbed his eyes with the back of a grimy hand and grimaced as the crusty dirt irritated his blistered face. "I've heard gossip that they need to protect Rome from hordes of invaders called the Visigoths." Through the still-opened door, she saw a small, dull flash of distant lightning as it licked the base of the western sky. An end-of-summer storm was gathering. "You're a lucky man. It'll be pouring rain in a while, but if you behave, I'll let you stay here until it quits," Cynde said as she leaned the broom against the wall and reached to hand him a tankard of ale.

"Thank you for your kindness; I promise I'll be good!" the stranger said, grinning weakly as he tipped the drink to his lips and drank greedily until it was empty.

"What's your name?" she asked, handing him a chunk of

well-cooked meat left over from earlier meals.

His response came between indulgent mouthfuls of the dried-out venison. "My name is Magnus of Rau. I traveled here from Gaul."

"Well, I knew you weren't a local. Your speech is very strange. Where is Gaul?" she continued, picking up some wooden bowls from another table.

The young man explained that it was many days of travel south, across the treacherous arm of the North Sea, as he chewed on the stringy scraps of meat.

"I would never venture across the great sea; I'm afraid the horrid monsters it shelters would be waiting to swallow me up!" she said with a shudder.

"I didn't worry about mythical beasts beneath the waves. My threats were tangible. The authorities in Gaul were going to arrest me," he said offhandedly.

She paused momentarily, collected her thoughts, and looked at him with a piercing glare. "So, the law is after you. What are you, a murderer, or a thief?"

"That's not giving me much of a choice," he mused.

"I'm serious. Which one? If you don't answer me this instant, I swear I'll yell, and you won't have another chance to respond!" A sudden unease gripped her as she glared at the stranger.

"Neither I swear," he said quickly. "I am but a traveler, an adventurer."

"Hogswallow," she answered, "add liar to that list!" Pushing past him between the benches, determined to raise an alarm.

"All right, please stop!" His arms darted out involuntarily, one grabbing her elbow and the other clutching the dishes before they fell. "Wait to sound the alarm. I'll tell you whatever you want to know."

Cynde stiffened in his grasp, "Let me go," she hissed.

"Will you let me explain?" he pleaded. "Please?"

"Let me go now!" she said, spitting the words out.

He released his grip with a loud sigh. Surprised to be let

go, she recovered quickly, though still uneasy. "Say your piece or say goodbye!" she threatened while looking fiercely into his eyes.

He looked away and paused, "I have been labeled a criminal," he said, bowing his head, "but I've harmed or stolen from no one."

"Are you saying you're innocent, perhaps a victim of mistaken identity?" she stated flatly.

"No, I'm guilty of daring to be a true Christian."

"A what?" Cynde asked. The boy didn't have time to answer before faint sounds of conversations and laughter reached their ears. Cynde recognized one of the voices and said, suddenly grinning. "That's Father Osric, and he's with soldiers."

"Please let me continue my explanation later. I pray thee," whispered Magnus, looking so sincere that Cynde almost laughed at him.

"Be certain of that, Magnus of Rau," said Cynde as she turned and yelled loudly, "Father, Dwig, I need help; we have guests arriving. The soldiers are returning from their search for the Picts!"

A short, portly man shuffled into the room through a curtain in the back wall in a few moments. He was followed closely by a small, blonde-headed boy looking maybe twelve years old. "Who's he?" the man asked, pointing a beefy finger toward Magnus.

"He's just a traveler. I've already fed him, so we can see to the Romans now." Cynde said.

Magnus quietly asked, "Is there anything I can do to help?"

"Yes, help Dwig bring some wood in," she said, hurrying to grab the last dirty plates as the first soldier walked in.

QUEST FOR THE SCROLL

Chapter 2

The Test

Magnus turned and quickly followed the boy through a dingy curtain into a dimly lit room at the rear of the inn. He could see piles of straw and mats laid out - simple beds but welcoming for an aching, weary traveler like himself. He wished he could lie down, but first, he would fetch firewood for that lovely girl. The boy disappeared under a loose deer hide on the outer wall, and Magnus hurried to keep up.

Dwig moved quickly between the cone-capped houses of the Celtic village toward the decaying timber-framed ramparts encircling the town. They had formed a necessary defensive perimeter in earlier centuries. "You may need to repair these if the Romans continue to depart," Magnus uttered, trying to start a conversation, but Dwig said nothing.

Once clear of the houses, they jogged along a well-worn path leading downhill, across a wooden bridge spanning a creek, and then up into the nearby forest. Now Magnus didn't even try to say anything as they ran. He wanted to talk to the boy, but it was taking all his concentration just to follow him into the woods. It was hard for Magnus to see with opaque storm clouds spreading across the face of the moon, and twice, he nearly collided with low-hanging branches as he sped down the path.

Finally, the boy stopped and bent over as he picked up branches from a large pile between two trees. Magnus again spoke to the boy: "If you fill my arms with wood first, I think I can carry enough, so we only have to make one trip!"

"Fine," Dwig answered, dropping his load of sticks into Magnus's outstretched arms. Sporadic bursts of lightning illuminated the forest, and the wind suddenly increased. The storm encircled them in a tightening grip as undulating branches projected demonic shadows.

In the intermittent flashes of fire across the heavens, Magnus could see that the haunting scene was affecting the boy. His eyes were wide with fear, but he stayed focused on his task. Dwig worked frantically, pulling the largest pieces he could lift from the pile and thrusting them into Magnus's arms. Soon, they were both loaded and walking quickly back toward the inn. "Where are the soldiers from Dwig?" said Magnus, hoping the boy would feel like talking now that they were headed back to the safety of the inn.

"Seaford Downs, it's their barracks," Dwig replied in a strained voice as he struggled under his own load of sticks.

Seaford Downs was the larger coastal city where Magnus had first stepped onto English soil two days before. He remembered seeing a large monastery enclave being built inside the Roman fortress walls with the surrounding infantry dormitories. Hurrying through the town in a desperate effort to remain unnoticed by the local authorities, he imagined that they must have agreed on a deal with the legionnaires to be able to build the church inside the walls of the fort.

"Is that girl your sister?" Magnus asked, remembering how silly he must have looked when he stumbled through the door and stared at her. She was beautiful.

"Yes," Dwig said as he wobbled across the bridge.

"What is the name of your village?" Magnus asked.

"Hastell Cenllys," muttered Dwig with a groan of exertion.

Magnus didn't ask any more questions. Dwig obviously wasn't capable of extended conversation. They were close enough to the inn to hear muted sounds now, and they trudged the last steps in silence.

Magnus was breathing heavily and felt the first large drops of rain splash on his face as he stepped through the doorway into the firelight. The bellow of conversations suddenly stopped, and all heads turned toward him as he carefully followed the boy between the tables of armed men and deposited his load of wood next to the stone fire pit. Dwig had really loaded him down, and the muscles in his arms felt as if they were burning. There was an uncomfortable silence as Magnus straightened and tried to rub the pain from his biceps. Thunder crashed close now, and he heard rain begin hitting the roof in sheets. He sheepishly glanced around the room at the stern stares of twenty battle-hardened Roman legionnaires. Their captain sat in shining armor and fur-trimmed robes, glaring at him across the table. Magnus felt the color rising to his face. He had never felt comfortable being the center of attention. Smiling widely, he fought to keep his emotions under control so as not to betray his fear.

A large, jovial man in a simple brown robe next to the captain suddenly stood and declared. "Thank you, sir, for your service to the emperor's troops. You must be a good man because God held the heavens closed long enough so, you wouldn't get washed away!" He then emitted a booming laugh that seemed to shake the building.

Magnus saw smiles crease on the soldier's faces, and the return of easy conversations quickly erased any tension in the room. He nodded gratefully to the monk who had broken the ice and silently gave thanks to God for finding shelter. Then he moved quickly around the room toward Cynde, who was busy filling tankards of ale. "Do you need further assistance? I still need to pay you for my meal." stammered Magnus.

"You've helped more than enough for the food and a night's lodging. Besides, you look well enough to expire before completing another task tonight. Find a space that suits you in the back, and we'll have that talk in the morning." She smiled and turned back to the other customers.

She had smiled. It had been the most beautiful smile he had ever seen. He knew instantly that the trip for firewood had been a test to see if he would try to escape from the soldiers. "Thank you, and God bless you," he whispered. He quickly turned and bent to exit through the curtain.

"Good night." The monk was smiling as he spoke and lifted his cup. Magnus grinned and offered a slight wave as he walked into the darkened sleeping area.

Looking at the rows of woven mats barely visible in the dim light, he stepped carefully to the most remote bedding. Sinking down into the soft straw, he rearranged the lumpy areas, pulled some furry hides over his shoulders, and fell fast asleep.

Suddenly, he was in an overgrown, disintegrating water garden. Magnus strained to see through the dense grey mist shrouding the dank ruins.

He was standing with his back against a solid stone wall at the edge of a large, reflecting pool. Looking across, he saw a wide stone path in the center with a series of tiled pools stretching into the distance. He looked down the walkway. Thorn trees and brush had sprouted everywhere, but he could barely see the outline of one enormous tree that dwarfed the others just beyond the last pool. That must be the biggest tree in the world! Looking in the other direction, Magnus saw carved stone columns and what had once been elaborate trellises littering the paths where they had fallen. They were being torn apart, collapsing from the pressures of growing vegetation, wind, and rain. He could see a dense layer of vines covering weathered stone lattice walls that encircled the garden. This place must have been spectacular when it was cared for.

Magnus stepped carefully through piles of loose stones and vines on the tiled walkway next to the pool. He noticed hexagonal-shaped stone pillars rising from the depths that provided a walkway across the water. Magnus hesitated for a moment and stepped lightly onto the first stone and then onto the next one. Everywhere, trees had fallen into the pools at odd angles. Noticing some bubbles rising to the surface next to one of the logs by his feet, he stopped and fastened his gaze on objects visible just below the water's surface. He noticed waterlogged leaves and a tree branch with air bubbles clinging to its surface. No, it didn't look like a branch. It was a nostril. The hair on his neck stood on end as he realized he was looking at the largest snake he had ever seen, and there were more of them. Magnus now realized that snakes were a majority of what he had assumed was just debris in the water. Some of them were as big around as his thigh. His blood ran cold as he noticed a lidded eye the size of his own open by his foot.

The water exploded beneath him, and Magnus sprang toward the next closest steppingstone as he swung his arm as hard as he could in a defensive arc. His forearm connected with something so solid that his fingers went numb, but he never looked back. The water began frothing in the pools, and dark shapes writhed below the surface as Magnus frantically leaped from one pad to the next. Just one more step, and he would be on what looked like a wide walkway between the pools. Magnus jumped for the edge, but something erupted below him and snagged his ankle. He tried to recover in midair but couldn't. Landing hard on his left arm, he felt it shatter as he pitched forward and skidded across a filthy slime-covered stone walkway. He stopped sliding close to the next pool. Magnus tried to lay motionless, but his heaving chest demanded air. He kept his eyes closed tight, hoping the vipers would settle down now that he was playing dead.

Where was he? This garden is infested with serpents, but for what reason? It seemed familiar to him. What was the best way to battle these huge snakes? Magnus searched his sensations and was relieved to feel his short blade pressing against his hip. That would help, but he knew there were far too many snakes to kill by himself. A judicious retreat was his only chance of survival. The turmoil in the water was gradually calming, and he risked a glance at his surroundings. Magnus lay uncomfortably tucked against a stone pillar. He could see the faint outline of the sun above, trying to burn through the blanketing gray mist. He also noticed his legs spread apart at almost a right angle, with one foot hanging perilously over the pool's edge!

A large head, the size and shape of a garden spade, began to rise next to his foot. Magnus watched until menacing eyes stared down at him from an arm's length above the walkway.

The reptile hesitated momentarily as a forked tongue danced obscenely in and out of its scaly mouth. Then it began a painfully slow arc toward his loins.

He wondered if it was searching for the tastiest spot to sink its fangs into. His rest period was over, and he realized he had to act now or die a coward's death. Immediately, he twisted away from the marble pillar and fired a snap kick with his left foot as he rolled to the right. Magnus caught the animal just below the head, and it jerked back in surprise. Thank goodness these larger snakes reacted more slowly than the smaller ones. As he rolled over the second time, he snatched the knife from its sheath and swung it towards a flash of green-gray above his shoulder. The blade struck home, severing the snake's body just before it bit his face. The scaled head smashed into his mouth with the force of a fist and rolled away on the stones. He tasted fresh blood from his smashed lip as he watched the viper's jaws snapping in a hideous final frenzy. Struggling to his feet, Magnus forced himself to run down the walkway toward the outer wall of the garden. He was in a cloud of pain, feeling several bones grinding back and forth in his bouncing arm. Waves of putrid water began to wash across the stones as an army of writhing bodies rushed to converge on him. He hurdled tables, broken pillars, and benches in an agonizing sprint.

Magnus reacted to any blur of color with a thrust of his knife as he ran. Twice, he made contact, but he forced himself to keep running without looking back. Several smaller snakes had crawled out of the depths and onto the pathway, causing him momentary delays. The blade in his hand constantly cut toward any threat. The exertion of twisting, jumping, and running was taking its toll. Magnus looked ahead and saw an outside wall of the garden. It was a crumbling length of stone trellis covered by withering vines. If he hit it hard enough, maybe his momentum would carry him through to the other side. Seeing no other options, he headed for one of the larger stone pillars that had fallen against a pile of rubble and was projecting toward the wall. Magnus scrambled onto the pillar. God help me! He prayed as he launched himself from the top at a full run. He pulled himself into a ball and closed his eyes tight as he hurtled toward the ornate stone barrier.

The impact nearly tore him apart. Magnus crashed through the wall in a mass of sound and flying debris. He was free from the garden but still falling! How far was it to the ground? His arms and legs flailed for purchase but touched nothing. A blind panic gripped him as he felt all the sensations of plummeting through space, and he forced himself to open his eyes...

He blinked in the dim gray light of a chilly English morning. He could just see one of the soldier's sleeping a few feet away. Magnus's entire body was soaked with sweat, and he was breathing heavily. *I'm at the inn*, he remembered as a wave of relief swept over him. Magnus laid back on the straw mat, smiling, and quickly fell into a dreamless sleep.

Chapter 3

Love

When Magnus awoke, the sun was shining through cracks in the dried mud of the exterior walls, warming and illuminating the sleeping area. He slowly decided it was too hot to fall asleep again. He sat up, looked around, and saw that he was alone. *The soldiers must have departed for their barracks. Thank goodness.* He still felt mentally exhausted and unprepared to answer a barrage of serious questions from the local military. *What about the girl?* He paused to vividly remember his first image of her. *Could it have been love at first sight? No, that would be too much to hope for. Besides, she might turn on him this morning if he couldn't convince her he was truthful.*

Magnus stood and shook straw out of the animal skins that had covered him the night before. He folded the hides into a neat pile and wandered back to the inn's great room. Cynde was there, busily sweeping the dirt floor clean of straw and scraps of food. He admired her work ethic.

"Afternoon. You missed breakfast and lunch. I was beginning to think you passed on," she said dryly.

"I'm sorry, but I hadn't slept well for a few days," he replied.

She turned her face away from him, thrusting her broom under a table at a stray piece of grass, and said, "No matter, I'll just tell the old ladies to stop knitting your burial shroud for now."

Was she smiling? Was that a joke? He couldn't tell, but he needed to speak plainly with her. "I may still need it if you don't believe my story. Right?" he quipped.

She turned and looked him coolly in the eyes. "Right," was all she said, without a trace of a smile.

He swallowed hard and began in a soft voice. "The truth is that I fled my homeland because I thought my family would be safer in my absence. The local bishop there declared me a heretic, and Jaral, one of my friends in the church, alerted me that I was to be condemned by the Holy Father and be jailed the next day. I would have suffered persecution, or perhaps even execution." Magnus said with his sadness very evident.

"What's a heretic?" Cynde asked.

"A man who refuses to recite church-approved dogma about God is one," Magnus said with a slight smile. "I don't care if I'm martyred, but my family doesn't deserve the shame or cruelties they were bound to receive from their 'good' neighbors."

"What could you possibly say that was so horrible they would kill you?" she questioned. "I consider myself an expert at reading people since I deal with both rough-hewn and smooth-talking patrons here every day. Somehow, I don't think you're lying."

"I told the truth, and they couldn't handle it," he answered simply. "I was a threat to their entire man-conceived doctrine and massive temporal powers because I told the truth."

She looked confused as she changed the subject. "Why did you decide to come here?"

"I had heard that Rome was withdrawing troops from your Isles, but I didn't know why. I hoped that I might be able to disappear into these hills where agents of the new Bishop of Tours won't find me," he said.

"I'd like that," she replied, turning away too quickly for him to see if she blushed. "How did you cross the English Channel?" she questioned, beginning to shove the heavy wooden benches back under the tables.

Magnus moved quickly alongside her to help push. "Well,

it wasn't a leisurely trip. I was on a small livestock ship, riding in waves as tall as I am. I made passage by hauling feed and water to the animals while crawling through the bowels of the boat covered in sheep waste. The crew treated me like I was less than human, and I certainly smelled the part. I can tell you truthfully that it's no longer one of my top choices for a job." He smiled.

Cynde laughed loudly.

"That's not funny," said Magnus grinning. "Well, maybe it is, but you're enjoying it too much."

"I'm sorry, but it isn't hard for me to picture you encrusted in stinky sheep dung!" she giggled.

"I'll take that as a compliment," Magnus replied with a wink.

Cynde suddenly changed her tone: "I've never met a man who can laugh at himself like you do. Are you ever serious?"

"Yes, but it's hard to stay humble if you take yourself too seriously, and humility is a precious commodity in this world," he said, thinking that often humility allowed him to pause and listen to God.

"I know that I haven't seen much of it in this village," she replied with a frown.

"What can I do to help you?"

"Well, we always need more wood," she replied with a shy smile.

Magnus spent the rest of the day gathering and stacking large piles of broken branches behind the inn. He was tired, and his throat was parched when he decided to take a break late in the afternoon. He entered the inn, and Cynde must have sensed how hot and tired he was. She handed him a jug of sweet cider before he even sat down. "That should help you revive," She grinned.

The sun was sinking rapidly into the horizon when Dwig suddenly ran into the inn and shouted, "Father Osric is back. Uncle Anut is dropping him off on the way back to his village!"

Magnus made his way to the doorway and peered out at the two men approaching on a wagon pulled by two horses.

Cynde smiled and said, "The one other humble man in England. Alright, Dwig, I'll start dinner; you bring in some wood for the fire."

"What can I do to help?" asked Magnus.

"Sit down," she commanded. "Tomorrow, you can repay me by gathering even more firewood, but you're not going to miss another meal under this roof." Magnus gratefully obliged and moved to sit at a table facing the doorway.

"Hello, friends!" Osric announced as he entered with his large arms outstretched as if he were trying to embrace the whole edifice.

"Good to see you, friar. To what turn of fate do we owe your quick return?" asked Cynde.

"We were on our way back to Seaford Downs when we met Anut, who was traveling this way. I joined him to see if I could convert that stubborn old Druid to Christ, but I fear it was to no avail," he said with a loud sigh.

"I do nothing of myself." The words were out of Magnus's mouth before he knew it, and he wondered why he had spoken, thinking, **"Then said Jesus unto them, When ye have lifted up the Son of man, then shall ye know that I am he and that I do nothing of myself; but as my Father hath taught me, I speak these things. And he that sent me is with me: the Father hath not left me alone; for I do always those things that please him."**4

The monk's mouth opened wide but remained silent, pondering the words. He suddenly looked extremely uncomfortable.

"I'm sorry. I didn't mean to interrupt..." Magnus stammered.

"You are quite right, my boy," Osric replied slowly. "My arguments for Anut's salvation were driven by my own self-will and justification. If I had expressed the qualities of the Lord as his instrument, it is written that I would have been victorious. Mind if I sit with you, my son?" Without waiting for a response, Osric grinned and immediately sat down across from Magnus.

"Please, help yourself," Magnus replied.

"I am sorry. I'm a little impulsive, but your insight is astounding," the monk said. "Are you a priest?"

Magnus sighed. He didn't want to be drawn into a deep conversation, but he could tell that this man was not going to leave him alone now. *Why couldn't he have kept his mouth shut?* "No, but I am one of the flock," he said politely.

"Where did you learn the words of our master?" Osric asked while pulling apart a roasted chicken that Cynde had just delivered to the table.

"I studied at Tours in Gaul," replied Magnus.

"Did you ever meet the great Bishop Martin of Tours?" asked Osric before stuffing a steaming handful of meat into his mouth.

His eyes opened in surprise when Magnus picked up a chicken leg and replied softly. "Yes, I was one of his miracles."

"What?" Osric bellowed. "You mean the stories are true about miracles being performed nearly four hundred years after Jesus, our Master, walked this earth?"

Magnus grinned but didn't answer until he had chewed and swallowed. "I'm originally from a small town outside of Paris. Do you know my story?" he asked.

"I've heard that Martin kissed and healed a wretched leper there, and I certainly would not believe that a healthy young man like yourself was once a loathsome leper," Osric replied with a sneer.

"I wasn't, I just looked like one. An illusion must appear real, or you won't believe it." Magnus answered. "Like Moses with his staff and leprosy!" Recalling what the Lord told Moses, **"And Moses answered and said, But, behold, they will not believe me, nor hearken unto my voice: for they will say, The LORD hath not appeared unto thee. And the LORD said unto him, What *is* that in thine hand? And he said, A rod. And he said, Cast it on the ground. And he cast it on the ground, and it became a serpent, and Moses fled from before it. And the LORD said unto Moses, Put forth thine hand, and take it by the tail. And he put forth**

his hand, and caught it, and it became a rod in his hand: That they may believe that the LORD God of their fathers, the God of Abraham, the God of Isaac, and the God of Jacob, hath appeared unto thee. And the LORD said furthermore unto him, Put now thine hand into thy bosom. And he put his hand into his bosom: and when he took it out, behold, his hand *was* leprous as snow. And he said, Put thine hand into thy bosom again. And he put his hand into his bosom again; and plucked it out of his bosom, and, behold, it was turned again as his *other* flesh. And it shall come to pass, if they will not believe thee, neither hearken to the voice of the first sign, that they will believe the voice of the latter sign."[5]

The monk looked puzzled. "What do you mean?" Osric asked with narrowing eyes. "He either chased the demons from your body, or you were healthy and pretending to be sick. Don't forget it's a grievous sin lying to a man of the cloth!" he replied, vigorously shaking a dripping chicken wing at the younger man.

Magnus held up his hands to emphasize his innocence. "Martin could see through the veil of human existence. He saw me as God had created me, and…I was healed."

For the second time that day, Osric's mouth opened but remained silent. He reached for more chicken.

They finished their meal together in silence, and Magnus knew Osric was deep in conflicted thoughts. Cynde had already removed the plates and bidden them goodnight before the monk spoke again. "A veil? What is the veil? How did he heal you? What about that paralyzed girl at Treves, the servant of Lupicinus that hung himself and died, and the others - the stories are all true?"

Magnus cleared his throat and answered, "Yes, they're all true. In fact, I have even met some of the others. The veil is the mist in Genesis that watered the face of the earth, and you know what it is like trying to look through a mist. It distorts and obscures the true image of the world just as it hides our vision of God's perfect creation. Bishop Martin saw through that and healed by understanding God."

This was too much for the monk. "Blasphemy!" he roared. "No man can understand God because we are all born sinners!"

The color was rising rapidly in Osric's face, and Magnus knew he had to diffuse the situation before the friar became violent. "Who told you that?"

"That's church doctrine, and not to be questioned by you!" the monk barked, slamming a beefy fist on the table.

"What if Bishop Martin questioned it?" asked Magnus.

Osric once again fell into an uneasy silence. Magnus knew that he must be wrestling with conflicting images of the great man Martin and the dogma imposed by the church.

"He saw a man in God's image like Jesus did. He told me that's the basis of all true healing. He identified only with the first record in Genesis where male and female are created in the image and likeness of a perfect, Loving God - and completely rejected the second record of mankind as material and fallen, after the veil of the mist." Magnus added quietly. He could see the man silently struggling to comprehend the ideas.

"Have you ever healed?" the friar finally asked.

"I do nothing of myself." Magnus began, again re-quoting the words of Jesus. "But God's grace has provided many divinely natural occurrences in my life."

"You mean miracles! Tell me everything about them," replied Osric as a thin smile replaced his frown.

Magnus considered all the conversations that had ended shortly after he began recounting his stories of healing. It made most people uncomfortable, but this was a man of the cloth. Maybe he could handle it. "I don't know where to begin. I've been instantly healed of minor nuisances like earaches, twisted ankles, and fevers, but some of the others are more like the time chunks of my foot began to fall off. That took a while."

"What happened? Which foot?" asked the monk as he tried to look under the table.

"I don't know, I can't remember; I was only about twelve

years old," answered Magnus, but I remember it was very colorful - orange, yellow, and purple with large blisters and a black line running up my leg."

"Blood poisoning," cried Osric as he identified the dreaded disease, "That's deadly. How did you survive?"

Magnus leaned closer over the table, "I remember it was a beautiful, bright fall day, and Father Martin had been praying for me too. I could feel harmony. I recall knowing that I reflected only the qualities of God, like Life, Joy, Strength, Perfection, Completeness..."

"That's it?" interrupted the monk, "You healed yourself by holding on to an image of perfection in your body?"

Magnus replied quickly, "No! Not of a perfect mortal man. I held on to concepts of Love, of Reality, Intelligence, of Substance, of ...God. A mortal man cannot be the image and likeness of God. I saw myself as a spiritual child of Father/Mother God!" Magnus watched as the big man suddenly rubbed his eyes and stared at him with a questioning look. Magnus leaned closer, "Were any of these concepts presented to you in your formal religious training?"

The monk sighed as he shook his head slowly and finally asked, "Does God hear our pleas and answer our prayers?"

"No, it doesn't work like that." answered Magnus, "You know the first record from Genesis, that God's work was done and that he created everything perfect? Jesus said that Life eternal was to know God and himself, whom God had sent. It is written, **"And no man hath ascended up to heaven, but he that came down from heaven, even the Son of man which is in heaven. And as Moses lifted up the serpent in the wilderness, even so must the Son of man be lifted up: That whosoever believeth in him should not perish, but have eternal life. For God so loved the world, that he gave his only begotten Son, that whosoever believeth in him should not perish, but have everlasting life. For God sent not his Son into the world to condemn the world; but that the world through him might be saved."**[6] We must see beyond our perceptions of a limited material reality and a God made in man's image. If God is omnipresent, omnipotent, and omniscient, he is everywhere, in everything, and is the only true substance of the universe. We have a Godly heritage. The Father/Mother of everything is God. As it says in the good book, **"The lines are fallen unto me in pleasant places; yea, I have a goodly heritage."**7

"But God is Un-knowable!" protested the monk.

"Martin didn't think so, and neither did Saint Paul in Athens when he stood in the midst of Mars' hill and said, **'Ye men of Athens, I perceive that in all things ye are too superstitious. For as I passed by and beheld your devotions, I found an altar with this inscription, TO THE UNKNOWN GOD. Whom therefore ye ignorantly worship, he declare I unto you. God that made the world and all things therein, seeing that he is Lord of heaven and earth, dwelleth not in temples made with hands; Neither is worshipped with men's hands, as though he needed anything, seeing he giveth to all life, and breath, and all things;'**8 You know?" Magnus ended with an easy smile.

Osric squeezed his eyes shut and wrung his hands nervously.

Magnus suddenly imagined what the friar was thinking. *As a monk he should not be listening to heresy — but if there was any truth in it. Of course, there wasn't but the man needed to gather more information to prosecute this misguided heretic.*

"What do you think God is my son?"

"God is Love" was the young man's simple reply as he thought, **"He that loveth not knoweth not God; for God is love. And we have known and believed the love that God hath to us. God is love, and he that dwelleth in love dwelleth in God, and God in him."**9

Chapter 4

Evil

Magnus stretched his arms wide and felt a couple vertebrae slip back into position as he breathed deeply. It had been his first good night's sleep in days, and he lay comfortably in the straw dozing. Osric had left after their lengthy discussion to return to the Abby, but Magnus wasn't worried. He knew the monk had been genuinely interested in his religious theories. In fact, he could not recall having had a more interesting debate with anyone. The friar had started the discussion with a healthy skepticism. That was understandable, considering the years of theological training based on an anthropomorphic God that he must have endured. Gradually Magnus had seen Osric's face soften as comprehension of God as an all-powerful, ever-present spiritual force replaced the man's belief of life only existing in matter.

He smiled when he remembered the monk's final statement: "For these ideas to be true, the entire universe, including mankind, would have to constantly express God — otherwise, there would be a moment when God's perfection didn't exist everywhere, and He wouldn't be everywhere."

"Right, you are!" Magnus answered and slapped the man's broad back. Osric had slowly risen from the bench, wearing a queer little smile. Then he just walked out of the inn without another word.

Yes, he thought happily, *someone finally got it!* Osric hadn't understood all of the concepts, but Magnus was sure that the monk would return in a few days with a head full of questions. Magnus rolled out of his cocoon of hides and straw and stood up. He smelled bread baking behind the inn and was famished after his long evening of conversation. He straightened up his sleeping area and hurried out to the fire, still smiling.

Cynde was bent over, stoking the fire, but straightened as she heard Magnus approaching. "Good morning, sir. I didn't think you'd be up this early after such a long night."

"I'm afraid we were carried away in a flood of ideas," Magnus replied.

"I tried to listen to your discourse, but I couldn't understand and fell asleep," Cynde confessed.

Magnus still felt filled with the Spirit and wanted to explain everything about God to her, but he knew she wasn't ready. Instead, he said, "If you ever have any questions, feel free to ask me." He hoped that didn't sound condescending, but he was aware that he might be the only person in this wilderness region who understood God to be spiritual. Possibly with the exception of Osric now.

"Why did you only talk of one God? Father Osric has spoken of a Trinity, three-in-one, like our three mothers," Cynde asked, moments later.

"Who are they?"

"The three mothers are the Earth, Sun, and Moon – and of course, we have other gods because there are so many things in this world to be maintained, and even three deities would not be able to monitor everything," she said.

"I believe God's work is already done!" he replied with a broad smile.

"Nonsense, has your God washed his hands of us? Do you think the trees would grow? The animals procreate without the guidance of the gods? Our druids communicate with mother earth, nature, and the spirits that inhabit her," she stated emphatically.

Magnus paused before beginning. "It is written that **'God saw everything that he had made, and behold it was very**

good.'10 The Creator's work was done. Plants and animals are his ideas. It's up to us to see and nurture all that is good in the world."

She fastened her eyes on him, and he knew that she was trying to detect any trace of dishonesty. "I see more evil than good, and I ask again, do you believe in the Trinity that Osric spoke of?"

"Honestly? No, not in the way he would have meant it." He paused and added, "I'll try to explain if you'd like."

She looked thoughtful and replied, "I like many gods better than one. They meddle in our affairs, but one of them is sure to be nearby when I need help. If you only have one, what do you do when he is busy with someone else? How many seeds are in the field, and how many stars reside in the heavens? One God couldn't tend to it all, right?"

Magnus watched her eyes sparkle as she asked the question. *If only I could gaze into her eyes forever,* he wished. He knew that she was sure he would have to concede on this material-based point. "Wrong. The one true God is everywhere, including throughout you and me."

"God within me?" She gasped out loud, "You're daft, mad, you're…"

"Absolutely correct and <u>not</u> crazy," he answered, smiling.

She stood with her hands on her hips, mouth agape, as she tried to process this stranger's ludicrous ideas. Frustrated, she turned on her heels, grabbed a pot from the fire, and said, "Whatever… breakfast is served."

Magnus knew the discussion was over for the time being and sat down beneath the welcoming limbs of a large tree next to the inn. Cynde handed him a steaming bowl and sat down next to him.

Smiling, she said, "Be careful. Fairies are living in this tree, and I don't know if they'll be kind to an unbeliever."

Ignoring the jab, he asked. "What are the villagers getting ready for?" He pointed at a group of women busily chatting and trading baskets with each other.

She answered: "Mabon, it's our second harvest feast and

only eighteen days away. Most of the crops are gathered by then, and we give thanks for our bounty."

"Gratitude is a beautiful thing," Magnus replied.

They had almost finished eating when Magnus asked, "What's your favorite feast of all?"

"Beltane, our May Day festival," she replied smiling, "The people light bonfires, and we drive our cattle through the smoke to protect them for the summer season, and the beings from the otherworld can communicate with us. Two of the Druids saw a dragon last year."

"What exactly is a Druid? I heard in Gaul that they are wizards that sacrifice people!" he finished.

She reflected for a moment and answered smiling. "Not anymore; I haven't heard of a human sacrifice in my lifetime! Father Osric says they are like your wise men. Many centuries ago, they were our religious and community leaders; now, there are not many left. The church displaced or absorbed most of them, although some continue to practice in secret. They are the custodians of wisdom and still perform some rituals. My Uncle Anut is one!" she announced proudly. "They tell us how the fight proceeds each year between Gwynn ap Nudd, a king in the otherworld, and Gwythyr ap Gwreidawl. Gwynn ap Nudd stole the betrothed of Gwythyr ap Gwreidawl. They are doomed to mortal combat on May Day until the end of the world."

"What happens then?" Magnus wondered aloud.

"Then neither one wins the girl's hand because it's the end of the world!" she replied, laughing.

They talked cheerfully about spirits, pagan gods, and the upcoming celebration as they finished their meal. Apparently feeling more comfortable, Cynde finally asked, "You're acquainted with my gods now. Why do you only have one?"

Magnus paused and looked out at the sun-drenched meadows surrounding the village. "There was a man who lived many years ago known as the Son of God. His coming was prophesied for centuries, as was his death. Still, during his time on earth, he healed many desolate souls of any disease instantly and performed other extraordinary miracles." He contemplated the prophecy of Jesus's birth, **"'And there shall come forth a rod out of the stem of Jesse, and a Branch shall grow out of his roots: And the spirit of the LORD shall rest upon him, the spirit of wisdom and understanding, the spirit of counsel and might, the spirit of knowledge and of the fear of the LORD; And shall make him of quick understanding in the fear of the LORD: and he shall not judge after the sight of his eyes, neither reprove after the hearing of his ears: But with righteousness shall he judge the poor, and reprove with equity for the meek of the earth: and he shall smite the earth with the rod of his mouth, and with the breath of his lips shall he slay the wicked. And righteousness shall be the girdle of his loins, and faithfulness the girdle of his reins. The wolf also shall dwell with the lamb, and the leopard shall lie down with the kid; and the calf and the young lion and the fatling together; and a little child shall lead them.'**11 His mother was a virgin, and his Father was God, Spirit. Thus, Jesus was both human and Divine. He understood his Father's will, the divine laws governing the universe. He even told his followers, **'Call no man your Father upon the earth, for one is your Father, which is in heaven.'**12 He was the way-shower to a new reality, a view beyond the dark, limited visions that mortal minds conjure up, and his Father is the one true God."

"Wow," but then she asked, "Why did he die if he was godlike?"

"He allowed himself to be put to death by a bunch of zealots to prove that even death was unreal. He lay in a tomb for three days and then came from it alive, wearing the wounds he had received at his execution, and an angel announced his resurrection," he said reverently, **"He is not here: for he is risen, as he said. Come, see the place where the Lord lay. And go quickly, and tell his disciples that he is risen from the dead; and, behold, he goeth before you into Galilee; there shall ye see him: lo, I have told you."**13 "He then commanded his followers to perform even greater healings and miracles than his when he said, **'Verily, verily, I say unto you, He that believeth on me, the works that I do shall he do also; and greater works than these shall he do; because I go unto my Father.'**14"

Her eyes widened as she asked, "Are you telling me that you, as his follower, can perform instant wizardry and remove whatever ails a person? Do you cast spells for love and evil curses too?"

Magnus couldn't help but laugh, "No, I try to reflect what God is, and there is no evil or carnal desire in Him. The only God is perfect, and his ideas are perfect. Otherwise, he would be fighting with himself." Praying quietly, as he thought; **"But Jesus withdrew himself with his disciples to the sea: and a great multitude from Galilee followed him, and from Judæa, And from Jerusalem, and from Idumæa, and from beyond Jordan; and they about Tyre and Sidon, a great multitude, when they had heard what great things he did, came unto him. And he spake to his disciples, that a small ship should wait on him because of the multitude, lest they should throng him. For he had healed many, insomuch that they pressed upon him for to touch him, as many as had plagues. And unclean spirits, when they saw him, fell down before him and cried, saying, Thou art the Son of God. And the scribes which came down from Jerusalem said, He hath Beelzebub, and by the prince of the devils casteth he out devils. And he called them unto him, and said unto them in parables, How can Satan cast out Satan? And if a kingdom be divided against itself, that kingdom cannot stand. And if a house be divided against itself, that house cannot stand. And if Satan rises up against himself, and be divided, he cannot stand but hath an end."**15 "Unfortunately, in my short life, I have found a lack of ears eager to hear how to draw closer to spiritual ideas. Mankind as a whole is too busy holding tight to the tattered shreds of the visible world and fearing the darkness of death."

Cynde spoke quickly. "I don't fear death. Our father god

has a cauldron of renewal of life, and all of our dead are recycled into this world again."

Magnus grimaced. "So, they are plunged back into the same struggles, the same domains. Life is more than being doomed to repeat the same mistakes, the same existence. Think of life as a ladder. As your understanding of God increases through different experiences, you move higher, closer to the true concepts of the universe. Jesus, the Son of God, was on the top rung, and yet he walked this earth to lift people up to higher concepts of reality."

Cynde answered, "This wall is real, this village is real, and the threats of barbarians are real enough. What could be more real than these?"

"Principles that are the cement of the universe and hold the stars in their place are! Perpetual Life is based on an infinite number of ideas made in God's image, including the promise of God's Love for you!" answered Magnus with a grin.

He watched Cynde's eyes redden as she replied, "God loves me? He can't, I try to be good, but then I fail. How could an all-powerful being tolerate failure?"

Magnus gazed at the innocence lurking behind the girl's hard, barbarian expression and asked, "How could a God, who created everything perfect, know you as anything less than perfect?"

"How did your One God create the world?" she demanded, pretending to rub her eye while wiping away a tear.

Magnus smiled, seeing how affected she was, and continued softly. "The record of Genesis states, **'In the beginning, God created the heaven and the earth.'**16 and it continues to include the earth and the waters, the night and the day, fishes, birds, plants, and all the other animals, including man and woman in His own image – in His own perfect image, with dominion over the fish, birds, and animals. It goes on to say, **'And God saw everything that he had made, and, behold, it was very good.'**17 In the first record of the creation, there is no mention of evil."

Cynde's mouth widened with astonishment. "No evil? That is ridiculous – oh, I get it. It was a big joke on me because you must believe in evil!"

Magnus straightened and looked at her solemnly. "I do not, and the record is true. We mortals are such egotists. We demand to know God as we see ourselves, full of strife and pride, rather than trying to understand the source of Life as perfect. I think most people would rather die wrapped in ignorance than learn!" Magnus quipped.

Cynde definitely did not look convinced as she asked. "No evil? Then where did it come from?"

"It didn't," Magnus replied with authority. "For evil to be real, there would have to be a place, a spot where an infinite God was not, and there isn't. What we think is evil is a lie about what life truly is. To see the real world, look beyond the physical. I know it sounds trite, but if you see the harmony and Love that is God, the ghastly aspects of life fade to nothing, and you receive healing. I've seen it happen numerous times." He smiled graciously, turned, and walked toward the woods, leaving the confused girl wondering if he was just pretending to be insane.

Chapter 5

Shamed!

Later in the day, more travelers, farmers, and craftsmen arrived at the village. They usually stopped at Hastell Cenllys on their way to sell wares to the abbey at Seaford Downs. Cynde enlisted Magnus's aid to help serve the extra patrons and locals that crowded the inn. As he moved about delivering drinks and food, he found himself bumping into and repeatedly apologizing to many of the customers.

Later in the evening, as the patrons imbibed more and more mead and ale, conversations became heated. Throughout the night, Magnus watched several boisterous people be summarily ejected by Cynde's father. It was still crowded when Magnus, who was carrying a large stack of dirty bowls, caught his foot on a stray scabbard projecting in the aisle between the benches. He fell heavily and struck several customers on his way to the floor. A roar of laughter filled the air as he scrambled to his feet while trying to gather the dishes.

"He's a pansy!" One drunk spat the words out in disgust. "He's as worthless as the runt of a pig's litter. I should put him out of our misery right now!" the man said in a rising voice while one of his spirit-numbed hands held tightly to his tankard of ale, and the other searched in vain for the hilt of his sword.

Magnus felt his face flush hotly. Searching through the crowd, he saw Cynde's father grinning widely, and Magnus knew that he was on his own.

"I say you're a coward! What say you?" the drunk asked in a patronizing wail.

"I think you had too much to drink and need to think about sleeping it off."

The man roared like a lion, finally whipping his sword into the air. "Kill him, Jarosh!" another man yelled.

Magnus hadn't expected that and, since he did not want to be the center of attention, turned to make a hasty exit.

The sounds of derision rose, and several patrons stood up to deliberately impede his progress. While saying nothing, he stepped purposely around them and continued to thread his way to the inn's closest exit amid a chorus of jeers and flying objects. A chunk of wet cabbage smashed into the back of his head, but he kept walking and was soon outside.

Minutes later, Cynde found him sitting at the edge of the village. Stray tears had left dark tracks on his cheeks. "Are you alright?" she asked, frowning, and followed quickly with: "You couldn't have been scared of that loud-mouthed drunkard?"

He stared into the distance and said in an unsteady voice, "No, but I won't allow myself to fight for vanity either."

"You just became the laughingstock of this town! Why didn't you fight?"

Magnus tried to calm himself. "I've tried to live the Golden Rule. I do to others as I would want them to do to me. Tomorrow that offensive clod will wake up, and I hope to be grateful that I didn't take advantage of him in an inebriated state."

"Will you challenge him when he's sober?" Cynde asked.

"I won't request some brutish contest just to amuse your friends," he said bitterly. He knew the villagers had been talking amongst themselves about her closeness to the new stranger. If he was ascertained a coward, their disdain would shower down upon her also.

Cynde's contempt for weakness showed itself. "I guess you've never been mad enough to kill a man?" she spat.

"Once," he replied, somewhat gratified to see the look of

surprise on her face. "Last year, I had trouble with a soldier, who just happened to be a nephew of the new Bishop of Gaul who hates me. I think it was just sport with him, or maybe his uncle promoted it, I don't know, but he would not leave me alone. I would be in the market, and he would ridicule me in public. Once at the abbey, he snuck up behind me and flicked my ears as though I were a mere boy. Another time I was studying at a table there, and suddenly he grabbed me from behind and started to choke me," emphasizing the attack with his cupped hands. "I was furious! The colors of the room faded to shades of gray, and I remember that time seemed to slow down to a crawl. Suddenly I was relaxed, yet I knew exactly where everything was in the room. I could picture the position of his throat in my mind. Before I reacted, though, he let go and stepped back laughing with some smart-ass remark, and my anger passed."

She looked interested now, and her questions came in a stream. "He was a trained soldier? Was he much older than you?" she said. "Did you ever fight him?"

"He was older, a head taller, and fairly stout," Magnus replied seriously. "One night, I ran into him on a bridge. I had been cutting and binding wheat in the fields for some friends of my parents and didn't get back into town until late. He had been carousing in the taverns and brothels that edged the fort and was full of himself along with who knows what else. He recognized me and screamed the most vulgar insults I had ever heard. Then he charged at me, saying he would 'Tear the worthless knave apart!' Rather than being afraid or angry, I seemed to be looking forward to the encounter, so I sprang toward him. People were gathering on the bridge to watch the spectacle. A skinny, unarmed kid being ravaged by a brutish soldier, but I surprised them and myself."

Cynde interrupted, "Tell me what happened."

"Just before he grabbed me, I stepped to the side, seized his wrist, and pulled it like a game of crack-the-whip. It threw him off balance, and when I let go, he careened across the bridge and fell flat on his face in front of a group of his fellow soldiers. They all were taunting him as he scrambled to his feet. One look into the man's wild eyes told me that the fight had progressed well beyond the bounds of civility. In the next instant, he pulled his sword and ran forward, waving it over his head and shouting that he'd cleave me in two! I started running to the opposite side of the bridge, but I didn't try to outrun him. I just wanted to stay beyond the reach of that blade." He smiled, remembering.

"How did you escape?" Cynde asked, frustration in her voice.

"Well, I didn't plan it. I just reacted," Magnus replied. "I sprinted toward the handrail, and I was sure he expected me to clamber up on the balustrade and dive into the water. At the last second, I reached out as if I was going to climb up and then dropped to my knees. He didn't have time to bring his sword down. As his groin crashed into me, I pushed up with all my strength. The people watching said that it looked like he vaulted over the side. Afterward, I remember how the crowd fell silent, staring down at the black water. He never turned up again."

"At the trial, I was acquitted since I was unarmed, and all the witnesses swore that I hadn't provoked the combat. The bishop was not at all pleased with the verdict. Shortly after that, he conducted a memorial service for his nephew, where he stated publicly: 'My predecessor Bishop Martin was a great man, but he was just a man unlike Jesus, who was the son of God and able to perform miracles. There is one citizen in our midst that misunderstands Martin's great teachings and let it be public knowledge now. That young man is viewed as an enemy of this church, as is anyone else who persists in attributing fanciful healings to Martin!' That's when I began making plans to leave Gaul, but I understood Martin," he added.

"You told Father Osric that there were others healed by Martin." she said. "Didn't the people remember them too? How could they say that the miracles didn't happen?"

"People have short memories, especially when they are

afraid of the consequences," Magnus replied flatly.

"I hope they have short memories. They're all drunk now, and with luck, the matter will be forgotten by the morrow," Cynde murmured unsteadily.

Chapter 6

The Orchard

The sun was still low in the sky the following day as Magnus sat under a tree at the edge of the orchard, eating an apple.

"Hey, young man! It looks like you've adapted well to the villager's hospitality."

Magnus smiled as he stood and waved. When Osric approached, he offered his portly friend a freshly polished piece of fruit. "I'm gathering firewood again for them, but there are tasty benefits."

Osric smiled widely, but before he ate, he asked a question. "What's going on with Cynde? She didn't speak two words to me back at the inn."

"I'm sure she's worried about last night. A drunk accosted me, and rather than fight, I took flight."

"Oh!" The monk said in a somber tone that proved he had assessed the situation correctly. "That could be serious with these people. They certainly don't understand 'turning the other cheek.' Remember the master's words as they were recorded? Jesus said, **Ye have heard that it hath been said, An eye for an eye, and a tooth for a tooth: But I say unto you, That ye resist not evil: but whosoever shall smite thee on thy right cheek, turn to him the other also.' 'Then came Peter to him, and said, Lord, how oft shall my brother sin against me, and I forgive him? till seven times? Jesus saith unto him, I say not unto thee, Until**

seven times: but, Until seventy times seven.'18 I'll talk to them on my way back. I'll tell them that you were under holy orders from the bishop to avoid trivial combat while you searched for evidence of the Picts in this region. That should quiet them down for the time being," he surmised as he searched for a good place to sit.

"Who or what are the Picts?" Magnus asked.

"Northern tribes of butcherous barbarians. They stain themselves blue and prey on our North and Central villages and farms without mercy. Don't worry; we haven't ever had raids this far south, though," after a pause, the big man continued, "Did you talk to Cynde about God?"

"Probably too much. Sometimes I get carried away preaching and telling people more than they are ready for, but you already know that don't you? What are you doing here? I assumed you went back to the coast?" Magnus said as the monk sat down in the tall grass under a tree.

Osric wiped stray apple juice from his chin and replied. "Nah, I started to, but my head was too full of your magnificent ideas. When I considered going back and resuming my duties at the monastery, I couldn't force myself to do it. I just wandered through the forests and meadows yesterday. Last night I could see every star in God's heaven, I felt his presence around and through me in the darkness, and I had no fears! I have you to thank, my friend, for that marvelous experience."

"Thank you for listening to my ramblings." Magnus thrilled at Osric's words, "I can take no credit for the wonderful ideas because they were not mine, but the Father's."

The big man continued, "Yet, those same stunning ideas brought to me a great torment; I now understand why our dear Master was called 'a man of sorrows', like the prophet said, **'He is despised and rejected of men; a man of sorrows, and acquainted with grief: and we hid as it were our faces from him; he was despised, and we esteemed him not. Surely he hath borne our griefs and carried our sorrows: yet we did esteem him stricken, smitten of God, and afflicted. But he was wounded for our transgressions, he**

was bruised for our iniquities: the chastisement of our peace was upon him, and with his stripes, we are healed.'19 He saw the reality, the vast harmony of God's creation, but mankind wasn't ready to accept his vision. I feel so sorry for the masses of people who know nothing of Spirit…, who are trapped in this false world of materiality, even as I myself was." He waved his arm at the panorama before them.

"Understanding God is the greatest gift that most of the world has never known. That's why Bishop Martin stressed spiritual education to his students rather than corporeal education. You have a humble servant's heart, my dear Osric. Of all the people I have shared the good news with, you alone have digested it. Thank you, my friend."

"All of the politicians and countries of the world ignore the realm that Jesus spoke of. His kingdom was truly not of this world – and they cannot comprehend. They still do not realize…" A large sob escaped the monk's throat.

Magnus was touched by the man's compassion and hurriedly said. "They will, brother Osric, they will. Truth cannot be ignored forever. Did you contemplate all last night, or did you get some rest?"

"I don't know, but it was all refreshing," Osric said, standing up. "Thank you for letting your light shine and giving me the most valuable gift in the universe." The monk grinned as he selected another apple from the tree and sank down heavily next to Magnus.

Magnus leaned back against the tree's rough bark, feeling the warmth of friendship. He was unable to think of an adequate reply for Osric's gratitude, so he changed the subject "I think I'll take some more of these apples back to Cynde. Maybe that will get her talking."

"Good idea!" Osric replied, as he stifled a yawn, "She's a bright girl. I'm sure she'll be able to handle anything you threw at her… eventually."

Magnus hoped that his friend was right. He knew Cynde was smart, but he didn't want to confuse her so much that she would retreat to her old ideas just because they were comfortable. He would have to gently coax her into his visions of reality and destroy the fears one by one. Inwardly, he had struggled, trying to deny and reason away his feelings for the girl. In those few moments of quiet, honest reflection beneath the tree, he finally knew from the pangs in his heart that he was hopelessly in love with her. Osric was already snoring deeply beside him. His eyelids closed involuntarily against the warm morning sun, and soon he too, was fast asleep.

Magnus gradually noticed that it seemed to be brighter here than it was before. With a violent start, he recognized the garden and remembered the thousands of serpents that infested it! There was something different now though. He heard people speaking faintly in the distance and struggled to hear what they were saying. It seemed like they were speaking English, but it was a strange dialect, and he couldn't understand many of the words. He got to his feet and silently drew his short sword from its sheath. Creeping slowly along the edge of the closest pool, he grew closer to the voices. His eyes scanned constantly for reptiles as he stared into both the dark, stagnate waters and the dense brush, but saw no movement. They seemed to be gone! How could that be? Did they consume each other or die of some disease? Somehow Magnus knew that the snakes had been expelled but remained wary as he moved among the garden's wreckage.

It smelled different than before. It was sweeter, like a day after rain. Then he noticed that the dank mist that had seemed impenetrable on his last visit had almost dispersed. It was nearly pleasant, unlike his last visit. He relaxed a little with a sigh of relief.

A rabbit suddenly darted out of the bush to his right. Magnus was so surprised that he sprang backward, stepped on a loose flagstone that tipped and launched him into the water with a monstrous splash. The water was warm and closed over him like a dark, mossy blanket. His weapon stuck in some heavy vines and was wrenched out of his hand. He recovered quickly, tucked his legs under himself, and kicked hard. His head broke the surface, and he found himself covered with a slimy mixture of moss and rotting plants. So much for the element of surprise, he thought. Struggling to the edge of the pool, his fingers clawed at the rocks in a desperate effort to climb out. It was like being in quicksand. The weeds in the water seemed intent on wrapping themselves around his legs and torso. His hands were covered in decaying, greasy vegetation that wouldn't allow him to grab anything firmly. Finally, after scraping his fingers violently against the rocks, they were dry enough for him to grasp the edge. I pray to God there are no leeches in here, he hoped as he paused to catch his breath.

He tried repeatedly to pull himself out of the pool. Straining, he was able to lift himself a few inches out of the greenish muck, only to slide back into the water defeated. The weeds seemed to tighten around his body with every effort he made. Great, a thousand vicious snakes couldn't kill me, but some passive weeds and a scared rabbit might. He considered the situation with uncomfortable amusement. Finally, resigned to his fate, he stopped struggling and rested as he clung to the edge of the pool.

He was watching a small, black water beetle swimming happily below his chin when he felt strong hands grasp his wrists. He looked up, but his hair was caked with algae that filled his eyes and blinded him. Despite his surprise, he forced himself not to resist the tugs. In a cacophony of slurping and gurgling noises, he finally came free from the watery snare and felt his belly drag across the smooth stones of the pathway. His liberators released his hands, and he clawed at his head, rubbing his eyes, and digging the slippery vegetation out of his ears. He blinked rapidly, trying to see who his rescuers were, and finally, they came into focus.

It was a strange gathering of people. So many more than he had imagined. They filled the area between the pool and the garden's wall, and others kept pressing forward, eager to see who had fallen into the water. Magnus could never hope to describe all the different clothing that he saw. There were none that wore garments similar to his. Some of the people had long, elegant apparel, while others were, in his eyes, practically naked. He wondered if some of them had painted their skin but then realized that they hadn't. This diverse group of people with brown, red, yellow, and white skin hues stood around him. Instead of trepidation, all he felt was Love. The crowd gave way as a woman with white hair and a flowing white gown walked toward him and offered her hand. Magnus knew this must be one of their leaders and struggled to his feet. He shook her hand with as much grace as he could muster. "Thank you for saving me." Magnus bowed as he noticed with dismay that a stream of dirty green water had poured out of his sodden sleeve and onto her clothes. She didn't react to the stained dress; instead, she gave him a loving smile like he was one of her dearest friends. Then she turned and walked away as the others busily began repairing the neglected garden.

One man was already mixing mortar to reset the loose stone that had thrown Magnus into the pool. Several others had rakes and were pulling plants and debris out of the water. Still, others were pruning the bushes and pulling weeds from between the stones. He saw beauty rapidly emerging from what had seemed to be an apparition of hopeless devastation on his first visit.

Magnus looked down the long line of pools and hedges toward the massive tree he had noticed on his last visit. With the mist thinned, it seemed even larger than he remembered. He was deciding on the best path to take toward its cluster of branches when something hit him on the shoulder.

"Ow!" he cried and opened his eyes just in time to see a large red object rolling down the hill away from him. He was in the apple grove as Osric awoke from a sound sleep beside him.

"What the…" Osric mumbled, rubbing his eyes.

"I'm sorry, but this tree threw something at me." Magnus apologized and pointed at the apple.

"It probably knew that you were sleeping on the job," Osric said with a grin.

Magnus couldn't argue, so he laughed and tried to remember the dream that was so vivid mere seconds ago…

"You know, your ideas make my heart burn within me," the big man muttered quietly as he recited, **"And they said one to another, Did not our heart burn within us, while he talked with us by the way, and while he opened to us the scriptures?"**[20]

"I can take no credit for the ideas; they are God's, as is everything."

"But what of the misery, hatred, and wicked ideas I experience each day?" the man said, his voice rising.

"Consider the source; if they are good and perfect, they belong to God. If it isn't Love, it isn't God," Magnus said. "I think of Jesus as the greatest alchemist of all time. He saw through the facade of material life and brought the harmony of God to people's perceptions and human experiences. Remember when he changed the water into wine? The story begins, **'And the third day there was a marriage in Cana of Galilee, and the mother of Jesus was there: And both Jesus was called, and his disciples, to the marriage. And when they wanted wine, the mother of Jesus said unto him, They have no wine. Jesus saith unto her, woman, what have I to do with thee? Mine hour is not yet come. His mother saith unto the servants, Whatsoever he saith unto you, do it. And there were set there six waterpots of stone, after the manner of the purifying of the Jew, containing two or three firkins apiece. Jesus saith unto them, Draw out now and bear unto the governor of the feast. And they bare it. When the ruler of the feast had tasted the water that was made wine and knew not whence it was: (but the servants which drew the water knew;) the governor of the feast called the bridegroom, And saith unto him, Every man at the beginning doth set forth good wine; and when men have well drunk, then that which is worse: but thou hast kept the good wine until now. This beginning of miracles did Jesus in Cana of Galilee, and manifested forth his glory, and his disciples believed on him.'21"**

That silenced the monk for several minutes as he laid in the sunshine, looking like he was reflecting on the story. "Well, I've got to be on my way!" Osric finally announced as he rolled onto his side to facilitate a large man's attempt at standing.

"So soon? Even though you've slept here all day?" Magnus asked with a wink. A small groan escaped the monk's mouth as he stood erect and grinned.

"Yes, but I'm on official church business. This was my time to reflect and solidify the ideas you've given me. Now I must report to the bishop that all is well; in fact, all is perfect!"

Magnus was shocked; he hadn't thought about Osric sharing his ideas on God so soon. "Whoa, not so fast, friend friar. I would prefer it if you kept our conversations to yourself for the time being. I'm not sure his Holiness will be as receptive as you are. Someday people may gather to share these ideas in small groups or even churches. For now, we need to nurture the knowledge, like sheltering a small flame, until it is strong enough to withstand the winds of opposition. Otherwise, it may be snuffed out!"

"Nonsense," replied the monk in his resonant, booming voice. "The bishop will be ecstatic. He'll love it. We need to proclaim the good word and let our light shine brightly as Jesus said, **'Ye are the light of the world. A city that is set on a hill cannot be hidden. Neither do men light a candle, and put it under a bushel, but on a candlestick, and it giveth light unto all that are in the house. Let your light so shine before men, that they may see your good works, and glorify your Father which is in heaven.'**22 There will be no more limitations of sin, disease, or death in this world. It'll be…the second coming!" Osric seemed to have shocked himself into silence with that final statement.

Magnus sprang to his feet and grabbed the monk's broad shoulders. He looked him straight in the eyes, saying, "Be wary, my friend; not everyone is ready to share the good news. I have tried to plant many seeds of truth in my life. Unfortunately, they don't grow well amidst the thorns of people's minds. Humans would rather wallow in self-pity, self-absorption, and self-love, which subjects them to sin, disease, and death in this material world, rather than rise upward in their thinking."

Osric paused with a look of deep contemplation. He then unleashed a smile that stretched from ear to ear and asked. "Do you think Jesus will need to return to a physical body? Or could his spirit, just his qualities, his Godlike thoughts, return to mankind instead?"

"I don't think the Christ needs to be contained in a body. He wasn't when he appeared to Saul on his way to Damascus," as Magnus reflected, **'I will pray to the Father, and he shall give you another Comforter, that he may abide with you forever; *Even* the Spirit of truth; whom the world cannot receive, because it seeth him not, neither knoweth him: but ye know him; for he dwelleth with you, and shall be** in you.'23 Do you remember where it says, **'But the Comforter, *which is* the Holy Ghost, whom the Father will send in my name, he shall teach you all things, and bring all things to your remembrance, whatsoever I have said unto you.'**24 The essence of Christ, the understanding of God is what heals, not a person," Magnus answered. "But please don't proclaim the news to everyone; they aren't ready for the revelation! I know from experience that all the different religions of men in this world: Jews, Pagans, Barbarians, even many Christians, serve the same gods. The people of this world all worship matter - mankind's material, limited concepts of Deity. In truth, we need more followers who recognize an unlimited spiritual Life and practice the healing works that Jesus commanded that we do, before it can be safely presented to the masses." After a moment of hesitation he added, "The world didn't listen to our master even as he performed countless miraculous cures. Why would they listen to us?"

Osric replied with a slight air of indignation, "You worry way too much for a young man. His holiness is dedicated to God, and I promise I'll explain it only when he's in a receptive mood."

Magnus could see that the big man wasn't about to listen to any of his logical arguments.

"This is going to be great, Magnus! I'm sure he'll want to see you immediately to help teach the brethren! I must return to the monastery now, but I'll see you soon! Oh, and I'll be sure to tell the villagers on my way back that you were under strict orders as the bishop's agent not to quarrel with the local rabble-rousers!" he promised as he swallowed Magnus inside of a massive bear hug. Then he turned and sauntered out of the orchard whistling a beautiful hymn. A man without worries.

Magnus, on the other hand, was praying desperately to remove a growing knot of fear that had gathered deep in his stomach. Slowly, he began to pick up fallen tree limbs. Magnus gathered the branches that had fallen in the orchard onto stacks for firewood for the rest of the afternoon as he concentrated on praying for protection, especially for Osric.

Lost in his communion, time passed quickly. The sun had almost set, and it was growing harder for him to see the tree limbs hidden in the tall grass. He struggled to clear his mind of any dark images of possible pain or suffering by understanding that all creatures, including jovial monks, are entitled to enjoy continuous harmonious experiences. He knew that the qualities of God were always present because God is everywhere. Then an idea came to him, **"What shall we then say to these things? If God be for us, who can be against us?"**25 *If the one true God is with you, who can stand against you?* he thought to himself. Immediately, his fear retreated somewhat, and he smiled at the small victory.

The sun had settled beneath the horizon before Magnus finished his mental search for relief. *Lord, I think it's finally time for me to head home. Thank you for your protection of everyone, including my new friend friar.* He continued praying as he walked toward the village, but abruptly stopped in his tracks. He heard a man's laugh that was quickly stifled in the distance. *That's strange; most of the villagers have been staying close to home to prepare for the coming feast. Who would be hunting tonight?* he wondered as he silently crept into the woods toward the direction of the sound. *Why do I care who is hunting? They might mistake me for a deer and let loose an arrow! I should just go back to the inn.* Ideas crowded into his mind, but he kept climbing up the hill, moving farther away from the promise of safety. He could see nothing but a darkened valley when he reached the top. The moon hadn't risen high enough to provide light, but he could hear some muffled voices and the sounds of twigs breaking that echoed through the depression. There were a lot of men down there, not a tiny hunting party. Magnus was confused for only a moment, and then he realized that it had to be raiders!

Chapter 7

The Horde!

Struggling to draw air into his lungs, Magnus forced himself to keep up the pace. Dodging tree limbs and rock outcroppings, he was running as fast as he could now after having crept quietly away from the hilltop. *They must be Picts trying to claim lands occupied by the Romans,* he supposed as he raced towards the village.

He passed the outer ramparts and tried to cry out but couldn't. His throat was constricted by exertion, but he didn't slow down until he was at the inn's door. He kicked at it violently. Cynde immediately threw open the door, and he knew that she must have been waiting for his return. Before she could ask him any questions, he croaked: "Raid, barbarians in the valley beyond the orchard!"

Her eyes filled with disbelief for only a moment, and then she ran past him, calling out for the darkened village to evacuate. The paths filled with people almost instantly. A few of the younger men ran toward the animal pens and shooed the chickens, cows, pigs, goats, and sheep out of their confinements. Other inhabitants rushed to grab what precious possessions they had and began running down the steep hill behind their homes, toward the forest on the next rise.

Magnus took a series of deep breaths to recover from his sprint and then struggled to carry the pots and furs that Dwig and Cynde's father thrust into his arms, as they gathered other valuable objects. Cynde returned, grabbed her own collection of odds and ends, and cried: "Follow me!" Obedient as well-trained soldiers, the three men didn't hesitate and followed close behind her, first down the hill behind the village and then up toward the darkened woods on the hilltop.

The villagers were all breathing hard as they reached the tree line above the village. They dropped their bundles and sat down in small groups to rest after the rapid climb. The moon had risen high enough so that they could see the outline of their homes while remaining hidden in the thick, brushy foliage. Despite the story told by Osric that afternoon, every one of the villagers except for Cynde remained suspicious of the cowardly stranger. They believed he was a bad influence on Cynde and her family, and maybe this exodus was one of his tricks. Still, none of them so much as spoke a syllable as they sat silently in the thick blanket of leaves and brush.

An hour passed, and some low murmurs began to pass through the group. Magnus leaned over and whispered to Cynde: "I know what I heard."

She made a quick motion with her hand for silence. *Apparently, she still believed him.* Moments later, Magnus was almost relieved to hear a chorus of yells as invaders attacked the empty village. Their shrill war cries filled the night air. They had taken enough time to completely surround the cluster of houses. It was clear to all the frightened residents that it would have been a bloodbath if they had not been warned by the stranger. The livestock that had been left behind in haste were charging through the buildings as the savage band of marauders frantically tried to round them up. Fires erupted and quickly engulfed the town as flames shot into the air. Showers of sparks began to ascend into the night sky like millions of hungry fireflies fed by the thatched roofs.

Magnus could see the awe and disbelief reflected on the faces around him in the pasty white light of the moon. As he looked back toward the buildings, he saw the raiders bathed in light from the fires they had set. *Their bodies were colored blue!*

One older man murmured, "Picts," and spat on the

ground in disgust. Magnus knew from Osric that the savages had been attacking villages in central England, but how did they get this far south? He could see what looked like quarrels breaking out between the vandals. They seemed both confused and furious about how they had been tricked into attacking empty dwellings.

Several sword fights ensued, with the losers lying in grotesque positions, some with missing limbs. *If they can't kill us, they'll kill each other. What fools!* Magnus thought. One squat man with huge broad shoulders strode back and forth among the pillagers trying to redirect their efforts from fighting amongst themselves. *That must be their leader*, he decided.

The villagers silently watched, glued to the unfolding spectacle. Finally, a larger man with a lion image on his shield challenged the Pictish chief's authority. A circle of painted bodies quickly formed around the two combatants as threats and insults were hurled back and forth. Soon blades flashed in the firelight, and the crashing sounds of metal on metal drifted up to the invisible audience on the hilltop.

Both fighters were skilled, but the chief's larger opponent seemed much stronger as he rained down blow after bone-shattering blow onto the smaller man's shield. The chief swung his sword wildly and finally connected with his opponent's cheek, but it was only a glancing blow. After briefly stepping back and licking the blood streaming down his face, the huge warrior resumed his attack. The first strike was a huge arc that began behind his back, swinging over his head, splitting the chief's shield in two. The blade never stopped moving as it arced again to the right side and swung instantly across to his left. Magnus watched as the once-mighty chief's head rolled into the frenzied mob, and his decapitated body sank to the ground. A hush fell over the Picts briefly, followed by cheering and violent dancing. With their blood thirst sated, they soon became quiet as they searched methodically for any prizes left in the town worth carrying away.

Within an hour, the raiding party was gone, without riches, without slaves, but with a new chief to lead them. The villagers watched the glowing remains of their homes with a mixture of sadness and gratitude as they drifted off to sleep under the stars.

Chapter 8

Restoration

In the morning, Magnus awoke to find Cynde gently shaking him. "Magnus, the villagers are ready to start rebuilding, but they don't want to begin without thanking you first." She offered her hand and helped him up.

One by one, the line of people passed. Some clasped his hand in theirs and hugged him, while others just nodded. Appreciation showed in all their red-rimmed eyes. When the last villager had passed, Cynde surprised Magnus by grabbing him and kissing him on the lips. Instantly, extraordinary happiness engulfed him in a heated wave of emotion he felt throughout his body.

"What do I owe that distinct pleasure to?" he stammered.

"You saved our lives. You're my hero!" She smiled, and he felt helpless.

Searching for words, he said, "I'm no hero; I couldn't protect your village."

"You saved all our lives; the rest will be replaced," she said with confidence while taking him by the hand and leading him down the hill toward the smoking ruins.

When they reached the village, Magnus saw that the residents were concentrating on assessing the damage to their homes and ignoring the blue-toned, blood-caked bodies that lay where they had fallen. Flies were already starting to swarm, and he decided to take on the distasteful job of disposing of them. He smiled when it occurred to him that he was the most qualified. *These guys didn't smell as bad as the sheep he had cared for on the boat.*

Magnus figured that the quickest method of burial would be to pile rocks over the bodies at the foot of a cliff close to the orchard. Permission to do so was quickly granted by the grateful village elders. He located two rafter poles that were charred but still usable and lashed his blanket from the night before between them.

Magnus decided to give the honor of the first trip to the decapitated chief. He pulled his makeshift sling next to the body. The guy's arms were as thick as Magnus's thigh. He grabbed one of the man's wrists and pulled. Gobs of reddish-brown blood spurted from the severed neck as Magnus struggled, rolling him over onto the blanket. Then Magnus looked for the head. It wasn't anywhere in sight. Had the interlopers taken it with them? Just then, Magnus heard a girl shriek as she ran and hid behind his legs.

He looked up and saw a boy about nine years old struggling to carry the grisly prize. *That's much better than snakes and frogs to scare his little girlfriend!* Magnus smiled as he remembered his own childhood. "Let me have that young man," he commanded.

Reluctantly the boy surrendered the head and ran off, chasing the laughing girl. Magnus winced as he lifted it by the hair, and his other hand closed the vacant blue eyes. He placed the head on the blanket, grabbed the poles, and began dragging the man's remains out of the village.

He decided to move all the bodies out of the villagers' sight first, and initially, he piled their remains just outside of the decaying ramparts that ringed the village. Then he began ferrying them to a cliff base a good distance from the community. There were four cadavers in all, and two of them were little more than boys. *Perhaps they were related to the deceased chief,* Magnus considered. After arranging them side-by-side, he began covering them with the large rocks scattered around the area below the bluff.

Magnus worked through the heat of the day without a pause. He was sweating profusely and coated in streaks of rock dust and warrior's blood. The gruesome task destroyed any desire to eat or rest; he just wanted to be done with it.

He was returning from the makeshift graveyard late in the day when he spotted soldiers. They were helping the villagers to rebuild. Magnus could see that a lot of progress had been made, and several of the homes now had newly thatched roofs.

As Magnus walked through the houses, he saw the captain growling at several of his men. "Why isn't this wall finished? Are you fools, or do you just not care?"

That doesn't give them much option to answer, thought Magnus. He called out. "Hello sir, thanks for the helping hands."

The captain looked startled at the vision of Magnus covered in dried blood and dirt. "We saw the smoke this morning, and the bishop requested that we provide a final act of Christian charity to these less fortunates," he replied, looking irritated.

"Final?" Magnus questioned, as he suddenly knew the captain was lying. *They couldn't have seen the smoke at night, and it would have taken a full day for the soldiers to travel to Hastell Cenllys. Did the captain know that the village would be attacked?*

"Rome is being attacked by Visigoth barbarians from the east, and the emperor has personally recalled our legion from this cursed land to repel them. The troop ships sail in two days," replied the captain with a fierce pride that somehow softened his demeanor.

"You were speaking of Christian charity, is Osric about?" Magnus asked.

"No, I'm afraid the bishop had some urgent duties for him to attend to at the abbey. He'll be tied up for some time."

"Too bad we could use his mirth around here," Magnus replied with a grin as he hurried toward the inn. He didn't feel like grinning. *Something was not right.*

Cynde and her family had been working hard alongside several of the legionnaires all day. The thatched roof was already halfway replaced as she and her brother scurried around the rafters attaching the twisted grass bundles formed by the others. "You've done a great job! Now let me take over while you feed these hungry legionnaires," yelled Magnus.

"Alright," she replied as she swung down from the nearest bare rafter and dropped lightly to the ground.

Magnus and Dwig continued working in the sparse light provided by the cooking fire until all the soldiers were fed. They had covered the sleeping areas first so that they could all rest in the dry and were almost done with the main hall. After a quick meal, they retired to their beds, exhausted.

In the morning, the captain woke Magnus with a firm shove of his foot. "Young man, his Holiness the Bishop sent a message last night requesting that you accompany us back to the abbey. He is celebrating the mass tomorrow and would greatly appreciate your attendance!" The man was smiling, but Magnus felt an underlying hostility.

"I would be honored to visit him, but there are still so many repairs to do in the village, and I must help the villagers restock their stores of food before winter."

The captain's grin widened as he showed rows of white, even teeth. He replied slowly. "He also said that if you hesitate, I should insist," as he placed a hand firmly on the hilt of his sword.

Magnus understood the implied threat. If he refused, he would be bound and beaten on the walk back to the abbey. He quickly agreed to the kind invitation and began to gather up his few belongings. A soldier suddenly snatched his sword and dagger away from him. Shaken, he asked Captain Claudius if he could have a moment to say goodbye to Cynde. With an animalistic sneer, he acquiesced and motioned Magnus away with his hand.

She was gathering ingredients from clay jars to prepare breakfast when Magnus approached her. "I've been invited to accompany the legionnaires back to Seaford Downs to meet with the Abbot-Bishop," he said, trying to sound cheerful.

Cynde immediately looked like she sensed that something was wrong. "No, you can't leave, there is too much to be done here, the rebuilding…"

Magnus made sure that Claudius was behind him and pressed a finger to his lips silencing her. He pulled a worn leather roll from his tunic and shoved it into her hands. She immediately pushed it up under her corset to conceal it. "Relax, Cynde. I'll only be gone for a day or two." He kissed her on the cheek and pulled away.

Reaching up, she removed her red scarf and tenderly wrapped it around his neck. "I'll miss you, be careful." Confusion danced in her troubled eyes.

"You too, Sweetness," he replied and turned to join the soldiers.

~

Cynde's father came to her side. "What's happening?" he asked.

"They're forcing him to go to Seaford Downs to see the bishop. Do something, Father." she said with reddened eyes as her heart raced.

"Do what? He'll either be back, or he won't. Don't spend time worrying about things you can't change," answered her father as a middle-aged man and woman stepped into the room.

"Men are always so pragmatic," the lady said.

"Uncle Anut, Aunt Sephia! What are you two doing here?" Cynde cried as she hugged them tightly.

"And young girls are always too emotional," her aunt replied with a slightly crooked grin. "We left our village as soon as we heard of the attack," she then added, "I saw that boy pass you something. What was it?"

"I don't know," Cynde said, pulling the package out. She moved to one of the benches and unrolled it carefully. Inside were a collection of gold coins, several small pieces of frankincense and myrrh, and a small scroll.

"Let me see that!" Sephia demanded, and then in a more subdued voice, "Please, Osric taught me to read some Roman symbols when he visited us in the past."

Cynde surrendered the spool to her aunt with mild

reservations.

"Why this was penned by a man named Mmm aa arr tt tinn," she pronounced each syllable painfully slow as she struggled to remember the sounds that accompanied the ink scratching's at the bottom of the parchment. "Martin," she finally said quickly. "I wonder why your young friend treasures this document?" asked Sephia, quickly adding, "Do you want me to hide it for you until he returns?"

"No, no, I'll keep it for now," replied Cynde. Grabbing the roll of parchment before her aunt could read any more. Involuntary chills rose through her spine, but she didn't know why.

"Well, I certainly hope your dashing admirer returns from the bishop soon. I can't wait to meet him personally," her aunt purred.

Chapter 9

Arrest

Notwithstanding the fact that he was under armed guard, Magnus realized that it was a beautiful day. The troupe strode down the dusty pathway two abreast. Magnus was paired with what he perceived as the group's largest and probably the meanest-looking soldier.

The brilliant rays of the sun danced across the late summer leaves that would soon turn into myriad shades of red and gold. Reflecting on the good in his life, Magnus inadvertently began to sing a hymn:

"God leads me, above life's pains, in an atmosphere of love.
Daily trials and distress, my thoughts ascend above.
Mortality fades like a dream, reality appears.
I understand a little more; God's will replaces my fears.

"Flesh and blood are parodies, not the substance of creation.
Infinite ideas, solid and firm, fill the universe with wisdom.
My heart overflows with happiness, dark forces fall away.
I feel Love, Life, and Truth; God's leading me today."
One of the soldiers suddenly announced loudly,
"The man is daft. He thinks the captain is God!"

This brought on a loud round of guffaws until the captain barked, "Silence!"

A fierce glare from Captain Claudius also silenced Magnus for the remainder of the journey.

They arrived at the abbey well after dark, and Magnus was billeted in the soldiers' barracks. He moved between groups of the legionnaires, asking many of the men about Osric, but received no replies other than negative grunts and cold shoulders. Exhausted from the long march, he finally crawled into an unoccupied spot and fell asleep.

He was awakened by a guard's prodding the next morning. After a quick trip to a drafty privy, he was immediately marched to the dining hall. Seated prominently next to the captain, he took his breakfast in complete silence. Next, the captain escorted him into the newly constructed cathedral.

Local parishioners were filing in the large double doors at the front of the church as a choir of monks sang a melody of Psalms. The captain chose two seats toward the front and roughly motioned for Magnus to be seated. Mass was a relatively new invention of the church, having started around 394 A.D. Magnus watched closely as the Abbot-Bishop performed the sacrament ceremony. He was a wizened little man, covered head to foot in the flowing robes of his religious post. From the color of his nose, Magnus realized that the little man must enjoy the sacramental wine a little too much. The lines of the faithful formed up to the Altar, and one by one, they drank from a golden cup and ate a biscuit. Magnus sat quietly in the pew with no real desire to participate in the ritual, but once again, the captain seated next to him insisted. Magnus patiently stood in line with the faithful to gain a blessing. He noticed the bishop's eyes glint maliciously as he gracefully offered the bejeweled cup to Magnus. He took a small sip and a dry biscuit and hurried back to his seat in the pews.

After the service, Magnus was forced to tour the abbey accompanied by two armed guards and an unfriendly monk who didn't say much and seemed to have no personality, but Magnus did notice that the man walked with a pronounced limp. For the rest of the day, they climbed countless stairs, walked through bunk halls and large galleries that were being vacated by the troops, and toured much of the farming areas surrounding the buildings. Soldiers were everywhere in the compound, busily packing equipment and preparing to move out the next day. Gazing past the village, he could see several large ships at anchor in the harbor. Golden sheaves of grain stood everywhere in the fields, awaiting the threshing floor. He realized that this was a very prosperous parish with plenty of provisions for the coming winter months. Unfortunately, he never spotted Osric in the groups of monks strolling through the grounds and hallways. *Where could he be?* He wondered.

Later that evening, he was ushered into the bishop's massive private office. It was a huge room lined with stone buttresses, smooth plastered stone walls, and a huge fireplace blazing on a relatively warm night. Magnus couldn't help but think it was a few degrees warmer than Hades. The bishop sat at a single large table in the center of the room. He rose from his chair as Magnus was escorted into the great hall by two guards and forced to kneel. In the flickering light of the hearth, the man's shriveled face looked sinister. He welcomed Magnus with a wide, toothy grin, but Magnus saw no warmth in his eyes. "What do you think of our edifice?" he asked.

"It's very impressive; you have done a wonderful work here," Magnus said as he tried to stroke the man's ego.

"The church does good work everywhere, young man. Father Martin should have taught you that in your formative years!" he said with a mocking expression.

"I do know that to be factual," Magnus replied, lowering his eyes.

"What do you think of me, young man?" A thin smile played across his face.

"Sir, I don't know you, but you put God first as the leader of this edifice, and for that I respect you."

"You answer well, for I am the leader and builder of this region. We were fortunate enough to be able to trade the fruit of our labors for a stake to this land and re-purposed building materials inside of these fortress walls. Now tomorrow, when the troops depart, it will all be mine to build even greater. I have long admired Pachomius the Great, who founded a monastery in the year 321 in Tabennisi, Egypt. Did you know that Pachomius set up a formal organization for the monks? Before that time, monastics were living in individual huts or caves. He created the communal organization, in which monastics live together and share their property in common under the leadership of an abbot or abbess. Pachomius bore the burden of the community's administrative issues himself. His community called him Abba, as 'father' in Hebrew— from which the title of Abbot was derived. I have assumed that title and am currently endeavoring to build the grandest abbey in the entire world here! You see what I've created so far, and I know that our possessions will continue to grow." He took a long breath and continued. "What I do not need in this region is anyone who dares to deny church doctrine. That would foster conflict and subversion amongst our monks and our present and future parishioners I will not tolerate that - do I make myself clear?"

Magnus was looking away, considering a parable about avarice, **"And he said unto them, Take heed, and beware of covetousness: for a man's life consisteth not in the abundance of the things which he possesseth. And he spake a parable unto them, saying, The ground of a certain rich man brought forth plentifully: And he thought within himself, saying, What shall I do because I have no room where to bestow my fruits? And he said, This will I do: I will pull down my barns, and build greater, and there will I bestow all my fruits and my goods. And I will say to my soul, Soul, thou hast much goods laid up for many years; take thine ease, eat, drink, and be merry. But God said unto him, Thou fool, this night thy soul shall be required of thee: then whose shall those things be, which thou hast provided? So is he that layeth up treasure for himself, and is not rich toward God."**26 "Yes sir," replied Magnus softly.

"What do you think the blood of Jesus is, young man?" the bishop rasped.

It was just what Magnus had feared would happen. Osric had presented his ideas, and the bishop immediately knew they were a dangerous and revolutionary threat to his power; even if he understood some of the ideas to be true, he could not permit his subjects to consider praying to God themselves without the aid of priests.

"What do you think God is? What do you think the flesh of Jesus is, young man? Is it the bread we shared this morning?" The man pressed the question.

With a loud sigh, Magnus decided to answer truthfully. "It is said that no flesh shall see God and live, so I think that drinking the blood and eating the flesh was a metaphor for following Christ's pathway in healing the sick and raising the dead as he instructed us to do, **"Heal the sick, cleanse the lepers, raise the dead, cast out devils: freely ye have received, freely give."** 27 Then he added to it, **"And the Lord said unto Moses, I will do this thing also that thou hast spoken: for thou hast found grace in my sight, and I know thee by name. And he said, I beseech thee, shew me thy glory. And he said, I will make all my goodness pass before thee, and I will proclaim the name of the Lord before thee; and will be gracious to whom I will be gracious, and will shew mercy on whom I will shew mercy. And he said, Thou canst not see my face: for there shall no man see me, and live."**28

"Our Lord Jesus Christ spoke to you directly?" the little bishop's eyes widened in mock amazement. "Perhaps like he spoke to Saul?"

Magnus remembered the words of Saul (Saint Paul). **"At midday, O king, I saw in the way a light from heaven, above the brightness of the sun, shining round about me and them which journeyed with me. And when we were all fallen to the earth, I heard a voice speaking unto me, and saying in the Hebrew tongue, Saul, Saul, why persecutest thou me? it is hard for thee to kick against the**

pricks. And I said, Who art thou, Lord? And he said I am Jesus whom thou persecutest."29 "He spoke to his disciples, and I was taught by Bishop Martin, who followed him with healing works." Magnus replied quietly.

The bishop's eyes narrowed as he spat out his next words. "I've never believed the lies told in legends about Martin or that anyone other than Jesus and his disciples should attempt spiritual healing. So then, are you saying that I am not a true follower of Jesus?"

Magnus wisely chose not to answer.

"Again, I ask, what do you think of me?"

"I do not judge others; I only wish to express God's will." Magnus murmured, keeping his thoughts to himself, **"Ye judge after the flesh; I judge no man. And yet if I judge, my judgment is true: for I am not alone, but I and the Father that sent me."**30

"I believe you know my cousin, the present Bishop of Tours?" the man queried.

Magnus felt an involuntary shiver quake his spine. *This diminutive clergyman was related to his tormentor?*

"He sent me a dispatch which described you and mentioned your sudden disappearance from his region. He does not seem to hold you in very high esteem."

"I left Gaul because I feared persecution..." Magnus stammered.

"I understand," the little man said as he held up his hand for silence. "I've recently spoken several times with your new friend Osric. He explained quite a number of your fanciful ideas in great detail to me! He has a very simple mind and is easily impressed with fables of healings and spiritual realms," he said as he slowly waved his hands over his head like a mystic. Pausing, he crouched, putting his hands on his knees, and looked Magnus directly in the eyes. "Unfortunately, I feel you Gnostics would destroy our church if we allow you to spread your venomous theories of anyone being able to communicate with God." Leaning closer, he continued. "I have a word for your radical ideas young man, heresy! I see now that my cousin was correct in his assessment of you! Did you intend to bewitch all of my monks with this nonsense, and do you think that we have lost our true mission of following Christ?"

Magnus fought to maintain his composure as the man's spittle, tinged with foul breath, sprayed his face. "Yes," he finally answered defiantly, as a slight grin creased his lips.

"Do you think that's funny? Take him!" shrieked the bishop as he lost every bit of poise he had maintained and turned away, enraged.

Magnus tried to recover. "No sir, I only…" Then a heavy lance struck him in the head, and the world exploded in a shower of stars.

Magnus awoke shivering on a cold, filthy wooden floor. He reached up and winced as he touched the mound of dried blood in his hair. The guard had nearly crushed his skull. *Good thing he had a thick one,* he supposed and grinned again. He was in pain, but he definitely would remember that the little despot had no sense of humor. He was locked in a square stone room with a rough wooden floor. There were no furnishings except for a foul-smelling wooden bucket and a small pile of filthy rags and straw that he knew was the restroom. A large round hole served as a window. It was almost three meters from the floor and was nearly a meter in diameter. The window was also the source of the frigid morning air. The ceiling was rough wood supported by heavy wooden beams. He guessed that he must be incarcerated in the church's bell tower since he had noticed only one round window on the grounds.

Struggling to roll onto his knees and get up, he almost passed out. The world was still spinning as he stood upright and leaned against the wall. *What have I gotten myself into now?* he wondered as he crossed his arms, trying to stay warm. When he thrust his cold hands into his clothing, he knew he had been searched. The coins that he had kept in a small pouch were gone. Thank God he had the foresight to give Cynde the scroll. His heart ached as a flood of feelings about missing her assailed him.

Hours later, the sun had finally risen high enough to warm

the room to a tolerable level. Magnus paced the small confine as he prayed to God for guidance and freedom. He was careful not to trip over the waste bucket as he strode back and forth. He looked at the sun's rays streaming through the window and decided to try looking out of it. Running from the other side of the room, he was able to leap up and grasp the edge. He struggled to climb up the rough stone wall and thrust his arms through the opening, frantically grabbing onto the rocky exterior. His heart sank into his belly as he drew himself onto his elbows. It looked like the only escape from this window would be to another dimension after a swift trip to the rocky courtyard six stories below.

It was a beautiful view, though, and he gazed out at the main buildings of the church. He saw a walled courtyard with a few shade trees and the quiet village with a harbor beyond. Several large ships still lay at anchor as they awaited the legionnaires. He watched the inhabitants go about their business until his arms began to cramp. Sliding reluctantly back down into his cell, he turned his thoughts back to prayer and shouted out loud. "God, tell me what to do."

"Magnus, over here in the floor," a faint voice replied.

Chapter 10

Revelation

Magnus looked quickly around the room until he noticed a hole the size of his thumb next to the wall. He crouched down on his knees above the knothole in a floorboard. "Who are you?"

"It is Osric my friend. Yes, I should not have been so headstrong and listened to your warning." The booming voice drifted up through the small hole.

"Are you hurt? What happened?" Magnus asked as he stretched out prone on the floor to hear better.

"My pride is definitely bruised, but my commitment to the Lord stands strong," the monk announced defiantly. "I returned to the village and found Cynde in a group of women doing chores and trading gossip. I told them about you being an agent of the bishop and under direct orders not to harm loathsome drunks while secretly searching for the Picts. Gazing at the bright blue sky, I decided that I should go back to the monastery, so I started walking to the next hamlet. I had almost dawdled too long, and the glowing edges of the sun were retreating from the sky as a small huddle of conical roofs appeared on the horizon. Shuffling down the well-worn dirt path to the village, I reflected the words of Jesus, **"And these signs shall follow them that believe; In my name shall they cast out devils; they shall speak with new tongues; They shall take up serpents; and if they drink any deadly**

thing, it shall not hurt them; they shall lay hands on the sick, and they shall recover."31 It felt as though the words were palpable, solid, and speaking just to me as I hurried through the bright golden sunshine of the afternoon. It didn't take long for me to glimpse a small huddle of conical roofs. The smell of cooking fires touched my nostrils, and I realized how hungry I was. As I sauntered into the village of Clitson, I was assailed by a throng of scruffy kids who surrounded me and pulled violently on my robes for attention. Smiling broadly, I lifted two of the smallest ones up and cradled them in my arms. The other children ran ahead, shouting, "Osric is here!" I, too, was feeling like a little child in the realm of Spirit as I considered the following statement, **"And Jesus called a little child unto him, and set him in the midst of them, And said, Verily I say unto you, Except ye be converted, and become as little children, ye shall not enter into the kingdom of heaven. Whosoever therefore shall humble himself as this little child, the same is greatest in the kingdom of heaven. And whoso shall receive one such little child in my name receiveth me."**32 I proceeded on toward a shabby hut at the other end of the community. A white-haired lady beamed and held her arms wide as I approached. She was an older widow whom I have ministered to for years. After a tender hug, she began cooking an extra portion of her meal for me. As I ate, I tried to explain some of your new spiritual ideas to her, but she just smiled blankly at me, like a mother trying to calm an overly imaginative child. I finally gave up and was feeling somewhat defeated as I settled down to sleep.

"But what happened, why are you imprisoned?" Magnus interrupted.

"I'm getting to that, the next morning I hastened towards the abbey to share my newfound knowledge with the other brothers. I remember being grateful that you shared the elusive keys to life's myriad questions with me. Jostling along, I maintained my customary sluggish gait."

Magnus heard him laugh loudly.

"I felt as if the love of God was enveloping me, and I struggled to recollect all my experiences from these last glorious days. I also thought about your urgings for caution but then dismissed them completely. I was not a child and not about to hide the Truth. That was my downfall."

"What happened at Seaford Downs?" Magnus hesitantly asked,

"I watched the sun settle slowly in the western sky and realized that I would barely arrive in time for the evening meal. How should I address my brothers in Christ? Always the assembled monks ate in silence and then retired until vespers, the evening prayers. It was unheard of for a friar to address the entire room. If I broke the tradition, though, I would have the attention of everyone during dinner, and I felt this was vital information for the brotherhood."

"Tell me you waited," Magnus urged.

Osric didn't respond but continued. "I thought, what about the bishop? Normally, he eats secluded in his chambers. Should I wait to gain an audience with the Holy Father before sharing my news with the others? I finally decided that I shouldn't because I couldn't contain myself that long. Besides, I was sure the Abbot-Bishop would be so grateful to receive the good news in any form. I crested a hill, and spotted the abbey and fort framed by a spectacular blazing sunset. Nodding greetings to various brothers, I hurried through the maze of stucco hallways to my monastic cell. Once there, I washed the day's road dust off with my pitcher and basin, put on a clean robe, and headed off toward the dining hall. The sun was very low on the horizon and waning rose-colored light from the ten large windows washed throughout the gallery as I entered. The other friars were gathering bowls of stew and chunks of coarse brown bread from a large serving table next to the kitchen. I worked my way through the lines of benches to the far end of the room and sat down next to a large unlit fireplace. I was far too excited to eat. Once everyone was seated and dining quietly, I clambered up onto an unoccupied table. 'Brothers!' I yelled. All their eyes turned toward me with mixtures of fear and anger, their sacred silence having been broken. 'You all know me, and I humbly beg you to forgive this unprecedented outburst, but I need to speak to you all in one gathering.'"

Magnus sighed, *could this story get any worse?*

The monk continued, "I told them in the past few days, I had spoken with a man who was taught and healed by the great Bishop Martin of Tours, and now my life has changed forever. I was a skeptic, and that I first wanted to prosecute you as a heretic, but that you prove your faith with your works as did our master Jesus Christ! You should have heard the uneasy murmur that filled the hall, Magnus."

"I told you to keep it to yourself," was all the boy could say.

"'Brothers, I ask only that you listen to what I experienced, and I'm sure that you, too, will begin to understand God!' Suddenly a cry of blasphemy roared from the back of the room. 'No, the truth about God and man!' I retorted and continued. 'Jesus once told a heathen woman: **'It is not meet to take the children's bread and cast it to dogs.'** My brothers, that woman told our master, **'Truth, Lord: yet the dogs eat of the crumbs which fall from their masters' table.'**33 Do you all remember that encounter?' Then I recited the full passage, **"And, behold, a woman of Canaan came out of the same coasts, and cried unto him, saying, Have mercy on me, O Lord, thou son of David; my daughter is grievously vexed with a devil. But he answered her, not a word. And his disciples came and besought him, saying, Send her away; for she crieth after us. But he answered and said, I am not sent but unto the lost sheep of the house of Israel. Then came she and worshipped him, saying, Lord, help me. But he answered and said, It is not meet to take the children's bread and to cast it to dogs. And she said, Truth, Lord: yet the dogs eat of the crumbs which fall from their masters' table. Then Jesus answered and said unto her, O woman, great is thy faith: be it unto thee even as thou wilt. And her**

daughter was made whole from that very hour."33 We, too, are fed by the immortal ideas that he left us. In just this past day, I have come to understand that all of the heathen, and those of us who see this world as real or who look to the hereafter with the limited concept of God – worship the same God, a false God."

"Osric, you didn't actually say that?"

"I did and the response was, 'We don't worship as heathens.' Then I said, 'No, my friends, but this man named Magnus of Rau enlightened me with Martin's spiritual insights - that our God is not of this world like our great way shower stated, **'Jesus answered, My kingdom is not of this world: if my kingdom were of this world, then would my servants fight, that I should not be delivered to the Jews: but now is my kingdom not from hence.'**34, but God is still always here and all-powerful. Not in the way that this mortal world views power, but true, substantial qualities like Life, Love, and Truth that are expressed in our everyday experience. We need to leave the darkness of this world's limited deities and join in worshiping the one infinite spiritual God.' Then disaster struck."

"The bishop?" Magnus queried.

"Yes, at that critical point in my sermon to the faithful, I hear his crackling voice. 'What's the meaning of this?' He was followed by several of his personal guards. The little man looked furious and was visibly shaking. I said, 'Your Holiness, I beg your forgiveness, but I needed to tell…,' but he held up his hand and stopped me." The monk continued in a nasal whine. "You need to say nothing! You have violated the sanctity of this evening meal with your misguided rantings. Guards, escort this unruly monk back to my office!"

"My friend, I am so sorry." Magnus's voice broke in.

"I'm not," Osric answered abruptly. "I stood up for God. I was led back to the bishop's palace with the guards prodding and shoving me. Then they forced me to kneel on the flagstone floor as if in supplication. My knees were throbbing in pain when the little man eventually arrived, carrying a worn leather pouch. 'What say you for yourself, monk?' the bishop demanded as he caressed the pouch. I swear Magnus, I tried to be diplomatic, I said, My Lord, I first beg your forgiveness for not directing this matter to you alone, but I believed that my good news dictated an immediate announcement to all the brothers. 'Pray tell me what good news that would be, my son?' The wizened little man's eyes were sparkling but with a cruel glint that I noticed. 'Could it possibly be news about a stranger in our midst who is preaching about spiritual healing?' I said, yes, exactly your eminence, but how did you know? 'Do you forget that I sit on God's right hand? I know everything because he knows everything.' 'Then why have you not blessed us with these words?' I asked confused. 'Because they are lies!' retorted the little twit."

"Magnus stifled a contemptuous giggle."

"I was stunned. I asked, 'Are you sure?' He went into a long tirade. 'How dare you question my veracity? I alone rule this abbey! I am master here! You will not interrogate me!' I said, 'No, my lord, please. You know that I am a faithful servant. What do you wish of me?' Even as I was pleading, these words sprang into my thoughts, **"Neither be ye called masters: for one is your master, even Christ. But he that is greatest among you shall be your servant. And whosoever shall exalt himself shall be abased, and he that shall humble himself shall be exalted."**[35]

Magnus spoke, "Those words are true, my friend."

"Then he opened the pouch and showed me a formal communication from his cousin, the newly installed Bishop of Tours, that said a dangerous heretic escaped his grasp and fled to this island. He told me that you are a threat to this community, to this region, and to the church worldwide. He said, 'Help me bait a trap for this miscreant, and together we'll bring him to justice. Afterward, when you have served your penance and recanted your affiliation with this vagabond, I will pardon you, and all will be forgiven, my son.' I tell you Magnus that random ideas suddenly flooded my mind. I felt blessed by the ideas you gave freely, I felt strengthened by the conversations we shared. The insights I gleaned in those brief encounters have bonded us together in an inexplicable way, my friend. You awakened something deep inside of me that is the opposite of the dark thoughts that had seemed to permeate and assault every aspect of my previous series of miserable life experiences."

Magnus couldn't hold back his tears any longer and vigorously swiped a sleeve across his eyes.

"You told me to nurture the concepts rather than proclaim them. Suddenly I realized that my own stubborn impetuosity had brought me to this critical juncture, and I couldn't suppress a small grin, even as I made a quick, solemn vow to God that I would never disavow the Truth.

I think the bishop thought that I was accepting his gracious offer, he smiled widely and thrust his ring hand forward, expecting me to kiss the large red stone and seal the bond. His wide smile evaporated when he sensed my decision. Now I wait to collect my glory in Heaven."

"Osric, you don't mean he is going to kill you?" Magnus cried out.

"Shhh, I hear guards coming up the steps. I'll talk to you later, my friend, and thanks for everything. I sincerely wish I had heeded your wise warnings."

Chapter 11

The Martyr

Magnus listened intently for a long moment. Then he heard a door squeak open in the cell below. Osric bellowed, "You certainly took your time. I've been bored to death in here," and then his booming laugh faded as he was led away.

Some minutes later, a rusty bolt slid back, and the heavy door swung open, revealing three barrel-chested guards filling the stairway. "Here's your lunch!" the first one snarled and dropped a bucket while almost spilling the contents.

The guard behind him threw a tall, splintered wooden stool into the room. "So, you can see the festivities this afternoon!" Laughing, they slammed the door shut and bolted it again.

What did they mean? Magnus wondered. He grabbed the stool, stood up on it, and peered out of his window for a long time. Columns of soldiers were marching out of the fort's main gate and down to the village. The ships still sat quietly in the harbor, and he could see small boats ferrying soldiers in gleaming armor out to them. Other than that, nothing in the view had changed noticeably.

He spent the next hours alternating between looking out the window and forcing down the rancid gruel dinner. Finally, he climbed up to the window and saw a procession of monks, along with a few guards, entering the courtyard. He saw one of the monks was being led by the others. A thick rope was tied around his wrists. It was Osric! They led him to a large tree in the center of the courtyard and, throwing the end of the rope over a stout limb, pulled as a group until his feet could barely reach the ground. Then his brown robe was ripped away by the guards until his mid-section was bare in the sun.

Despair swelled in Magnus as he prayed urgently to help his friend. *Father, please! He doesn't deserve this. He's good!*

As he watched, Magnus saw the little bishop arrive and address the group. The man's scratchy voice drifted up to his ears. "For the unconscionable crime of heresy and blasphemy toward God and his loyal servants, I condemn you to be flogged until you recant your words. Do you understand my charges?"

Magnus watched Osric closely and saw him nod slightly. "Do you retract your vile statements?" the man continued.

"No, brothers, listen, it's true; God is Good. He…" The crack of the cat-o-nine-tails stopped the monk's proclamation mid-sentence.

Magnus saw the bishop make a motion for the guard to continue the assault and watched helplessly as dark red lines formed around Osric's ample midsection, accompanied by the big man's shrieks of pain.

"Stop! Osric, don't suffer — they're just words!" Magnus shouted down from the tower. All eyes turned toward him, and the guard with the whip paused to catch his breath. Magnus could see Osric's broad face, flushed with exertion, break into a wide smile.

"Words worth living and dying for my friend!" he said in that great booming voice and then laughed loudly.

The little tyrant was clenching his withered fists in a blind rage. That bitter old man was going to do something drastic to regain control of the situation. Motioning to the guard to continue, he turned his back on Magnus. Magnus couldn't watch and fell to the floor of his cell, racked with despair.

The rhythmic whipping began again in earnest, and the monk's protests of pain rose and fell. Osric's cries seemed to fill his cell. Magnus tried but couldn't block out the noise to pray. He couldn't shut out the sounds of his friend's torment, and hot tears rolled off his face in torrents. After what seemed like an eternity, the monk's weakened moans dwindled to silence, and Magnus knew that his friend Osric had been martyred.

Later, Magnus awoke shivering violently in the damp night air. His head felt like it had split wide open from the hours of anguish he had endured. *Was he guilty of causing his friend's death with his words?* Praying about it, he eventually decided. *No, it had been the monk's own decision to defy the orders of the bishop.*

One thing he understood clearly, *he had to escape, or he would suffer a similar fate at the hands of that little, wrinkled egomaniac!* Slowly he forced himself to calm his hatred and fear of the situation, remembering the passage, **"For though we walk in the flesh, we do not war after the flesh: (For the weapons of our warfare are not carnal, but mighty through God to the pulling down of strong holds;) Casting down imaginations, and every high thing that exalteth itself against the knowledge of God, and bringing into captivity every thought to the obedience of Christ;"**[36] *God, tell me what to do,* he struggled to pray, until he once again, fell asleep…

He didn't feel much better when he awoke the next morning determined to find a way to escape. He decided to examine his surroundings methodically to find a weakness in his prison. The door was solid oak and bolted securely from the outside. The walls were fitted stone. The masons that built this tower had been skilled, and the rocks were laid tight. Magnus pried and poked at every joint he could reach until his fingers were bleeding, and he sank to the floor in another wave of despair.

Somehow though, he couldn't remain on the floor in defeat. He stood up. Something was telling him to move and investigate the window view again. Obediently he followed the urgings. Using his stool, he clambered up to the window again. Looking out, he saw that the troop ships were gone from the harbor, and he briefly hoped that the merciless Captain Claudius was susceptible to seasickness. Magnus then squirmed around until he could sit with some difficulty and look straight up the tower wall. It looked smooth and unscalable until he noticed a small hole in the mortar, a little larger than his thumb, directly above his window. Excited, he squirmed back to a prone position, leaned out farther than he had dared previously. There he saw his escape path. Holes that the masons had used to anchor their scaffolding as they set their stones were spaced every few feet.

He pulled himself back into his cell and jumped off the stool. Then he removed his tunic and tied a sleeve around the leg of the stool. *Tonight, he would escape.* He smiled as he thought about it. The Lord hadn't leveled his prison with an earthquake as he pondered Saint Paul's experience. **"And at midnight Paul and Silas prayed and sang praises unto God: and the prisoners heard them. And suddenly there was a great earthquake so that the foundations of the prison were shaken: and immediately all the doors were opened, and everyone's bands were loosed."**37 He was sure that many of the monks would see his sudden disappearance as a miracle rather than sleight of hand. *Too bad Osric hadn't been able to slip away before his gruesome fate.*

Magnus waited until he heard the haunting sounds of the monk's evening prayers drifting up from below. Quietly he grasped the free arm of his tied tunic, stepped on the stool, and raised himself to the window. As he peered out, he saw no movement in the courtyard below. It was a dark night, shadowed beneath dense clouds, with just enough light to locate the holes in the masonry, exactly what he needed.

He pulled himself up and through the opening so that he was sitting with his legs inside the cell. Then he lifted the stool up, untied his tunic, and put it on. He used both hands, wrenched two legs of the old oak stool free, and stuck them inside his shirt.

He let the remnants of the stool fall soundlessly into the pile of dirty rags that he had arranged below the window.

Grabbing one of the legs from his shirt, he reached out as far as he could, found the first hole, and shoved the hard oak leg into it. Then he gingerly stepped on it, testing his weight. It held. Mouthing a silent prayer, he grabbed the other leg from his shirt and swung unsteadily out of the window. Hanging by one precarious peg and then another, he began his laborious descent.

Several times he stopped and hung by both arms, trying to search and listen for any movement below. Hearing nothing but the muffled chants of the monks, he continued down until he was about twice his height from the ground. Blindly, he dragged the stool leg repeatedly across the face of the wall seeking another hole. Exhaustion crept in, and he decided that the masons must have patched these holes for aesthetics. Gathering his courage, he kicked away from the wall and simultaneously pulled the other leg out as he dropped straight down onto rough flagstones.

Magnus allowed his left leg to collapse when he hit and rolled over several times to dissipate the force of falling. Clambering to his feet, he tucked the two stool legs back into his shirt and sprinted as soundlessly as he could toward the fort's outer wall. A squat oak tree was growing next to it, and he climbed up until he grabbed a lower branch extending over the elevated walkway that ran inside the defensive wall. Hand over hand, he moved until he could drop onto the walkway. Quickly rolling himself over the wall, he hastily fell into the dark shadows outside the compound, landing beside one of the guards that had led Osric into the courtyard.

The sentry's face registered surprise only for a moment, then his hand was on his sword. It sliced the air only inches from Magnus's nose before he could react. Immediately he dove to the ground and quickly rolled several feet away. He was unarmed except for the two stool legs tucked in his shirt, which he quickly retrieved as he scrambled upright. The guard's next move was a thrust, which Magnus parried to the side with one leg as he delivered an overhand blow to the man's helmet with the other. The stool leg wasn't heavy enough to do any real damage, but it had to hurt. Magnus looked into the man's eyes and realized that all it had done was make the guard furious. The sentry was done playing around now and held his weapon with both hands, raising it over his head to deliver a death blow.

Magnus stood with his back against the rough stone wall, looking desperately for a way to escape. As the sword arched down, Magnus lunged forward, spun past the guard, planted his hand on the man's back, and pushed as hard as he could. The momentum of the heavy swinging sword helped carry the guard off balance, and he crashed into the rock wall headfirst. This time the man crumpled to the ground as Magnus dashed toward the safety of the darkened village streets. *I can't believe that move worked again!* As he remembered the life and death struggle with his soldier/tormentor on the stone bridge in Gaul.

Chapter 12

Flight!

Magnus moved as silently as he could, creeping through alleys and staying away from open windows and doors. Then a neighborhood dog on its nightly rounds gave chase. Thankfully he didn't encounter anyone else on his short trek through the town. He did, however, hear the sleepy residents swearing oaths blindly at the barking mutt as he ran toward the river in a futile effort to elude the dog. Then he heard a bell ringing at the abbey announcing his escape. Without hesitation, he ran the length of the nearest dock and dove headfirst into the dark water.

Icy fluid closed over him, and bitter cold stabbed at every pore in his body. He swam through the liquid darkness as far as he could before surfacing for air. Turning back toward the village, he could see several figures emerging from their homes. The dog was still barking at the end of the pier. Magnus knew he needed to find a safe haven before the locals organized, and he started paddling in earnest toward the opposite shore.

Water poured out of his clothes as he struggled up the muddy riverbank with his teeth chattering. He clawed at the sparse weed clumps to prevent himself from sliding back into the mire. Finally, as he gained firmer footing, he rushed toward the nearest tree line. Just as he reached the forest, he saw a rowboat filled with people leaving a wharf on the opposite shore. The hunt was on!

Branches and briars scraped at him as Magnus moved swiftly through the darkened woods. He caught a glimpse of the North Star and hurried eastward deeper into the wilderness. Hours later, a limb finally snagged his shin. He pitched forward and fell heavily atop a large, rotten log that burst apart into clumps of decaying sawdust. He stifled a sneeze that might betray him as he scrambled to his feet and pushed on. The sky had turned opaque now, and a light rain was falling sporadically. He walked for several hours more, trying to keep the wind at his back for a general sense of direction since he couldn't see any stars.

Peering into the gloom, he noticed a large fallen tree ahead of him. It was leaning almost parallel to the ground. He slowed his pace as he walked toward it, looking at its large mass of branches and hearing running water. Erosion had weakened its base to a point where the tree had toppled across a creek. Sliding down the bank to investigate, he found that the tree's main trunk had fallen atop a smaller ravine and formed a cave large enough for him to crawl into. He dragged in some larger limbs that had broken off and laid them down in line with the ravine. He then laid smaller limbs perpendicular to the large ones to create a wooden mat over the mud and trickling water. Magnus then gathered armfuls of dead leaves that blanketed the ground beneath the broken limbs and filled the little grotto. It was starting to rain heavily as he burrowed into the pile. He smiled; he was safe and hidden by foliage. The rain would conceal his tracks. He thanked God with a very short prayer for his deliverance and fell asleep.

When Magnus awoke, he was surprised to find himself dry and comfortable, although he could hear the gurgle of last night's rainwater as it traveled beneath his bed of leaves through the ravine. He crept quietly out of his hastily constructed lair and searched for signs of pursuers, but found he was alone in a moist but sunny forest.

His belly growled in protest. Finding food was an immediate need. Then he would plan his escape from this dreadful land of savages and despots. He began scavenging for anything edible and found a few stale nuts on the forest floor but little else. Finally, hours later, he stumbled into a meadow that lay hidden in a small valley between two tree lines. The ruins of an ancient roundhouse sat at the edge of the forest across a small creek. As he looked around, he saw stalks of wheat scattered between the wild grasses and dried weeds. *This must have been a farm field,* he reasoned.

Magnus removed his tunic and spread it on the ground. The air was cool after the rain, but not cold. The sunshine warmed his back as he worked at both eating and gathering seed heads onto his shirt. He picked for an hour until he had a large pile of grains and had eaten his fill. Then he wrapped and tied his bundle and crossed the stream to search the old ruins for any usable items.

Magnus crawled over a small pile of rubble that had been the main doorway. Their upright supports had failed, and the rotting roof timbers lay flattened at odd angles like the spokes of a giant wheel. Scraps of thatch were everywhere and obscured most of the floor, but Magnus could see that much of the previous resident's belongings lay in matted, musty piles around a central fire pit. Most of the hides and wooden utensils had succumbed to the elements long ago, but several clay pots were relatively undamaged. These he transferred his grain heads into. He then began to search the dwelling methodically by pitching the moldy piles of thatch outside the wall, and digging into the decaying mass beneath with a broken tree branch.

There was a lump under a bone-white, mostly hairless deer hide that was lying in a spot farthest away from the door. As he pulled it up, he gasped at death's grisly smile. A partially mummified human form grinned back at him. He sheepishly smiled back while thinking, *Well, here is at least one soul who passed on peacefully in this land!* He was about to replace the hide when he noticed an elaborate golden torc draped across the form's shrunken breast. The necklace was a large plate festooned with intricate leaf and animal designs. "Something this beautiful shouldn't remain hidden, my silent friend," Magnus said quietly, wiping away the thick coating of dust and gently lifting it from around the shrunken neck. It was heavy, and Magnus was sure that it was solid gold. He turned it over in the waning afternoon light but saw no additional markings.

The shadows were getting longer, and Magnus realized that further investigation of this remote homestead would have to wait. He quickly grabbed his tree limb and swept his footprints away on the dirt floor. If his pursuers discovered this abandoned farm, he didn't want them to know that he was in the area. Gathering up his grain pots, another empty pot for water from the stream, and the golden torc, he headed for his hideout.

He had almost waited too long. Shadows crawled quickly up the trees and across the ground as he searched desperately through the hills for his refuge. In the twilight, he finally saw the downed oak tree and burrowed deeply into the pile of leaves beneath it. *Next time he would mark a trail,* he decided. Grabbing some seed heads from one of the pots, he rolled them around in his callused palms until the grains came free.

Munching on handfuls of grain and drinking from his water jug, Magnus reflected on his busy day. Last night he was pursued as a heretic, hungry, penniless, and without shelter. Now he was fed, warm, and cozy in his retreat. He also had in his possession a golden necklace. He wondered, *What will tomorrow bring?* as these words scrolled through his head. **"But my God shall supply all your need according to his riches in glory by Christ Jesus."**38

The following day Magnus awoke to the muffled sounds of people talking. He hoped that he hadn't given away his position by snoring. As he lay motionless, he could hear them moving around. They were probably sitting on the trunk over his head, but he couldn't tell what they were saying. *He'd been careful to walk only on the rocks in the stream, but had he left muddy footprints?* He quietly cursed himself for being too careless the night before.

Eventually, he couldn't hear the voices anymore, but he continued to lie still. He imagined that they had been legionnaires who were waiting to arrest him. Gradually, as he felt the day warm, curiosity subdued his sense of fear. He crawled out of his cave, crept from beneath the branches, and stood up. Then he remembered: *Two days ago, was the soldiers' departure date. Surely none of them would dare defy the emperor's orders to leave this land.* Thankfully, he was alone.

Searching, he found three sets of footprints. The interlopers had followed the creek bed and probably only stopped to rest at his tree before continuing. Not knowing who the men were, Magnus decided that it might be risky to venture into the woods and possibly be spotted, so he stayed hidden in his pile of leaves for the next couple of days.

On the third day, the weather had turned cloudy with light rain showers that raised a dense mist through the forest. Magnus imagined that no one would be searching for him in such low visibility conditions, so he decided to revisit the remote homestead. First, he gathered a large pile of similar-sized stones from the streambed. These, he shoved awkwardly into his tunic and marched off toward the clearing. Each time he counted ten paces, he dropped one of the rocks to mark a path back to his hideaway. When he reached the clearing, he dropped the remaining rocks near a large, forked tree he would easily recognize among the others and headed straight for the ruined dwelling.

After several hours of scavenging through the musty remnants, Magnus found only a few useful items, including a rusty axe head and two more usable clay pots. Other things, such as a corroded iron sickle and two hoe heads, crumbled apart in his fingers as he pulled them from the dirt. Finally, he reluctantly moved toward the mummified remains and began probing the surrounding area. Dragging his staff through loose dirt next to the wall, it hit something. Getting down on his knees, he dug with a broken potsherd until he unearthed a large bundle of hides bound with leather thongs. Carefully, Magnus unwrapped the stiffened animal skins and gazed upon the prized possessions of the deceased warrior.

A long sword with an ornately carved hilt lay encased in a

leather-wrapped, weathered wooden scabbard. Next to it was a dagger in a brass sheath. There was a bronze Celtic war helmet complete with two curved metal horns and decorated with elaborate carvings. A round bronze shield covered with similar designs lay beneath it. The remaining items included a small, stylized bronze figurine holding a spear and a shield and a well-preserved leather bag filled with handfuls of ancient gold coins showing warriors on horseback. *This man had not only been a warrior but a very rich one.*

Magnus walked unsteadily away from the ruins of a solitary soul's life, struggling under the weight of the dead man's treasure. Magnus felt confident that God had led him to this isolated tract of land. He had been well-fed on his last visit. Now, he was well-armed and abundantly rich by peasant standards, without any guilt for disturbing the man's cache of valuables. There was obviously no one else to mourn the old man's passing or to care for his worldly possessions, but one issue was bothering him. Pausing at the creek to fill the pots with water, Magnus pondered the question. *The Celts are a very social society. Why had this one died alone?*

Magnus worked hard to restore the corroded weapons over the next couple of days. He rubbed the edges across damp stones in the creek beside his hiding place. Back and forth, he scraped until the steel was covered in a thick, rusty liquid. Then he wiped them dry in clumps of grass and repeated the process. Eventually, Magnus was rewarded with the sun's glint reflecting off nearly every portion of the steel blades. The axe head was too heavily pitted to shine, but he did raise a keen edge to it and fitted it onto a whittled oak handle that he shaped from a dead branch.

Now he wondered what he should do. His prayers over the next couple of days didn't reveal a salutary solution. He didn't have enough provisions stored to survive the coming winter, although he might be able to kill enough venison if he fashioned a bow and some arrows. Worse was the fact that he couldn't start a fire to cook anything without revealing his presence with the smoke, and he didn't relish dining on raw flesh for the next four or five months. He also desperately wanted to see Cynde and his new friends at Hastell Cenllys, to at least say goodbye before he fled from this isle. He finally decided, without a discernable sign from the Lord, to begin his return to the village in the morning. *Perhaps Anut could travel with him to an eastern kingdom where he'd find passage back to Saxony and then trek onward into the barbarous regions of the East. Or maybe it would be safer for him in Hibernia, (Ireland), across the sea to the west.* His plans held no promise of a long life, but they prolonged the possibility of happiness.

After another night's sleep buried safely in the leaf pile, Magnus prepared to depart for the village. Thinking he might need to return to this sanctuary again, he decided to leave some items hidden beneath the tree trunk. Filling his pockets first, he sealed the remaining grain into the pots with a thick mixture of mud and grass, forming air-tight corks. Along with the pots, he left the axe, helmet, and shield. He decided to take the golden torc as a gift for Cynde and put it on beneath his shirt. After fastening the sword and dagger to his belt, he stuffed the bag holding the coins, along with the figurine that he had decided to give to Dwig, into his tunic and set off toward the morning sun.

He supposed that the village would lie to the northeast of his campsite. With the sun showing through the colorful leaves rapidly transforming into their medley of fall colors, Magnus found his way easily to the cart path that connected Seaford Downs to Hastell Cenllys in a few hours. He watched and listened intently for several minutes before summoning his courage and crossing the open expanse. He quickly worked his way up, scaling the steep rocky ridge that edged the road on its north side. Then he followed the hill on a course parallel to the path. Forward progress was hard as he stumbled through thick brush and around briar patches, but he dared not descend to the public pathway. Pausing to look around, Magnus found that he could observe much of the road below from this higher vantage point. Seeing a group of travelers approaching from the west around noon, he flattened himself into the forest floor.

As they drew closer, Magnus could see two monks leading the procession. The early afternoon sun glinted off breastplates and edged weapons on the men that were following. *Soldiers, but they should have been recalled to Rome days ago unless the bishop had kept a company of men behind to search for him!* Magnus quickly crawled on his belly behind a nearby tree.

Peering through a tangle of vines, twigs, and leaves, he continued to monitor the group's advance. When they were no more than a stone's throw away, he realized they weren't legionnaires at all, but Saxons! These were large, heavily muscled men with light-colored hair and features, and they immediately reminded him of the Pict raiders that had attacked the village. Their armament was the same - lances, broadswords, daggers, and shields. Peering down, he saw that the largest man carried a shield with a lion on it. *Why were these supposedly peace-seeking monks, leading foreign savages through the countryside?* Magnus wondered, and then he noticed that one of the friars had a pronounced limp!

He knew that man. It was the monk that had led him through the abbey before he was imprisoned. Had the bishop imported these mercenaries to search for him?

He decided to shadow their progress, hoping to find the answer without being spotted. Magnus waited until the men had passed on a safe distance. Carefully, he made his way down through the thick brush to the roadway and began to follow.

They reached a fork in the road and turned away from Hastell Cenllys. *Thank goodness,* as Magnus breathed a sigh of relief. *Maybe they weren't looking for him after all. Otherwise, they would undoubtedly have searched the village.*

He trailed the group at a safe distance for the rest of the day. They eventually turned off the main road and onto a side pathway that grew increasingly narrow, a foliage ravine walled by thick tangles of brush and trees. As the fall sky began to darken with the last rays of the sun turning into rich shades of pink and violet among high clouds, the group appeared to reach its destination, a strange rock formation atop a hill, with a large bonfire burning next to it. Surrounded by droves of people, it was the focal point of what appeared to be a local festival or celebration. *This must be Mabon!* He realized.

Instead of confronting the crowd of Pagans, the lame monk moved toward several men dressed in white robes at the center of the congregation. Magnus realized that these were Druids from Cynde's colorful descriptions. He could tell that introductions were being made as he observed their exaggerated gestures.

Looking at the rock formation, he realized that it was man-made. Three large rough stone pillars supported a large flat rock. To Magnus, it looked like an enormous three-legged stool. Focusing on the smaller group, he tried identifying faces in the dancing firelight. Expecting them all to be strangers, he was surprised to first recognize Anut, the man that he had seen on the wagon with Osric, clad in the white robes of a Celtic priest.

Magnus decided it would be best to withdraw from the vicinity before he was noticed. *Anyway,* he thought, *Cynde would be able to get the information from her uncle about this twilight meeting.*

Magnus walked under a full harvest moon towards the village. The autumn air was crisp, and he shivered in his light tunic. There wasn't enough light to walk through the forest, so eventually, Magnus moved closer along the edges of the path, trying to stay in the shadows while stopping periodically to listen for threatening sounds. Several times he had to dart into the sparse foliage and remain silent as groups of villagers passed, talking happily on their way home. He tried to spot Cynde or someone else he knew as they walked by, but he couldn't see well enough in the dim light.

It was nearly daylight when he finally approached the village clearing and saw the group of thatched roofs suspended in a sea of gray, early morning mist. Idly, he wondered if any of the residents might know the identity of the body, he found in the ruined house.

Chapter 13

Magnus's Return

Magnus crept through a dense thicket that had grown to encompass some of the buildings. He moved silently, not wanting to alert the villagers' watchdogs. Pulling himself beneath the prickly vines of the last line of bushes, he heard a cock crow as streaks of daylight began to spread in the eastern sky.

Trotting quickly to the rear of the inn, he ducked behind a stack of firewood and sat down in the shadows. He waited about ten minutes before he heard someone stirring inside. Moments later, Cynde emerged, carrying a pot toward an outside firepit.

"Psssst, Cynde!" Magnus hissed.

She stopped, dropping the pot. Turning with fearful eyes, she hurried into Magnus's uneasy embrace. She looked exhausted from the prior night's festivities. "You're in danger!" she stammered. "Inside...," her voice trailed off.

Magnus understood immediately. The bishop had stationed church guards at the inn. He kissed her quickly on the lips and said: "Come to the orchard in the canyon, go back to the farthest rock wall, tomorrow afternoon. Do you still have my pouch?"

"I kept it well guarded. What is it?" she reached beneath her bodice, intending to hand it to him.

"Not now, I'll tell you later." he smiled. Reluctantly releasing her, he scurried off beneath the tangled brush on hands and knees like a large rodent.

The canyon was shaped like a huge horseshoe. As the centuries had passed, water had softened the fertile soil, allowing it to erode down and away from the white limestone walls that now surrounded apple trees like a tall, solid white fence.

It was mid-afternoon the next day when Magnus could see men, far in the distance, shadowing Cynde's progress. Luckily, they knew if he was trapped in the box canyon, they could take their time apprehending him, so they lingered at the entrance between the two rocky ridges. Cynde drew closer, and Magnus let a handful of small rocks cascade down to grab her attention.

Looking up, she saw him partially concealed behind a bush, motioning toward some vines to her left. Quickly stumbling across the loose stones at the bottom of the cliff, she located her own red scarf tied around a vine that had been cut at its base. The scarf was the one she had given to Magnus before the soldiers had taken him to Seaford Downs. Magnus was turning in a circle with one arm outstretched. He looked comical, but she understood what he wanted. Grabbing the rough vine, she rotated, tightly wrapping it around herself, and then looped it through itself in the semblance of a knot.

Magnus turned and began climbing over the ridge. As he did, several men started shouting, and he knew he had to hurry. Rushing through the trees, Magnus glanced at the forked limbs where he had scraped the bark off and threaded the vines through, knotting them together. The soft green wood would provide enough bearing surface for the vines to slide on. Reaching a wide crevice on the other side of the hill, he tugged on the vines to make sure Cynde was attached and then ran forward and leaped onto a small bough suspended on the end of the vines.

~

Cynde hadn't known that she was being followed, and the men's shouting surprised her. They must be the men from the inn. Trussed about with the rough vine, she knew she couldn't free herself quickly enough to run away. So, she reached down, gathered as many small stones as she could in the crook of her left arm, and stood, ready to repel the attackers, as she felt the vine stiffen slightly.

She saw a man come from between two trees and pitched the largest stone overhand straight at his head. Disappointed, she saw it fall well short of its target as the man began running toward her. Cynde was taking aim for another throw when she felt the vine suddenly tighten, a moment later, she lifted into the air. She watched as her would-be captor stood below and opened her arms, raining rocks down upon the man's curses.

~

Magnus landed at the bottom of the crevice with a soft thud. Reaching out for two large flat stones standing on their edges, he tipped them over onto the ends of the log and gingerly stepped off. After making certain that the taunt vine was securely anchored, he began running back up the hill.

Suspended above the orchard, Cynde watched as a group of four angry men gathered below her. Kicking her legs, she was able to swing close enough and grab the woody bush that Magnus had hidden behind. Holding to the branches with one hand, she loosened the vine and un-wound herself from it.

They met at the top of the hill in a quick embrace. "We must hurry. They'll be on their way up here." Magnus said, taking her hand and leading the way through the trees.

"Where are we going?" She asked.

"The only place that I know is safe," he replied, heading away from the orchard canyon and down the far side of the ridge. "What was the gathering for, and what was Anut doing there?"

"That was our Mabon feast that I told you about. I was there most of the day and well into the evening. What does your scroll from Martin say?" she inquired as they trotted along.

Stopping mid-stride, Magnus turned abruptly. "How did you know that it was from Martin?"

The intensity that shone from his eyes was unsettling to

her. "My aunt started to read it, but I stopped her and have kept it next to my heart since that day," she added quickly.

"She only read who it was from?" Magnus demanded, stretching his hand out for the leather pouch.

"Yes, I took it back because I was immediately uneasy. I still don't know why," she stated, digging at her bodice. She handed the pouch to him and said, "Here it is, safe like I promised."

"Good, there are other names listed that need to be protected," he said, then began telling her of the scroll's contents. "Martin knew his ideas were far too radical for the organized church. This manuscript contains some of his essential concepts on God and healings. He called it his Keystone document. It explains the ideas that hold mankind's concepts of this world together. It also contains the name of one of his relatives. Conchessa of Kilpatrick, and her husband Calphurnius, who is a decurio."

"What is a decurio?" she asked quizzically.

"He is a member of the local council of the community and is involved in administration, finance, and judgements. It is considered an honor to be one."

"A town father, huh?"

"Yes, I suppose. Martin wanted me to contact them if I needed help, but I don't want to endanger them."

"Where is Kilpatrick?" she wondered out loud.

"About three weeks walking north of here, on the Antonine wall – north of Hadrian's Wall. It's an earthen works wall," he added.

She had heard about Hadrian's Wall, the great stone wall and fort system that stretched across the expanse of Briton, from sea to sea. It had protected them from the onslaught of Pict warriors attacking from the northern regions in years past, but she hadn't known about the wall located further north. "Have you met them before?"

"Once, shortly before Martin passed. I was nine when Martin presented this scroll to me. Later on, that same day, Martin introduced them to me in Tours. They were traveling back to Briton on official business and had their son, Maewyn Succat, with them. I remember it well because he was about eight years old, and after they left, Martin told me that he had a clear vision of the boy becoming a saint. He seemed like a normal child to me, but I guess it's possible. Maybe Martin gave them their scroll that day too."

"Can you tell me what the magical letter says?" she teased.

"I'll be happy to read it to you when we reach a safe place." He winked.

After an hour of walking, they arrived at another, smaller stone cliff. The stench of death still hung heavy in the air. "I don't like your choice of accommodations," she said, looking at the rocks piled in rows that covered the remains of the dead barbarians.

"While I was searching for enough limestone to cover those poor souls, I noticed a cleft in the rocks back here," he replied, crossing a small trickle of water, and following it between boulders as tall as two men.

A jumble of smaller rocks filled an area that looked to Cynde like a small courtyard. Magnus found one that suited him and sat down, motioning to Cynde to sit beside him. The air was cleaner here. Reaching deep within his tunic, he withdrew the pouch and opened it. Pulling the roll of yellow parchment out, he began to read:

I, Martin, humble servant of the one Lord, do hereby set my hand to this document with my prayers for all of mankind. I have been blessed with a lifetime of service to others. I have healed many suffering mental and physical ills, including the great nemesis of death. These were not miracles. They were the result of my conscientious and continuous communion with God. For prayer to work, you must look at the spiritual evidence hidden beneath layers of human thought and emotion, and strive to understand God's perspective. Every one of my life's questions has been answered through a broadened spiritual understanding.

What separates us from the eternal and everlasting spiritual reality that is God? What holds this conglomeration of material experience together for all people and creatures? I believe that it is a false sense of history, for in the sage words of the apostle Paul, **"For I am persuaded, that neither death, nor life, nor angels, nor principalities, nor powers, nor things present, nor things to come. Nor height, nor depth, nor any other creature, shall be able to separate us from the love of God, which is in Christ Jesus our Lord."** [39]

The Lord is infinite, and the only history in an eternity is now. No before, no after, just now. In my own experiences, if a man truly realizes for a moment that he cannot be separate from the Kingdom of God, false historical images pass away, and he is healed.

If mankind would strive after this knowledge, perfection would become increasingly evident in all of our lives. With God realized as each individual's only father/mother, mortals would see God as their one true relative, the only creator. If you perceive everything and everyone as spiritual ideas, discrimination disappears. There is no gender, age, race, or human history to hate, all becomes Love.

When material history is seen to be a lie — all anger, resentment, fear must pass into the nothingness that spawned them. Reality then appears as harmony, health, and purity untouched by the lie of an existence separate from God.

Remove this keystone of material history, and the façade of a limited life crumbles, replaced by limitless unfoldment. I can best illustrate this with a parable of two young boys:

Cain was raised with a belief in a material mother and father. He is continually exposed to fear, sickness, and death. He believes he is entirely separate from God and cannot fathom infinity. He sees mental and physical violence from his father, witnesses its marks left on his mother and siblings, and listens to stories of past violations heaped on his family by others. He becomes a bigot and spews hatred towards others of different faiths, skin color, and social status. Cain believes in a world driven by both good and evil, including people possessed by evil. Challenges to health, prosperity, intelligence, and joy have been handed down to him through generations of ancestors. It is that inheritance that he passes to his own offspring.

On the other hand, Abel was raised with an understanding that God was his father/mother. Speaking to God directly, with unselfish motives, he receives God's perfect ideas. He experiences growth in Love,

Wisdom, and Harmony. Perceiving the spiritual reality that is obscured by the mist of mortal existence, he sees evil, the devil, as unreal because, as Jesus announced, it is a lie when he said, **"Why do ye not understand my speech? even because ye cannot hear my word. Ye are of your father the devil, and the lusts of your father ye will do. He was a murderer from the beginning, and abode not in the truth, because there is no truth in him. When he speaketh a lie, he speaketh of his own: for he is a liar, and the father of it. And because I tell you the truth, ye believe me not."**[40]

Abel is victorious as our master, his disciples, and myself have been at healing disease, fear, and even death, through an understanding of God's allness and the universe as spiritual — not material. God could not be omnipresent if evil lurks in any part of the universe. Otherwise, he would be a house divided against himself, as it is recorded, **"And Jesus knew their thoughts, and said unto them, Every kingdom divided against itself is brought to desolation; and every city or house divided against itself shall not stand: And if Satan cast out Satan, he is divided against himself; how shall then his kingdom stand? And if I by Beelzebub cast out devils, by whom do your children cast them out? therefore they shall be your judges. But if I cast out devils by the Spirit of God, then the kingdom of God is come unto you."**[41]

Abel's inheritance is peace, perfection, and an infinite supply of spiritual ideas that he can demonstrate in his own life. He understands that God is All, and as a reflection of God, he is himself unlimited by any material laws or restrictions. Remember how our master walked on water? **"And when even was now come, his disciples went down to the sea. And entered into a ship and went over the sea toward Capernaum. And it was now dark, and Jesus was not come to them. And the sea arose by reason of a great wind that blew. So, when they had rowed about five and twenty or thirty furlongs, they see Jesus walking on the sea, and drawing nigh unto the ship: and they were afraid. But he saith unto them, It is I; be not afraid. Then they willingly received him into the ship: and immediately** *the ship was at the land whither they went."*[42]

Their two lives are opposites. Which one will prove to be true? Cain holds the tatters of ruined, limited lives and beliefs around him as he walks through a dismal existence with fleeting promises of happiness. Abel is free of mortal encumbrances and shares the unlimited joys of the universe with others. Which experience do you aspire to?

The latter legacy I intend to leave with my flock. It is the heritage of salvation for this world, as it is the Kingdom of God discerned by mankind. I have no material roots! I wish only to bless this world as an expression of the Love of God. **"And thou, child, shalt be called the prophet of the Highest: for thou shalt go before the face of the Lord to prepare his ways; To give knowledge of salvation unto his people by the remission of their sins, Through the tender mercy of our God; whereby the dayspring from on high hath visited us. To give light to them that sit in darkness and in the shadow of death, to guide our feet in the way of peace."**[43]

This verity pertains to all races, creeds, and creatures upon this earth. As people struggle to free themselves from the lures and anchors of mortal reasoning, realization occurs. As beliefs in sin and materiality wash away, they find 'at one ment' with all the ideas of creation in the Mind of God. Mankind must see itself as not removed from God. With no material history to bind them, man and woman become free to discover their true origins. Earthly yearnings subside as they discover that they themselves are the perfect images and likenesses of God. Strive to perceive materiality through the lens of Spirit. Discern the Heavenly qualities expressed in corporeal ideas. Learn the opposite of what the world is teaching you. Study the Laws of God, which protect and guide. Heal yourself and others on this earthly plain. Be Deity reflected.

I humbly petition God daily to be a better example for others of freedom from material limits. A vocation that sorely needs to be nurtured in this coarse world. I am leaving copies of this document with a few of the receptive minds that I have encountered on my life's journey. This knowledge is my most valuable possession, and I bequeath it to all generations that must follow. With people, there is always dissension. The only balm for this irritation are spiritual concepts. Mankind must understand that they have never fallen from God's grace, for God, being infinite, knows nothing opposed to himself. This is the only solution for harmony and healing in this world!

Awaken my children to the latent joy and power of Christianity. You are not mortals. You are spiritual creatures! Beauty lies beyond the Adam dream.

> *Humble servant of the one Lord,*
> *Martin of Tours*

> *Magnus,*
> *One copy of this treatise resides with my relatives, Conchessa of Kilpatrick, and her husband Calphurnius. They have promised to help protect and nurture these ideas with others. If you need assistance, contact them.*
> *Go with God's Love and protection, my son.*
> *Martin*

Magnus rolled up the document and carefully replaced it in the leather pouch. "So, what do you think of it?" he asked.

"I don't know why there is such a fuss about it. It's just his funny ideas," she replied.

"Ideas are what build and destroy the kingdoms of men!" he said, smiling as he motioned to her to follow him.

Cynde complied, ducking to pass below a protruding rock, which had obscured an opening in the cliff face. Blinded by the sudden immersion into dank darkness, she raised her hands above her head and stood up slowly.

"Are you alright?" his voice gently chided.

"Yes, just give me a second to adjust." She was beginning to see outlines form from the sparse light provided by the entrance. Suddenly she saw a small glimmer in the gloomy confines. "What is that?"

"It is a gift for you, my dear," he said gallantly.

"Why?" was her reply.

"Because I care about you, and you're always on my mind…" he answered in a confused voice.

"I'm sorry, but I'm not used to receiving presents of any

type. Father and Dwig have never given me a gift, and I've only received a few over the years from my Aunt Sephia."

"You should be showered with offerings throughout your life. You are incredible!" Magnus replied earnestly.

"What is it?" she asked without much emotion.

"Here, let me show you." He moved behind her and slid the ornate plate across her breast, carefully fastening the gold clasp on her neck. "Now, go back outside into the sunlight and take a peek." He sounded in good humor, despite her apparent reservations.

"It's really heavy, but very well," she said impassively. As she stepped outside, she stopped abruptly and stared. "Oh my God! Oh no. It's too beautiful! I can't accept this. Magnus, where did you find this?" her words came in a flood as she gripped the torc and spun around.

"You deserve it, and it's yours. I found it in a deserted ruin of a house, and I have this gift for Dwig too," he added, showing her the figurine.

"No, it's too much. Take it back… Take it off so I can see it."

Magnus complied, gently unfastening, and lifting the neckpiece.

"Oh my God! It's so beautiful, but I really can't accept it, can I?" she said, holding and examining it with trembling hands. Looking at the back, she pointed and asked, "What is this mark?"

"Looks like a small capital R, I didn't see that before," Magnus said and continued with a grin. "You know that I have a heart of gold! Now you will always have a piece of my heart with you!" he said, smiling. "I wanted to give you something to remember me by, and you can always sell it if you need to. I'm sure God led me to this and to you," he said, pointing at the torc but looking into her eyes.

"I do love it and could never sell it… but wait, to remember you by? What do you mean?" her face clouded over.

"I need to leave," he answered gravely.

She knew why he had to leave. In a solemn voice, she

asked, "What are you going to do? Where will you go?"

"The sailors that brought me here told me stories of Hibernia, an island to the west. It sounds like it might be remote enough to offer me sanctuary from the bishop. If I can make it to the western coast, maybe I can find a ship to give me passage."

"Do you think we'll ever see each other again?" she asked, crossing her arms, and fighting obvious emotional pains.

"You could come with me…"

She could see his timid smile radiate. "You want me… You're asking me to…"

Magnus took a large breath and began to recite the words he had forced himself to memorize. "I've never lied to you, and I never will. You're too perceptive for that. I'll always stand behind you for support, beside you for sharing life's loads, in front of you to protect you from any threats – but I will never stand over you in judgment - just with and for you, always. From the first moment I saw you I knew I wanted to be your best friend forever. If the world passes away, I will still be thinking of you. I can't be any more truthful than that… You've seen it deep in my eyes - but I'll understand if you can't leave your family, your home." He finished breathlessly, dropping his head, as a slow stream of tears began to well in his eyes."

Gathering her composure, she stated defiantly: "I love you too, Magnus of Rau," before stepping to him and folding into his arms.

Chapter 14

Exodus

In the morning, Cynde retraced her steps to the top of the ridge and gazed over the orchard. Smoke from morning cooking fires wafted slowly up in the still morning air from the village beyond. She hoped that her father and Dwig hadn't worried too much about her absence as she continued her journey back to the inn in a looping path that wouldn't reveal Magnus's hideout. Absent mindedly, she reached up and caressed the heavy golden torc, now hidden beneath her clothes.

As she approached the houses, she heard some of the women shouting greetings to her. Several of them ran up and asked where she had been, expressing fears that monsters or barbarians had abducted her. She recognized two of the bishop's agents as they watched her with looks of intense disdain, but still maintained a respectful distance.

After quieting the women, she continued to the inn, entering under the stern gaze of her father. "Where and with whom did you spend the night?" he demanded.

She didn't answer right away but first marched through the bedding areas to ensure they were alone. "Where is a secret, and you know with whom," she replied evenly. "I am of age, father, and I love him!"

The frank revelation still stunned him. "I'll not have you running off with that, that... criminal!"

"He is not a criminal. He's a hairy-sick," she said, struggling to remember the word Magnus had used.

"Heretic! Is the term young lady."

Cynde spun around, searching for the source of that voice in the main doorway. "Aunt Sephia, why are you here?"

"I came to try and talk sense to my niece, but I hear that the battle is lost - you're in love."

Cynde didn't try to deny it, falling suddenly silent.

"It's alright, I understand. Deep within this shriveled old breast beats the heart of a young maiden. I want to help. Your uncle is here too." She motioned towards the door.

Anut stepped inside, looking uncomfortable. Cynde dismissed his apparent unease and returned her aunt's gaze. Dropping her voice, she said: "Fine, we are in love. We need help to escape to Hibernia."

"I'll not hear of it! You're not leaving with that renegade!" shouted her father.

Cynde was surprised when her aunt suddenly leaped to her defense. "Brother, she is past prime age. She must decide her own fate!"

Her father looked as if he had been physically stricken. His braggadocio gone, he began to stammer: "Sister, you're in favor of this? Why?"

With a toss of her hair, Aunt Sephia answered him. "I need to go to the granary to pick up some wheat for Anut. Accompany me dear brother, let me explain how a woman's mind works in these matters." Tugging on his sleeve, she pulled him outside with a passing wink to Cynde. "I also need to visit Aunt Giffin today. The poor old thing must be terribly lonely. I'll bet you haven't seen her in a month. She probably needs more firewood before the weather turns."

Cynde watched through the opened door as Anut followed them outside without a word and began unloading his tinker's wares from worn bundles. He laid assortments of cookware, jewelry, and other items in rows on hides spread across the ground. In the next minutes a small group of curious onlookers began to gather, bringing things for him to repair and haggling with him over prices.

Cynde busied herself cooking and cleaning with her brother, while waiting for her aunt and father to return.

Dwig was washing dirty bowls in a tub of fresh water when he blurted out: "Why are you leaving us?"

"Oh Dwig, you can't believe that I want to leave, but Magnus needs my help now." She didn't know what else to say. She wasn't even sure of everything she was feeling. At a loss for words, she fell quiet, hoping everything would turn out for the best.

Dwig continued to work in silence.

The day passed slowly. When her father and aunt finally returned, the chores were done, and supper was cooking. Anut had once again wrapped his various wares up in the dusty hides after a profitable day. Cynde noticed that the subject of Magnus was carefully avoided throughout the evening meal and in the polite evening conversations that followed.

In the morning, it appeared that even the bishop's agents had lost interest in him, for they were nowhere to be seen. Cynde inquired with several of the village ladies and received the same answer: "They left to return to Seaford Downs yesterday afternoon. Guess they lost interest in your friend." they all replied with a wink.

Cynde was ecstatic. Soon after her morning chores were complete, she took Dwig, who she could tell was still feeling melancholy, and left to tell Magnus the excellent news. On the way, they talked about the possibility of her and Magnus being able to live near the village rather than fleeing the country. Cynde also chided her brother about what girls he was interested in. Looking backward often, she scanned the area with as much nonchalance as possible, looking for any evidence that their progress was being watched, but saw no one.

"Magnus, I've brought Dwig!" she called as they neared the cliff face. She didn't want him to be surprised. Scampering and sliding through the loose stones on the steep pathway, they arrived at the cluster of boulders. Threading her way through,

Cynde led Dwig back to the small cave. It was empty except for the sleeping mound that Magnus had fashioned out of armloads of soft grasses. Cynde blushed inadvertently and walked rapidly back out into the sunshine.

Looking at the ground, she and Dwig tried to find tracks but could see nothing among the scattered stones. Disappointed, they began retracing their steps to the village.

They were nearing the top of the hill. As they walked past a large dead tree, someone suddenly grabbed Cynde from behind. "Aayaahaa!" she screamed and brought a fist around in a wide arc. It caught him in the temple and knocked him to the ground.

Rubbing his head, Magnus looked up, grinning. "I suppose if that was a test, you passed."

Cynde was still standing in a defensive position and breathing hard. "Don't ever do that to me again!" she declared.

"I'm sorry, but I couldn't resist. I stayed up here to make sure you two weren't followed to my Secret Hiding Place!" He loudly enunciated the last three words to make his point.

"You don't need to hide! The bishop's men have left the village! That's what we came to tell you," she exclaimed.

Chapter 15

The Discussion

Magnus looked unconvinced but changed the subject. "Dwig, I've got something for you." Digging into his pouch, he withdrew the bronze figurine.

"Wow! Where did you get this?" the boy asked, carefully turning it over and examining it from every angle.

"There is a ruined house in the forest that I found. I want to ask Anut about it," he answered.

On the walk back to Hastell Cenllys, Magnus described the remains of the little farm in the forest. Cynde and Dwig listened intently, asking many questions. He continued to talk as he watched for threatening forms in their surroundings. In less than an hour, they stood in the shade of the woods on the outskirts of the community.

"I'd appreciate it if you two would make sure that the bishop's guards aren't waiting to welcome me with leg irons," he quipped.

In a short time, Dwig returned to escort Magnus back to the inn. "We didn't see any visitors other than our aunt and uncle," the boy said.

As they entered the building, they found Cynde and her father busily preparing dinner along with a small gathering of villagers. *It looks like I'm having a welcome-home dinner,* Magnus realized. Anut and Sephia were helping, seated near the rear wall as they plucked chickens. Feathers covered their clothes and the floor around them.

"Anut! Magnus has a question for you," Dwig blurted, pulling the bronze figure out absent-mindedly.

No subtlety there, thought Magnus, but before he could frame a non-confrontational question, the tinker excitedly spoke to Dwig.

"Where did you find that?" Anut said, dropping the chicken and hurrying over to the two young men.

"He gave it to me," Dwig replied, poking a skinny finger in Magnus's direction.

Magnus didn't want to lie to Anut, but the man's sudden interest in the figurine made him cautious. "I found it in the forest."

"Where?" Anut demanded as he clasped Magnus's forearm so tightly that it hurt.

"Ow! In the ruins of a farm in the forest," Magnus replied, as he pried himself free.

"When you escaped from the bishop." Anut finished his sentence without acknowledging the discomfort he had caused. "Do you know where? Can you take me there?"

"Maybe, but first, I need to know why, and second, I need to know what you're meeting with the monks and mercenaries was about."

Anut's brow furrowed deeply in concentration, then his eyes widened with surprise. "You were at the Autumn Equinox celebration?"

"Only at the beginning of your meeting with that group, I left and returned here before I could be spotted. What did the warriors want?" Magnus demanded.

"They visited at the behest of the bishop. Brother Leo introduced them to us. They will protect us from the Picts now that the last centurions have been recalled to defend Rome from the hordes of Visigoths."

"Brother Leo is the monk that limps?" asked Magnus.

"Yes."

"Did you notice the largest warrior's shield?"

"Yes, he is also the chief of the band, with a golden lion

adorning his shield," Anut stated loudly.

Now Cynde's father quickly joined the conversation. "A golden lion you say?"

Magnus announced: "Remember how all you villagers watched him slay his predecessor as his band of cutthroats set the fires and pillaged this hamlet? He carries the same shield, although he's bathed and lost his blue tint!" Mouths dropped open, and silence ensued for several moments after Magnus's revelation.

Then conversations rose quickly. "You're right!" Cynde's father shouted above the others. "By the gods, I didn't remember… But why?"

"Why would they destroy our village?" an older woman cried.

All eyes turned to Magnus for answers. "They pretended to be Picts to threaten you. I don't know why the brute with the lion shield killed the former chief, but you were in danger. Now they are pretending to drive the Pict invaders away. I don't know if they are Picts, Saxons, Romans, or Britons – but I am sure the bishop is involved. Whoever they are, they want to give you all a sense of security, to make it easier for you and your countrymen to accept the church's doctrine and continue to fill its coffers."

Sephia looked away and kept plucking as Magnus spoke, but Anut pushed forward and addressed him directly. "Where is Rodarik's farm?"

"Who?" Magnus asked.

"The farm that you found. The one with Dwig's figurine. Where is it?" the tinker insisted, his face inches from the young man's nose.

"Why?" Magnus could have answered directly but decided to egg the man on a bit.

"Because if you don't, I'll thrash you within an inch of your life!" the man screamed, turning a deeper shade of purple.

"I need to know why an abandoned farm is more important than your meeting with a terrorist who burned this community!" Magnus replied, trying to match the man's tone and arrogance.

Suddenly Cynde sprang between the two men. "Stop it, you idiots," she hissed as she pushed them apart. "Stop teasing Anut." she said evenly to Magnus and, turning to the tinker commanded; "And you, answer him."

Hanging his head slightly, the older man first looked around at the others and then awkwardly back to Magnus. "I had no idea who the man with the lion's shield was. That was the first time I met him. I had no idea that he attacked these homes, and I offer my sincerest apologies for that," he then continued as though he was confessing a great secret. "Rodarik was a friend of my father's, a druid and one of the greatest warriors this land ever produced. He fought to preserve our heritage," he said, bowing his head and striking over his heart with a clenched right fist. "He was my teacher," he added.

"If that's true, how could you not know where he lived?" asked Magnus, perplexed.

Anut coughed nervously while he looked around at the group, whose numbers were gradually increasing, but then continued, "Rodarik stayed true to the old ways, our old… you would call it, religion. When the church arrived with its new teachings, he continued leading a resistance that was begun by our forebearers. Gradually we, the younger people, drifted away lured by the impressive promises of the church. The abbot promised us rich rewards in the next world and the protection and benefits of the religious community in this one. Rodarik grew disgusted with us," he announced loudly, motioning to the villagers around him. "He left to pursue a solitary existence rather than dishonor himself. I will be in your debt if you can take us to his remains, so we can properly bury him with the great honors he deserved." Anut hung his head in an apparent show of shame and deference.

"It is a good day's walk from this village. I will lead you there tomorrow, but no one in this village must betray me, or you may never find the body of Rodarik." Magnus stated flatly.

Mummers of acquiescence spread through the small group until they were all nodding their assent. Sephia just smiled as she continued to pluck feathers.

Chapter 16

Rodarik's Farm

In the morning, Magnus awoke to the smell of freshly baked bread. Cynde and the other ladies in the village must have begun kneading dough well before daylight.

When Magnus pulled himself upright and peered through the doorway, he noticed that the villagers were in a festive mood. Several kids were chasing each other in circles, and their parents talked freely, with a great amount of animation.

"There you are my boy. Grab some biscuits, and let's get started," Anut proclaimed when he saw him. Magnus had surrendered the corroded remains of Rodarik's long sword and dagger to the villagers the night before, and now strapped on a handsome new blade that Anut provided for him. Several other men were standing close by under a tree.

Cynde ran forward, stuffing a folded cloth filled with warm bread into his hands, and gave him a quick peck on the cheek. "Good luck!" She said, and hurried back to where more loaves were baking.

Soundlessly, Magnus turned and began walking westward out of the village. The other men fell into step behind him, and they strode away in the cool early morning mists of the English countryside.

Magnus nibbled at his stash of biscuits throughout the journey. Several times the group stopped briefly at streams to rest and re-fill their animal skin flasks. It was late in the afternoon when they finally reached the clearing that held the ruins of Rodarik's home. He noticed a sense of reverence pass among the men as they glimpsed the jumbled rocks and roof beams at the far end of the field. Magnus paused outside the circle of stones and let the others pass inside. One man carried a large sack, and the others held digging implements. Magnus watched as they carefully began to excavate around the Druid's remains. In about an hour, they carefully loaded the mummified carcass into the sack. Several small items that fell off were gingerly gathered up and placed gently into the bag. At the end, Anut spoke. "Should we camp here tonight?" he asked the group.

"I have some wheat hidden not far from here if you would rather sleep away from this place. I also have some more of Rodarik's possessions there." Magnus knew that most of the bread had been eaten and noticed the men's nervous looks in the direction of the bagged corpse.

"That would perhaps be wise. We will leave Rodarik here for tonight," Anut said, answering for his uneasy companions. They quickly gathered their belongings and followed Magnus across the field and into the forest.

The darkness threw shadows around them as twilight edged closer. The trees had less foliage than when Magnus had visited before, but enough to shade the trail. He had difficulty finding the stones that marked his pathway, since they were sometimes hidden beneath the blanket of newly fallen leaves. The men remained dutiful, following him in patient silence.

After about an hour's trek, Magnus finally spotted the downed tree that marked his hiding place. He led the group to a spot a short distance away and told them to set up camp there. Then he returned in the gathering darkness and disappeared beneath the tree's branches, crawling under the trunk, and feeling along the cold mud walls for his grain pots. He found the first one towards the tapered end of the hollow and began dragging it backward towards the opening. His knee found the rough handle of the old axe close to the entrance, and he closed his hand around it. *Maybe we'll need it for cutting firewood or bedding?* he thought, pulling it back through the opening. Standing in the creek, he lifted the clay pot up and over the bank with one hand.

A large shadow of a man looked down on him. Magnus couldn't tell who he was in the faint light, but he saw a glint of metal in the starlight and raised his other hand instinctively to protect himself. "Clang!" The axe reverberated in his hand as he ducked beneath the embankment's edge. A sword had glanced off his axe. He heard the other men shouting as he stumbled back into the creek. Another figure ran up behind his attacker. *Are they going to kill me here?* Magnus hadn't considered the possibility. Then the shadows merged and struggled until he heard a gurgling sound and felt a warm spray of liquid across his face. In scant moments, his attacker collapsed beside him in the creek bed with a thud.

"Are you all right, boy?"

Magnus heard the voice of Anut and responded hesitantly. "Yes… I think so. What happened?"

"Varnos almost killed you, but he can't hurt you now," the tinker replied matter-of-factly.

"Why?" was all Magnus could think of to ask.

"Well, I suppose he assumed this was your only other hiding place for Rodarik's belongings. So, he was going to kill you and take them," replied Anut.

"Very hospitable of him. You can tell I make friends easily," Magnus said with a nervous laugh.

"You don't have any other treasures hidden, do you?"

The man's tone wasn't humorous, and Magnus suddenly felt uneasy. *Was there anyone in this country he could trust?* "The only things I have are grain pots, an axe, a shield, and a helmet, and I was going to give them to you," he said truthfully.

"See that you do!" Anut's shadowy form said, stooping and grabbing the grain pot as he turned and walked away.

Magnus was still shaking when he pulled himself up and over the bank by grabbing onto dried clumps of grass. He had tried to wash his face and hands in the puddles he found in the stream, hoping it hadn't been pools of Varnos's blood.

These men are like animals! I can't trust any of them. How can I envision them as God's children? he kept thinking. Looking ahead, he saw that a large fire was now crackling, and prone forms were gathered around it. Grasping the shield and helmet tighter, he walked into the light.

"The gopher has emerged from his burrow!" One of them said, and they all guffawed loudly until they saw what he was carrying. "The armor of Rodarik!" Another said reverentially, and they fell silent.

Magnus laid the items beside the fire, and the others quickly gathered around, stroking the heavily pitted metal.

"Can you repair it?" one of the men asked the tinker.

"Not strong like new, but I think I can preserve it," Anut replied, grinding an edge of the corroded bronze helmet between his thumb and forefinger.

Magnus felt exhausted. He made one more trip back to the creek for another pot of grain and the axe. Returning to the group, he gave the pot to Anut and curled up close to the campfire clutching the axe. Everybody seemed to understand that he wouldn't surrender Rodarik's axe tonight. The raw scar across the rusted metal from the sword strike shone silver in the firelight as he closed his eyes and fell asleep.

Magnus felt the cold creeping into his joints in the early hours of the dark autumn morning. The fire had died to feeble coals struggling to throw off heat in the damp, cool air. He saw one of the other men stirring the ashes and blowing into them to ignite the broken limbs piled onto the charred mass. As Magnus saw the first flames lick the side of the wood, he fell asleep again.

"I feel like a large red target is painted on my back Osric! I know that someone is going to betray me." Magnus said as he motioned at the sleeping forms around himself.

"Don't worry, my son, the good you do is an image, a truth that will live forever since it is truth. Their attempts to obliterate you, or the facts you espouse, will not prevail since destruction is only capable of untruths." Osric's voice rumbled, and he smiled widely.

Magnus didn't understand and began to argue. "How will I know if I've finished my mission in this world? They can rob me of my life, my expression!"

"Your mission? Ha, ha, ha!" Osric let go a booming laugh that Magnus feared would wake the sleeping men. "You have no mission other than to express the qualities of God, and you'll be doing that here or hereafter my friend. Life is eternal."

"Hereafter? That's right, you're... dead!" Magnus stammered. Osric's smile suddenly grew brighter and was replaced with sunlight.

"That must have been a hell of a dream, son," Anut said, staring down at him.

"Beyond my imagination," Magnus replied as he forced himself awake and struggled to his feet. He could see that the other men had dragged the body of Varnos onto the creek bank and were covering it with stones.

Anut saw him looking at the hastily constructed crypt and said: "That'll keep the dogs away from him till his relatives come back for the body, if they come back," he added.

"Why wouldn't they?" Magnus asked.

"Well, he died like a dog, without honor. They probably won't want to remember him. I really don't know what possessed him to try to kill you like that, not with the rest of us about," the tinker said as he began leading everyone back toward Rodarik's farm.

The men systematically worked their way through the ruins for the next few hours, digging through the clutter with sharpened sticks, but found no items of real value. Filthy with dust and tired from the exertion, they began the long hike back to the village with Rodarik's remains and possessions well before noon.

"Did you speak with my friend Osric much?" Anut asked as they walked along the dusty path in the autumn sun.

"Quite a bit. He was a prodigious person."

Anut looked confused but continued. "A bit of a buffoon, but he had a good heart. That's always the ones that die too young, the good ones. The rest of us worthless bastards fight through life until the gods have no choice other than to receive our tarnished souls."

"You shouldn't think of mankind like that. You've made choices every day to be good, Anut. Cynde wouldn't love you if you weren't a good man," Magnus exclaimed.

The tinker only grunted and walked on. Magnus wondered about the man, knowing that most people say more with their silence than with their words.

By the time they returned to the village, the sky was a vibrant display of colors, tinged with white, yellow, light blue, cobalt blue, and dark grey. Shafts of sunlight fell towards the ground in streams of light like folds in a piece of delicate fabric. Magnus slowed his pace until the others were ahead of him and stopped to admire the view. He loved the dramatic lighting and colors emblazoned in these English sunsets. *Maybe I should be an artist, so I could try to capture the best of these?* Ahead of him, he heard the first shouted greetings as the group entered the town. The returning men must have displayed their trophies to the crowd for a few minutes because gaiety and frivolity filled the air. Then the noise stopped almost immediately. There was a long silence, followed by mounting pitiful wails and sobbing.

Magnus turned on his heels and walked away. He didn't know where to go, but he didn't want to face the family of the dead man. Undoubtedly, the residents had assembled a large potluck dinner to celebrate the homecoming, but none of them would be having a good time tonight.

Magnus felt his way through the gathering darkness, following a narrow trail to the orchard. Stumbling through the tall grasses, he searched gently around the tree trunks with his feet. In time, he located half a dozen apples that had fallen from the branches. It was too dark to see if they had worms, but he ate around the soft spots, enough to fill his belly. Unrolling his blanket, he curled up next to one of the trees and fell asleep.

He slept fitfully, and only for a brief period before the cold temperatures invaded his thin coverings. Magnus awoke shivering. The rising moon was providing marginal light, illuminating his exhalations in a series of dense silver clouds.

Quickly draping the blanket over his shoulders, he hurried back toward the quiet village.

Moisture hung in the chilly air as he walked quickly between the houses. A chorus of neighborhood dogs announced his arrival, but he ignored them and walked straight to the inn. Embers still glowed in the fire pit, but no flames provided light as he groped his way between the benches.

"I suppose you don't care that I was worried to death!" Cynde's crisp accusation was palpable as it hung in the darkness.

"Sorry, I felt I could not face Varnos's family," he replied in a tired, strained voice as a dark shadow moved quickly in front of him.

"This isn't only about you anymore," Cynde jabbed at his chest with a boney finger. "You must think of me too. I've been beside myself with worry, not knowing if another assassin had taken you from me. You need to grow up and ...and be thoughtful!"

"I'm sorry, it won't happen again," he replied, rubbing the pain away where she had poked him. "Wait, what did you say, another assassin?"

"Yes, after you left yesterday, one of the patrons at the inn mentioned that the bishop put a price of twenty gold coins for a traitor's head, but he didn't have any more details. I worried all day that it was you, and then when you didn't show up, I just didn't know what to think," she said as she wrapped her arms tightly around him in the dark.

Magnus absent-mindedly embraced her while his thoughts raced. *If he's put a price on my head, we'll have to move quickly. Now in fact!* Reluctantly pushing her away, he held both of her arms. "Listen, if that's true, they will be closing in on me. I've got to leave tonight."

"We need to leave tonight or as soon as possible." She corrected him with the sadness evident in her voice. "I'll wake Father, Aunt Sephia, and Uncle Anut. We'll form a plan," she said flatly as she turned and strode away.

Magnus raked an iron rod back and forth through the

ashes in the fire pit. He was rewarded as they gave off an increasingly soft glow to the room, even as the chill of the fall night continued to invade its recesses. Magnus placed several small logs atop the exposed coals and watched as small flames flared and licked the wood. Then Cynde led the little group in, and hushed voices began to finalize an escape plan.

Anut and Sephia would continue to Seaford Downs the next day to conduct his regular business and gain information about the failed attempt on Magnus's life. He would then drive his horses and wagon to a remote seacoast enclave that the locals called Clataguay, where he would arrange passage to Hibernia on one of the fisherman's ships. "I should be able to make the trip and other arrangements in three days," he announced.

"Great." Cynde agreed. "Tomorrow, father and I will gather provisions while you continue to hide," she said, pointing at Magnus. "We'll leave as soon as it is dark, before the moon rises, and travel on an inland course to meet him." she motioned, indicating her uncle. Nods of agreement concluded the meeting, and they all stood. The others moved toward the inn's sleeping areas while Magnus left through the rear door, skulking toward the orchard and the safety of his cleft in the cliff face.

Quite a take-charge girl. He realized, smiling.

Chapter 17

Delayed

In the morning, Anut and Sepia began loading their wagon before breakfast. Cynde's father was visibly distraught as he stomped through the inn, grumbling loudly. She tried her best to ignore him as she gathered a few more items for her trip with Magnus.

Cynde heard him exit the inn with a loud verbal "Humppff" into the early morning light. She knew he was angry that his daughter was leaving. She remembered him saying that she was turning her back on her family in exchange for a life with a worthless vagabond. She heard the man's breath suddenly come in loud, short gasps, and ran out the door after him. As he rounded the edge of the inn, she saw him clutch his chest and fall to his knees. Dwig had been outside re-filling and carrying water pots to the inn. He quickly rushed to his father's side along with Anut and Sepia. They all grabbed him by the arms and waist, carefully dragging him through the doorway, and into the strawed sleeping area.

"What happened to father?" Cynde wailed as she covered him with blankets.

"He just collapsed." Dwig wheezed.

Cynde reacted immediately. She was off, racing through the village. Ignoring the remarks and stares of her neighbors, she hurdled some low shrubs and sprinted towards the orchard.

Magnus was seated, praying, when Cynde rushed in and gasped. "Father is sick!"

Magnus forced away initial feelings of panic and instead, quietly listened for God's guidance.

"Please help him. I know you can!" Cynde cried in a stricken voice.

~

"I am," he said. "Let's walk back to the inn."

While they walked, Magnus battled the theories of mortal life that assailed him. He tried to see Cynde's father as a perfect child of Spirit, completely separate from a material history or situation. He prayed to understand that mortal sickness was not a reality to a spiritual God. Cynde remained respectfully silent as she wrestled with her own fears.

As they approached the inn, Magnus felt a great sense of calm envelop him, and he entered first. He walked directly to the sleeping area, where he found the others.

"I can make a potion, but it will take me a day or two to collect the ingredients," said Anut earnestly.

"Let me sit with him awhile," Magnus said. Turning around, he motioned with his finger for Cynde to come closer. As she knelt over her father's still form, he whispered: "He's alright. Please leave us alone."

She backed away and quickly ushered Dwig and the others out, saying with a forced smile: "Breakfast is ready. I guess there's more to eat for you three!" Throwing a worried glance back at Magnus, she disappeared into the main room.

Magnus sat down and repeated the Lord's Prayer aloud over and over, earnestly trying to understand all of it clearly. He concentrated mostly on one line: "Thy will be done in earth, as it is in heaven." Magnus knew that a loving God could not cause suffering, and he struggled to see how this man was expressing the qualities of God in his earthly existence. Patience with his children, kindness to strangers, life, love, caring.... Thoughts of joy and gratitude continued replacing the dark fears that he had reluctantly entertained - including the fear that he would be attacked or arrested by the villagers.

He knew that he was in his right place, supporting Cynde and her father.

He was surprised that Cynde's father could lie nearly motionless for two days, but he did. Magnus told him to reflect on the good tasks in his life that he hadn't finished yet, such as working with Dwig and supporting Cynde in her decisions. "You know your daughter may want to come back here someday."

Occasionally Cynde would try to bring him a drink or some food, but the man refused most of it. Reclining next to him in the straw, Magnus told him about the healings performed by Jesus and Father Martin. He helped him pray to God to continue supporting and blessing others with his life. At one point, the man made an effort to speak, saying his name was Bynelld and that his family had always lived in this valley. They didn't chat much after that, but he listened quietly to the ideas on health, life, and spirituality that the young man was espousing.

Anut and Sephia tried diligently to visit with the sick man, pleading and arguing loudly with Cynde, but she respectfully refused their repeated requests. Magnus heard her repeatedly tell them, "I trust Magnus to care for him."

On the second night, Bynelld woke Magnus early in the morning and said it sounded like a thousand rumbling wagon wheels in his ears. He whispered that his blood was pumping too rapidly, and his heart felt three times its normal size and ready to burst. Fighting panic, Magnus again began repeating the Lord's Prayer out loud. The time passed slowly, but the man calmed and became more peaceful as the boy continued his prayers. Suddenly, Bynelld said that he had felt a painless release of pressure, like fluid squirting through a hose inside of his chest. Magnus realized that the danger had passed and smiled as the man thanked him, and then fell quickly into a restful sleep.

"And all flesh shall see the salvation of God."44 Magnus thought, *Bynelld's a perfect reflection of health and peace.* He laid back down overflowing with gratitude to God, as he too, fell asleep thinking. **"As it is written in the book of the words of Esaias the prophet, saying, The voice of one crying in the wilderness, Prepare ye the way of the Lord, make his paths straight. Every valley shall be filled, and every mountain and hill shall be brought low; and the crooked shall be made straight, and the rough ways shall be made smooth; And all flesh shall see the salvation of God."** 44

Cynde was grinding wheat into flour with a mortar and pestle when Magnus arose the following day. "All right, I wouldn't believe it if I hadn't seen it with my own eyes. How did you do it?"

"Do you mean your father?" he asked.

"Of course, I mean him. I've seen many a person in this village taken ill and die of milder complaints. I had a devil of a time keeping Uncle Anut away from you two. He was ready to give father a variety of potions. What did you do?"

"Your uncle, like most people, is always ready to treat matter with matter. Hippocrates was the 'Father of Medicine', trying to promote health through material science. He died in 370 B.C. Subsequently, Jesus and his followers proved that health could be achieved spiritually, but mankind continues to ignore the laws of God and is focused only on manipulating their bodies. God is everywhere but unperceived by most people. Bishop Martin taught me that even a small glimpse of the Truth about a person made in the image of God can cure sin, sickness, and sometimes, even death. I prayed, seeing beyond his material limitations and situations, to perceive the likeness that God created. You try to understand what the person really is, a spiritual being. You see him as untouched, protected, a spiritual idea that remains perfect, so the illness or accident couldn't have occurred," looking around, Magnus suddenly asked. "Where is he?"

"He took off before daylight, saying that he was going hunting with Dwig and also that he hadn't felt so good in years. I really don't understand a word that you were saying, but I do want you to know how grateful I am." She caught his neck with both hands and gave him a deep kiss.

Shaken, he quickly turned a deep shade of red and stammered. "I'll, uh, I like your rewards system here!"

Smiling, she repeated the act. Backing away, she said, "We better be going. We are three days late now! Anut and Sepia left this morning after they saw father up and about."

"What about your father?" Magnus asked.

"It's all right. We had a good talk before he left. He listened to me!" she said proudly, gathering up bundles of supplies.

Magnus didn't wait for more details but ran to collect his own belongings, and together they set off without any fanfare other than some waves and shouts from the villagers.

Taking her hand in his, Magnus said: "I wish I could put into words how you make me feel, but it's like trying to describe sunshine."

Cynde blushed and smiled wider as they walked through the bright light of a crisp fall morning.

Chapter 18

Treachery

"That miserable fool!" The bishop screamed. "It was a simple job, dispose of a scrawny boy, and you hire the only idiot in the village incapable of completing the task! I have enough problems to deal with. Swaingraf here," the bishop pointed to the chief intently sharpening his sword in the corner, "killed my friend Chief Ruel, after the failed attack on Hastell Cenllys to kill the boy. I can't blame Swaingraf because Ruel made a mess of the raid, attacking an empty village! That miscreant boy escaped me after I killed one of my finest monks for listening to his drivel and taking it to heart. The Romans have pulled out all their troops, so I now must deal directly with that ass, King Joedel. He's revisiting the abbey tomorrow, planning on forcing me to swear an allegiance and pay exorbitant tributes to him! Now you say the boy has escaped me again!" he hissed breathlessly as he stamped back and forth in his office.

Chief Swaingraf couldn't resist a smile while whistling a tune as he pulled a stone over the edge of his blade.

"Stop that whistling, this is serious." the man spat.

"My liege, a single stroke of unfathomable luck was all that stood between that boy and the fires of hell the other night, and I could not kill him in the village where he is a hero. He will not be so fortunate the next time." Sephia cooed as she stroked the edge of the man's massive oak desk.

"Next time? If he has any sense left in his minuscule brain, he's fled the territory by now." the man replied sharply. Swaingraf watched as a thoughtful expression crossed the bishop's face. "On the other hand, do you know where he is?"

"I know where he will be," she replied with a cunning smile.

"Good, but this time I want to know the whole of your plan, and you'll be taking Brother Leo and my new enforcer here, Chief Swaingraf, with you!" he stated emphatically.

"Fine, as long as I don't share the gold with them," Sephia said with a wide mirthless grin as she glanced at the chief.

Swaingraf watched as the bishop shuddered involuntarily. *Such a waste of a man*, he thought. The bishop had explained to him why he hated dealing with savages like this woman. He had heard the stories of the Celtic female warriors' physical prowess, treachery, and beast-like ferocity, and this Sephia embodied them all. She had contacted the bishop, willing to work as his double agent and do anything for money.

"Fine, we have an understanding." The little man agreed, ignoring the warning of the chief's raised eyebrows. "Now, what do you intend to do?"

"My dear husband is selling and repairing trinkets outside the monastery today. Tomorrow he will head to the coast to arrange passage for our young interloper and my niece. I've told him that my cousin is sick in Leiswister, and that after visiting her, I will meet him on the coast."

"Where?" The man interjected.

"Clataguay, your Excellency," she said, giving a mock bow. "Although I plan to catch this renegade before he reaches the coastal trail and dispose of him in the countryside."

"Fine, fine, but make sure he's dead this time, and I need that scroll of Bishop Martin's that you saw! Remember the valuable parchment you held? It could poison people's minds against my church," the man replied grimly.

"I certainly will," she frowned.

"Also, my dear, secrecy is still a key point. I want no one to know what happens to the boy or his little girlfriend, and make sure none of the king's men see you leave with the chief. It might ruin any chance for a diplomatic solution to the king's proposal," he winked.

After she had closed the door, the bishop whispered to Swaingraf. "Don't worry about the gold, her portion will be yours. Follow, and keep an eye on that woman until you leave with her tomorrow."

Shaking his head slightly, the chief slid his sword into its scabbard, adjusted a plain monk's habit over his weaponry and left the room. *That man lies easier than he tells the truth,* he thought.

Leaving the abbey, he watched as she found Anut gathering his collection of trading goods into the dusty animal hides and helped him load them onto the wagon. They spent the night camping in relative safety just outside one of the monastery's rock walls.

Swaingraf checked on them periodically, hidden in his perch atop the wall. In the morning, he saw Anut trundle off. Smiling and waving goodbye to him, she carried her bag of belongings a few steps along the wall. Then she turned when he was out of sight, and hurried back to the entrance.

She waited at the large gate as a rag-tag procession of King Joedel's soldiers filed steadily through with as much pageantry as they could muster. They were followed by the king, dressed in bright clothes and furs, riding on a husky white stallion. Inside, monks lined the pathway to the bishop's quarters. As the king rode on, Sephia pushed several of them aside and strode toward the rear of the compound. Swaingraf swiftly descended a ladder and followed her through the enclave.

She found the monk named Leo in one of the remote barrack buildings that had been abandoned by the Roman soldiers. Leo was moving pieces on a Twelve Points gameboard (an early form of Backgammon). He stood as she stepped in. She heard the distinct clink of metal armor and weapons as the monk straightened. Grabbing the ceramic playing board, she threw it across the room, where it shattered against the wall. "We have no time for games. Where is Chief Swaingraf?

"Here I be." The chief uttered behind her.

"We leave now. Get me a horse," she commanded.

"But my men, I need to…," Swaingraf began.

"You need do nothing other than what I tell you," she snarled. "They are under the bishop's command for now. They are already in monk's habits and quietly surrounding the King's men as we speak. After they finish their job today, the monks will keep them drunk and entertained until we return. We leave now!" repeating herself and establishing her authority.

Leo was back at the doorway in a few minutes, holding onto a swayback mare that had obviously been retired from fieldwork. Swaingraf noticed her look of disdain at the animal, before she lightly scrambled up onto its broad back and nudged it forward toward the rear of the compound as the two men fell into step behind her.

~

The king stepped into the bishop's private office at that very moment.

"King Joedel, how good of you to visit our humble religious order again!" Opening his arms wide, the small man bowed deeply.

"Hogwash!" the king replied loudly in a gravel-filled voice as he sauntered in. "Your Roman protectors have run away and left your rich property unprotected. Join yourselves to my kingdom, or you might find your future is very short," he said in a thinly veiled threat.

The bishop made a small gesture, and the heavy door was shut by his guards.

"Certainly, certainly it seems to be the wise… Nay, it is the only course for us to preserve our tranquility," the little man said in a stammering voice. "And our good friends like you must share in the riches that the good Lord has supplied to us," he announced, quickly hurrying over to fill two tankards.

"That is my intention," the ruler said condescendingly as he lowered himself into the bishop's own chair.

The man of God appeared not to notice the flagrant affront. "Here, let us discuss the details over our own fruit wine. We make it inside these very walls. It's delicious, one of our finest products."

"I have not sampled your wine before. Is it good?" Joedel said as the man reached impetuously for one of the tumblers.

"Rest assured it is the best wine that you will ever taste in this world, my king," as the bishop proudly raised his own cup. "Live forever my king!"

King Joedel smacked his lips in delight and loudly announced his approval. "This is good sir! A trifle sweet, but very good." His huge hand cradled the tankard as he threw his head back for another large swig.

"Imbibe freely my king. Perhaps I can persuade you to allow my monks to share a barrel of this precious nectar with your guards during supper tonight. We have barrels upon barrels stored in our cellars." The man lowered his head and opened his arms in mock supplication.

"Fill my glass again, and you may," the king replied with a somewhat flushed face.

The bishop hurried over and filled the man's tankard up to the brim with a flourish. Then he dropped the empty decanter onto the desk and strode to the door. He slapped a flat hand against the wood, and an abbey guard opened it immediately. "Please instruct the monks to serve dinner to our guests, including the offering of our 'special' wine. The king and I are ready to dine now also." he added pleasantly.

The bishop watched the king drain the goblet and lick his lips as a small procession of monks entered carrying trays of food.

"A new decanter, please," the little man said as he seated himself across from the king. "And now I hope you will be well pleased with our other bounties King Joedel."

The king was sweating profusely now, but he smiled widely as cloths were removed from the various platters. Fruits, loaves of bread, vegetables, and a small roast hog were displayed. He immediately grabbed the whole hog and began sucking the meat off of its bones.

So much for royal manners, the bishop thought to himself as he timidly nibbled on an apple and a crust of bread. He smiled as he saw one of the monks refill the king's wine tankard.

The king coughed and looked physically uncomfortable now as he took a long drink and emptied the vessel again. Holding it up for a refill, he fastened ice-cold blue eyes on his host as sweat trickled down his face. "So, what are you offering me, or do I destroy this sanctuary and all the souls who are in it?" His speech was slurred.

The bishop replied with a note of disinterest. "I think we shall offer you..., nothing!"

The king shook with fury and turned purple with rage at this diminutive man's blatant insolence. "Whaaat? You dare refuse to compensate me for your protection? I'll see this compound in ashes. You'll rot in hell this night, little man!" He arose, slightly swaying, apparently intending to strike the bishop down. Suddenly strong hands gripped his shoulders and pushed him back down into the chair as if he were a child.

Now the tiny man flashed a withering glare at the king. "You'll not harm anything or anyone in this abbey tonight, but you and your soldiers are about to become a permanent part of it. We'll be constructing a new granary over your bones. Maybe, I'll name it after you!" he said and cackled gleefully.

Joedel's eyes were wide now. He dropped the tankard and clawed for the hilt of his dagger, but it had already been deftly removed by one of the monks. Quickly a cord flicked over the king's head, and he was lifted up by the neck as the final embers of life were choked out of him. The friar released one end of the garrote, and the king's body crashed to the floor.

"Too much wine. Poor King Joedel," the bishop said with a feigned sad sigh. "Chief Swaingraf left orders for you all to obey. Please see that our guests are disposed of efficiently after they each consume at least four tankards of our 'special' wine."

The large monk dropped his hood, revealing a wild mane of golden hair as he concealed the garrote in one huge hand. Nodding to the bishop, he led the other monks out of the office and toward the main dining hall.

Chapter 19

The Trek

Magnus and Cynde walked easily through the forests and glades, angling a bit north of the setting sun.

"Where do you believe this world is headed, Magnus of Rau?" Cynde asked with mock formality.

"Don't you know? Next will be the age of Dragons!" as he formed his fingers into mock claws.

"I'm serious," she said as a well-aimed finger brutally poked his ribs.

"Ow! Well, we've been through the stone, bronze, and iron ages, and we are now firmly headed toward an agricultural age where most people will be farmers producing food, if we survive these dark days of oppression," he added. "I would imagine that in a thousand years or so, more people will be skilled tradesmen producing inventions to make life easier for people. I heard the Romans recently built a paddle-wheel boat powered by oxen before I left Gaul. I even heard of a..."

"What will be next?" She interrupted, not giving him time to change the subject.

With a questioning look, he answered slowly. "I think an information age would come next, allowing everyone to share their ideas and knowledge. I hope people will grow out of their dogmas and clannish mentality, eventually." he winked at her and continued. "Do you, my dear Cynde, know what will happen during that period?"

"The end of the world?" she asked, suddenly serious.

"The world as we know it, perhaps. It will be the age of boundless energy and enlightenment when the world begins to understand and share the words and works of Jesus. Sin, sickness, and death will be destroyed throughout the world's populations."

"You say my beliefs are ridiculous…. Did you just listen to yourself?" she said, smiling.

"We are what we believe…, and right now I believe, no I know, that I am the happiest man on this earth," he announced, as he paused and began to kiss her.

"Stop it. I mean don't stop. I mean… I don't know what I mean. We need to keep moving." she finally said.

"You're right. We need to keep our minds on the task at hand," he replied, trying to clear his thinking. As he began walking, he decided to try to impart some useful information from the Bible. "Did Osric teach you the Lord's prayer or the Ten Commandments.?"

"No. Are those what you used to heal father?" She queried.

"Well, they are important parts,"

"Teach me," she said, smiling.

Glad to see her in a receptive mood, He began. "The Ten Commandments are a guide to living,

"God spake all these words, saying,

Thou shalt have no other gods before me.

Thou shalt not make unto thee any graven image, or any likeness of any thing that is in heaven above, or that is in the earth beneath, or that is in the water under the earth:

Thou shalt not take the name of the Lord thy God in vain; for the Lord will not hold him guiltless that taketh his name in vain.

Remember the Sabbath day, to keep it holy.

Honour thy father and thy mother: that thy days may be long upon the land which the Lord thy God giveth thee.

Thou shalt not kill.

Thou shalt not commit adultery.

Thou shalt not steal.

Thou shalt not bear false witness against thy neighbour.

Thou shalt not covet thy neighbour's house, thou shalt not covet thy neighbour's wife, nor his manservant, nor his maidservant, nor his ox, nor his ass, nor any thing that is thy neighbour's."45

After an hour of recitation and random questions, Cynde believed that she could remember the words and understand most of Magnus's descriptions of the meanings in the Ten Commandments. "Now teach me the Lord's prayer." She begged, and Magnus began to recite it. Magnus smiled as he saw her struggle to concentrate and commit it to memory.

As they walked, the landscape became increasingly spongy, finally turning into a muddy bog, mostly covered with a thin layer of stagnant water. Magnus held Cynde's hand tightly as they crept through the tangled undergrowth of the marsh. Vile, smelly, blackish slime sucked and squirted at their every step and soon coated their lower extremities in an odorous ooze of decay.

"Why did we decide on this route to the coast?" Magnus asked.

"Anut reasoned that it was the most direct course since we were traveling by foot. Also, I guess he thought we would be safer here than on a main road," she replied, twisting her ankles to release them from the sticky sludge.

Magnus couldn't argue with the logic, so he just concentrated on trying to stay upright. *At least there aren't many mosquitoes this time of year.* He was feeling grateful for that when his right foot suddenly slid on a mud-covered root, splitting his legs wide. He couldn't recover his balance and released her hand, just before he sprawled on his back, spread out like a filthy snow angel.

Looking down, Cynde didn't even try to stifle her laugh. She bellowed loudly, and grabbed a nearby tree to maintain her balance, laughing until she was weak.

Magnus groaned, feeling the cold, brackish water invading his clothing as mud enveloped his scalp. He was as helpless as an overturned turtle clawing at the air.

"Now that's funny!" Was all she could utter, extending him her hand. He grabbed it, and she pulled as he wiggled and writhed, producing a variety of grunts and slurping sounds. Finally, he got his feet beneath him and was able to stand. His sodden clothes clung to his backside, producing involuntary shivers as he pulled fingers through his hair, pulling out globs of sludge.

"Are you OK?" she asked with evident concern.

"Never better!" he replied sarcastically. "We need to keep moving, I don't know how far ahead of your friends we are."

"They aren't my friends!" she growled and then fell into an uneasy silence.

Quickly, he tried to apologize, "I'm sorry the stress, the mud, and these wet clothes,

forced me to lose my mind and say stupid things.

She squeezed his hand, and he knew he was forgiven.

They struggled along for another hour until the twilight dwindled away, obscuring the direction of the setting sun. Magnus's shivers had mutated into full-blown muscle spasms amid the wind and falling temperatures. He needed to rest and get warm, but how, in a swamp?

Finding a huge, overturned tree, he laid down on the trunk with the chilling moisture in his clothes pressing against him. "GAAAH, that's cold! Just give me a minute. We'll have to make a fire."

Magnus awoke feeling warm, he was still lying on the tree trunk, but Cynde had shed her outer clothes and covered him from head to foot. Pulling her scarf from his eyes, he was surprised to see a large fire burning next to him and Cynde sitting on an island made of tree branches.

Seeing his perplexed look, she brightened, "I built a raft in this sea of mud from dead branches that I pulled off this tree, and I found your flint and iron in your pouch for the fire.

Not bad accommodations for a swamp."

"Wonderful, but you better put your clothes back on before you get chilled."

"Are you sure?" she asked coyly.

"No, but you better before my moral restraints weaken. This is not a place for romance," he muttered, motioning at the darkened wetlands. "Especially with a man in a mud coiffure."

"I suppose that you're right. I just hope that we find that time and magical place soon." As she reached for her clothes.

Smiling, he slid off the log and laid next to her. After gathering her clothes and dressing, she snuggled into his arms, and they both fell fast asleep.

Chapter 20

Deceit Un-Masked

"Shhh." Cynde awoke with Magnus holding his hand over her mouth. The sun was shining brightly.

Sensing the urgency in his voice, Cynde brought herself awake quickly. "What is it?" she whispered.

"I heard voices, and they were close. They must have smelled the smoke from our fire. There's no place to hide here. We need to run now," he said softly.

"What if there was a place to hide?" Cynde asked quietly.

"In a swamp? Where?"

Without answering, she stood, and crept along the edge of the tree trunk toward the large root ball at its base. A smooth pool of water stood where the old tree had pulled itself free from the earth. Cynde stepped carefully along the edge so that she wouldn't fall in, holding onto the protruding dried roots. Bowing deeply, she crawled into a small, triangular hole close to the bottom and disappeared. Magnus smoothed their footprint impressions out of the mud with a stray limb and followed quickly into the dank, moldy interior of the tree.

"Hollow? How did you know?" he asked quietly.

"I found it last night when I was searching for sticks," she said as she stifled a sneeze.

They huddled together silently, trying to ignore the small insects that were now investigating their warm bodies. In the next minute, they could clearly hear voices, along with the sound of a horse plodding and slogging footsteps.

"There was a fire here. They can't be far away!" a man announced.

"But vhich vay?" Another man asked in a deep, thick accent. "Waters cover de ground, no tracks."

"They will head straight for the coast. Anut said that he would arrange for a boat and meet them at Clataguay."

Magnus felt Cynde shiver in rage as she recognized the voice of her aunt. He reached for her arm in the darkened space and held it tight.

"And vhat should ve do mit Anut if he is wit dem?" the foreigner asked.

"Kill him," the lady said coldly. "The fool is noble but not smart. He thinks power and wealth aren't as important as trifles like love and being good, and I'm sure I can replace him easily," she giggled. "He's a tired excuse for a man. Just kill him and that boy Magnus too. After, we acquire Martin's scroll for the bishop," she added.

Cynde and Magnus could tell that the group was moving away now.

"Und de girl?"

"Whatever!" The woman who had called herself an aunt laughed loudly in the swamp as Cynde silently cried into balled fists.

When they emerged from the tree, they shook the dust, beetles, and other residue from their clothes. Cynde's head was throbbing, and her face was covered with moist tracks from raw tears. He knew that she was furious and deeply hurt.

"We have to split up." Magnus finally said.

"No, why?" she stammered.

"You heard them, they'll take me alive if they can't find the scroll, but they...they..." The rest of the words congealed like a thick ball and choked his throat. Clutching each other, they stood and sobbed in the morning sun.

"Is there somewhere safe that you can go?" Magnus finally asked unsteadily.

"Anut's brother has a blacksmith shop north of here in

Riedrag." Then after a contemplative pause, she replied. "Or I could try to visit Calphurnius and Conchessa of Kilpatrick. The ones mentioned in the scroll."

Magnus quickly considered the options. "Don't go to Riedrag, Sepia might expect us to go there, but she shouldn't know about Calphurnius. Make your way to Kilpatrick. It is on the West end of the Antonine wall, at least twenty days from here. It will be dangerous for you to travel that far, but I don't see any other solution. Make your way there and stay with them. I'll try to rescue Anut from that she-devil."

Cynde said nothing, but her eyes darkened when Magnus referenced her aunt.

"Here!" he said, trying to change the subject as he handed her various items. "Take a good portion of the provisions, stay off the main roads as much as possible, and away from large towns. Take the scroll. Martin's manuscript will introduce you to them, and I'll meet you there as soon as I can."

"How will we get to Hibernia together?" she asked.

"I'll sail if I can, from Clataguay to Kilpatrick, and we can travel from there, or maybe Anut will know another way."

She hesitated, and he knew she didn't want to be separated from him. Finally, she replied, "Just be safe for me. I don't know what I'll do if something happens to you," her voice trailed off.

Magnus enveloped her in a hug, looked into her eyes, and murmured: "Life doesn't ever end. Our bond is permanent, and we'll be together in this experience or the next, and for always."

"Well, just be sure to come back to me in this experience," she stated emphatically and eagerly accepted his kisses. She embraced him for several long moments before pulling away and dutifully heading northeast.

Chapter 21

Outcast

Magnus struggled with every step, slogging through the viscous gooey mess. Putrid smells erupted from each sloshing footprint and engulfed him. He was exhausted, physically, and mentally. Sending Cynde away had been the hardest decision of his life. Several times he had paused in the swamp and seriously considered retracing his steps to try to find her. *No. Better, safer to stick with the plan,* he decided and hesitantly continued his journey. Magnus was lost in thought, when his foot slipped on a submerged root again, and he suddenly knelt in the ooze. As he did, a thick spear struck the tree next to him where his ribs had been a second before. "Thwack!" The flint tip shattered with the impact, and the shaft fell on top of him. *Who would carry a stone spear?* he wondered as he grabbed the wooden staff and hurriedly crawled behind the large trunk.

There was no visible movement among the thick swamp growth, so Magnus tried discerning different shapes and colors in the scene before him. A nearby tree had an odd root traveling up its trunk with a darker patch above. *A naked leg,* Magnus finally realized. "Hello, I see you. I mean, you no harm. Come out, and let's talk." He waited several minutes until the leg twitched, and he repeated his request.

Several more minutes passed until a small, dark head peeked around the tree. First, one eye, then two. The man was no bigger than a young boy and darkly colored, clothed in a ragged mishmash of deer and rabbit hides. Magnus remained still and said: "Please, I don't have much food, but I'll share it with you." The small man said nothing as he backed slowly away. Magnus then followed him at a respectful distance.

The smaller man watched him intently as they sluggishly meandered through the trackless swamp for half an hour. Then, seeming to make a decision about Magnus's character, he turned and quickly led the way to a small hill. Perched in the center was a crude, tiny shelter of mud-covered branches and leaves.

At least my feet will dry out here. Magnus hoped as he untied a bag and reached into it, drawing out some large pieces of dried venison. Placing the items on a small pile of dusty leaves, he spread his hands in an offering gesture.

The little man's eyes widened as he reached out a trembling hand for the provisions. Snatching up a portion of meat, he chewed greedily until it was gone.

Magnus waited, watching the man eat until one chunk went down noticeably slower, and he decided to ask. "What is your name?" The man looked at him with empty eyes until Magnus repeated the question, this time a little louder.

"Bolo me," the man muttered in broken English.

"Why do you live here?" Magnus asked as he scooped a few morsels of meat into his own hand.

Bolo looked up at him with a pulsating sadness in his eyes. "I here, no home." Looking down, he sat silent for a long moment, and then the dam shattered. "I here, no home!" The man suddenly wailed loudly. Then he sat sobbing uncontrollably, his body shaking convulsively. Tears rolled down his face. Dark streams appeared in the dust covering the man's naked chest and trickled down toward his waist.

Magnus reached out slowly, patting the man's shoulder lightly. The smaller man recoiled a bit. "I'm sorry," Magnus said softly. They sat like that for a few more minutes until the man calmed. "Why are you here?" He asked again.

"Slave, to trader, run away," the man said bitterly.

"So, you attacked me because you thought I came to

capture you, and take you back to him?"

"Yes." After a pause, Bolo muttered, "Sorry."

Magnus sat quietly, unable to imagine the horrors this man had faced, and now he was lost, trapped on an island far from his home, a lonely, terrified outcast. Bolo suddenly stood up and disappeared into the doorway of the small hovel. Magnus watched warily, wondering if the guy intended to fetch another spear to impale him. Bolo re-emerged, carrying a small pile of round, unleavened bread, which he offered to Magnus with some undisguised pride.

It was a little dry and much too tough but edible. "How long have you been here?" Magnus asked.

"Long time," was all the man said.

They sat and ate, drinking from a small spring that trickled from a cleft between two small boulders. *Not a bad hideout,* Magnus thought to himself.

"When you look on me, what you see?" the dark stranger asked him.

Magnus quietly struggled to see the real man beyond any taint of skin pigment. "A man that deserves better in this life," Magnus replied and then asked, "What do you see when you look at me?"

"A white man," the man's answer came in the form of a sneer.

Magnus understood. *This man thinks he can only see the world through his eyes, but you can't look at a man spiritually and still see his race. Bolo needed to perceive mankind spiritually as sharing one universal origin.* "You don't want to see me like that, do you?" Magnus stated as he earnestly prayed.

The man's lips drew back tight, exposing clenched teeth. Hatred showed in his eyes for a few seconds before dissipating. "No," he said dryly.

"I am going to try to escape from this land by boat. Do you want to accompany me?" Although he didn't want the added burden, Magnus felt he needed to offer the man a chance to leave the dismal swamp, as an expression of friendship.

The small man twisted his head to his shoulder as though it helped his thought process and suddenly straightened himself. "No, I stay here. Everything I need here…, safe here," he added defiantly.

Magnus opened his mouth to try a convincing argument and then shut it abruptly. *He wished that someday this would be a country where someone like Bolo would have the same advantages as everyone else to live safely and freely. Where people would ignore differences and embrace the totality of mankind. Maybe it was for the best that Bolo remained in the swamp. If he was smart, perhaps he should do the same and hide here for a while,* but he missed Cynde too much to delay his trip. They talked awhile about each of their families and homelands, which neither of them expected to see again. The conversation brought shared, bittersweet feelings to each of them.

Sometime later, Magnus untied his bag of meat again and carefully separated the contents into two piles on some clean, dry leaves. Then he wrapped one of the piles back up and offered the other to Bolo. The man smiled with gratitude, bowing deeply. Magnus then wound his cloak tightly around himself, said goodnight to Bolo, and laid down for a chilly night's sleep. The bushman quickly gathered the fragments of meat into his hands and crawled into the small framework at the top of the hill.

They had a small breakfast together the following morning, consisting of flatbread and dried apples. In the mist-filled morning, Magnus bid farewell to his friend with an awkward embrace and headed away in ankle-deep mud. Looking back once, he waved at a smiling Bolo, standing straight and proud with another flint spear at his side. Magnus turned and mouthed a sincere prayer for the man's future health and happiness as he sloshed a curving path away from the Sun's growing glow.

Chapter 22

The Coast

"Bam!" The door smashed into the wall, and a dust-covered Sephia strode across the floor of the musty fishing shack, stomping to a stop in front of Anut. "Where are they?" she demanded.

Chief Swaingraf and Leo watched with amusement from the door as Anut's immediate response was a dumb stare at his wife, accompanied by a slight shrugging motion.

Sephia didn't hesitate. She reached out, wrapped her fingers through the hair on her husband's head, and violently shook it back and forth. "I said, where are they?" she screamed.

"Ow. ow, ow, you bitch!" Anut howled as he blindly grappled to find her wrists in a futile effort to diminish the pain. At the same moment, Chief Swaingraf and Leo entered but remained near the door.

One of the other men in the room took a step in her direction.

"Sure, come over here, and you'll be next!" Sephia said in a low growl as she continued to yank on her husband's hair… and the man stopped in his tracks.

"Sephia, Sephia, stop! They aren't here yet! Stop! Stop!" Anut pleaded.

With a look of resignation, she released him, stepped back, and placed her hands on her hips. "Who are these men?" she challenged.

"They are local fishermen. They are friends." Anut replied while vigorously rubbing his scalp to remove the pain.

"Why are they here?" he pointed at the other two men.

Ignoring Anut, she demanded. "Fine! Which one of you cooks? My friends and I are hungry," she declared as she sat down and crossed her feet on top of the table. Reaching into a satchel at her waist, she pitched one of the bishop's small gold coins across it.

One of the older fishermen moved to a corner to gather wood while another began to rummage through a well-worn bag of salted and dried Mackerel fish. Still another grabbed a jug of hard cider and sat it on the table in front of Sephia.

She grabbed the container and tipped it back for a long drink that trickled down her chin, before offering it to her two thirsty companions. Then she turned again to Anut. "Where do you think they are?" she said in an authoritative tone.

"I'm sure they are close, maybe it's taking them longer to get through the swampy areas, or maybe Bynelld had a relapse, and it will take them another week," he replied sarcastically, not hiding the fact that he was furious with her. "Mark my words. They will be here by the by, but why are those men here?" he repeated.

"A change of plans that I'll tell you about later. Until our quarry appears, I want eyes scanning for them at all times. Husband, you take the first watch since you've been resting here awhile," Sepia commanded tersely.

Anut begrudgingly nodded his head as he displayed a dark scowl. He stood and grabbed himself a jug of liquor as he went outside.

"Don't let me catch you drunk out there, or you'll rue this day!" Sephia yelled loudly.

The fishermen cowered as they hurried to provide food to this fearsome woman, knowing full well who was in charge.

Swaingraf grinned widely as he continued to watch the spectacle.

"How many people are in this village?" Sephia demanded.

"Twelve," one of the men replied.

"What is the best shack in this collection of uninhabitable hovels?" she asked with a smirk.

The fishermen just stared at her with blank faces.

"Never mind, this will suit me just fine," she stated. "When you're done serving the food, move your things out of here. Chief, you, and Leo find yourselves suitable lodging elsewhere. Lord, I hope I don't have to spend too much time in this wretched place!"

The chief stepped out the doorway and followed Anut as he walked up the beach towards a derelict boat hull perched on a sand dune well above the other boats.

"Anut, you haf a real hellcat dere," he said as the tinker walked behind it and crouched down out of the cold breeze spilling from the ocean. Looking around he noticed the fittings and some of the wood had been removed because of dry rot.

"That miserable bitch! She should never have embarrassed me like that," Anut stated grimly. "Why are you here with her?"

The chief sighed and slid down next to him. "She make a deal wit de bishop. He order us to go also."

"Typical, she never tells me everything," Anut offered, as he handed the jug to the chief.

Swaingraf grinned watching the tinker obediently scan the hillside as the rough liquor flowed through his lips.

Chapter 23

Laying the Trap

Magnus felt better after the night's sleep on Bolo's mound, but still struggled to keep a good pace through the swamp. In two hours though, he was finally jogging on dry ground. *Quite a memorable trek,* he thought, as he filled his nostrils with the faint smell of the ocean. A little while later, he found a clear stream deep enough to wash the dried mud out of his hair and clothes. As he waited for his garments to dry he thought, *Now Father/Mother God, how can I save Anut?*

The wind felt stronger on his face as he marched toward the western sun, through fields of waist-high grasses dried rough with the fall weather. He could see a cart path on his right, winding its way down from the low hills to the north toward the coastline. Magnus trotted toward the nearest section and was soon walking easier. The late afternoon sun was gradually painting the meadows on either side of the road in a bright, white gold color. He walked along, thinking that he had never seen sunlight this vivid. He scanned the trees in the distance and the hills beyond them, aware that they were shining brighter and seemed closer all the time. Glancing around, he noticed everything growing brighter in an unearthly golden light. After a few more steps, he could hardly see at all. Squinting, he found himself immersed in blinding light. *This must be a million times brighter than the sun!* he contemplated, mystified. Dropping to his hands and knees, he cautiously opened his eyes and found that he could clearly see the dirt and pebbles of the road in the shadow cast beneath his body. Several small bugs happily walked to and fro, among sprigs of grass on the ground. Where his shadow stopped though, there was an unearthly, whitish golden curtain of light, obscuring everything around him, including the fingers and backs of his hands. Pulling his left hand back, he inspected it in his own shadow and thrust it out through the dense veil of light, where it disappeared up to his elbow. Pulling it back, he rested on all fours as he tried to examine all his sensations. He could actually feel the light laying across his back, like a heavy, fluffy blanket – but radiating heat into his skin wherever it touched his clothes. He could feel it pressing warmth into his fingers when he stretched them through the radiant curtain. Looking down, between his legs, he saw the light draping across his calves, obscuring his feet. Lifting his head, he tried to open his eyes to peer into the source, but it was too painful. He tried to pray in those moments, to know that he was protected by God, and striving to do the right things. Jumbled ideas seemed to cascade into his mind, but they were elusive, fleeting, and seemingly incomprehensible. After several more minutes, the light gradually dissipated to a tolerable level, and he was able to stand up and begin his journey once more.

Was that the same kind of experience Saul had on his way to Damascus? he wondered, recalling the transformation of Saul. **"And Saul, yet breathing out threatenings and slaughter against the disciples of the Lord, went unto the high priest, And desired of him letters to Damascus to the synagogues, that if he found any of this way, whether they were men or women, he might bring them bound unto Jerusalem. And as he journeyed, he came near Damascus: and suddenly there shined round about him a light from heaven: And he fell to the earth, and heard a voice saying unto him, Saul, Saul, why persecutest thou me? And he said, Who art thou, Lord? And the Lord said, I am Jesus whom thou persecutest: it is hard for thee to kick against the pricks. And he trembling and astonished**

said, Lord, what wilt thou have me to do? And the Lord said unto him, Arise, and go into the city, and it shall be told thee what thou must do. And the men which journeyed with him stood speechless, hearing a voice, but seeing no man. And Saul arose from the earth; and when his eyes were opened, he saw no man: but they led him by the hand, and brought him into Damascus."[45]

If I were more arrogant, would I have kept my eyes open like Saul (Saint Paul) and be blind now? He continued walking with the strange incident filling his mind. *What was that intense light trying to show me? Was it God?* He had heard no message, but maybe it was to show him that God was indeed with him. Speculations about the strange occurrence flooded his thoughts as he hiked on. In about an hour, he saw a thin strip of dark blue on the horizon. *Finally, the ocean.*

The sun had almost set by the time he reached the cliff's edge where the pathway descended a shear stone face, to the rocky beach below. Carefully peering over the edge in the gathering twilight, he saw a jumble of small buildings clustered a short distance from the base of the cliff, and white sea spray, spewing up like dancing ghosts on either side of a rough stone jetty pointed out into the sea.

This would be the village of Clataguay, he reasoned from Anut's description. Wooden docks extended from the jetty on either side, where a few hapless fishing boats bobbed up and down in the relentless waves. Smaller boats had been carried ashore and beached above the tide line.

He saw two figures resting with their backs against a boat hull and realized that it might be sentries.

Further down the beach, Magnus could see a small pasture with animals moving in it. *Probably Anut's horses are there.* Then he noticed the tinker's wagon parked next to a stone fence. There was very little natural cover on the beach, or the cliff face, with the exception of some scattered scraggly trees. *No good way to get close to the buildings. If they have watchers posted, I'd be noticed before I made it halfway there.* Sitting in the dark, buffeted by the coastal wind, enjoying the sounds of ocean waves breaking, Magnus devised a plan. He'd lure Anut away from the coastline. Somehow, he needed to separate him from Sephia and the bishop's agents. Hoping that the details of his plan would unfold, he lay concealed in the tall grass and fell asleep.

Magnus awoke shivering. He wondered why mornings always seemed to turn cooler right before dawn. There was dim light breaking over the hills in the distance and he could now see well enough to travel safely along the ridge. He began moving along the cart path that wound through the rugged coastal hills. Magnus walked for several hours before he finally found what he was looking for. A rickety wooden bridge spanned a wide chasm with boulders spawned from rocky spires, scattered, and eroded, far below. Water dribbled from small waterfalls between the rocks, forming a series of reflecting pools along the bottom. Shielding his eyes from the mid-morning sun, he scanned both directions and could see no other crossing points. *This will do nicely,* he decided.

There was a small farm clinging to the hillside on the opposite end of the bridge, with cows grazing inside an overgrown fence. Two children were playing on the far side. Magnus strode across it, making quick mental notes on its construction and structural condition. Limestone pillars had been built about a third of the way from each bank, with the deep chasm stretching between them. Three pairs of large oak logs had been laid end to end to bridge the gap. The ends rested on a bank, each of the sets of two pillars, and the other bank. Thick planks had then been pegged onto the logs to form the decking. It was still a solid bridge, although it showed signs of severe dry rot in several areas. *Needs to be replaced,* he decided with a mischievous grin.

As Magnus neared the second set of pillars, the larger of the two boys suddenly ran out onto the bridge. Turning, the boy found the edge of the planks with his toes and lifted his arms as if taking flight.

Magnus sprinted forward and clutched the boy's tunic from behind. "You really shouldn't play here," Magnus said breathlessly.

"Why not?" the boy replied with a sneer.

"Because if you have a careless accident, I know you don't want to pass that distress to him," Magnus replied, motioning toward the smaller child and his makeshift toys.

"I'm only playing." the boy said.

"Please play something safer," Magnus replied.

The boy said nothing, but he noticed that his demeanor had softened, and he felt confident that the boy had heard his message. "You have the love of your brother in this world and more than that, you have the priceless Love of the creator of this world. Share that Love, take care of him." Magnus said, taking a few small coins from his pouch and tossing them to the young man. The boy knelt on the dusty boards smiling and gathering the coins in earnest. Silently blessing the youngster, Magnus continued toward the farmhouse.

He found a woman in the back, busily collecting vegetables from what remained of a large garden. He thought she looked about thirty, but her hair was already turning white. She was dressed in a coarse fabric that resembled a sack.

"Good lady, might I have a word with you."

She looked up suddenly, not having heard his approach, and glowered at him. "Be on with it! What do you want?"

"Is your husband about?" he said with an innocent smile.

"I have no husband. Died near three years ago."

Magnus hesitated, not knowing how to respond. "I'm sincerely sorry for your loss, madam. I asked because I would like to rent space at your farm for several days, while I do some repairs to that bridge." he stated, showing her a handful of gold coins, with a genuine look of remorse.

The next day, Magnus awoke to the sounds of the boys playing outside. After a simple breakfast of eggs and bread, he found a quantity of thin hemp cord in a shack behind the house. Tying the ends of the cord to a low tree limb, he patiently braided them into a thick rope that could support his weight. Grabbing an iron bar from a pile of dusty tools and the finished loop of rope, he headed toward the bridge.

He tied one end of the rope near the first set of piers through a crack in the flooring and then fashioned a crude body harness on the other end. Slipping over the side, he went to work, driving the bar into cracks between the stones. Prying and chipping away, he created deep pockets beneath the timbers.

Dust fell from every crack and crevice of the bridge as he worked and sweat ran in brown rivers across his body. Magnus wondered when the seasonal fall rains would begin, converting the landscape from dry and sunny to a prequel of the coming sodden, grey winter.

He spent most of the next day in a nearby forest, fashioning two thick wooden beams, rounded on all the ends. These he drove upright into the pockets so that the centers of the bridge timbers rested heavily on the ends of the beams. After that, he spiked wooden blocks around the boards as braces and removed the rest of the loose stones from around them. Jumping back and forth on the decking above, he decided that it should be sturdy enough to support Anut's horse cart.

The following day he began rolling two heavy logs beneath the bridge. He wrapped all four ends of the logs firmly with ropes. The ends closest to the farmhouse he tied to a large tree stump obscured by bushes, on the bank close to the bridge. Then he threw the ends of the ropes nearest the center of the chasm up onto the bridge deck. Climbing back up to the bridge, he worked the rope ends through cracks in the rough floor so they would slide over the bridge's supporting timbers. After returning below, he began jacking, prying, and pulling the ends up so that the logs were suspended almost parallel beneath the two main bridge timbers nearest to the house. Magnus then double-checked his measurements with a length of chord and a small log swinging on the same arc. He made sure the suspended logs would strike the first set of pilings just at the wooden beams when the ropes were cut. He finished the job by covering the exposed ropes with dirt and branches.

After that, he fashioned two crude signs with flat rocks

and some red beet dye that he borrowed from the woman. He painted a wagon and one stick person, indicating a load limit for the bridge of one wagon and a driver, and stood them up with rocks at both entrances to the bridge. Several groups of travelers passed the farm later that day. Magnus inquired of each of them where they were headed and finally found a merchant making the trek down to the fishing village. "I've heard that there is a tinker there, and we have several pots and utensils that need mending. Could you ask him to visit us here?" Magnus asked, offering him a few coins. He was going to say: "Tell him Magnus says hello." but then thought better of it.

"Be happy to." the man muttered, pocketing the coins, and heading across the bridge.

Now, all I can do is wait. Magnus hoped that bridge would come down like the wall of Jericho when Jeremiah blew his trumpets. Then he headed toward the farmhouse for an early dinner and a good night's sleep, still thinking about the Bible story of Jericho. **"And the Lord said unto Joshua, See, I have given into thine hand Jericho, and the king thereof, and the mighty men of valour. And ye shall compass the city, all ye men of war, and go round about the city once. Thus shalt thou do six days. And seven priests shall bear before the ark seven trumpets of rams' horns: and the seventh day ye shall compass the city seven times, and the priests shall blow with the trumpets. And it shall come to pass, that when they make a long blast with the ram's horn, and when ye hear the sound of the trumpet, all the people shall shout with a great shout; and the wall of the city shall fall down flat, and the people shall ascend up every man straight before him. So the people shouted when the priests blew with the trumpets: and it came to pass, when the people heard the sound of the trumpet, and the people shouted with a great shout, that the wall fell down flat, so that the people went up into the city, every man straight before him, and they took the city."**[47]

Chapter 24

A Brawl

Magnus awoke to the sound of dogs barking in the distance. There was another sound too, a low rumble of wagon wheels.

Anut must have left the village well before first light! Magnus leaped to his feet, fumbling for his clothes in the dark shadows of the sleeping area. He scrambled towards the gorge's edge, carrying his shirt in one hand and an axe in the other. He dove behind the bushes next to the stump just as a wagon, surrounded by yellowish plumes of dust, lumbered into view on the opposite hillside.

Magnus watched with dismay as he noticed two figures seated on the wagon. Two other riders followed at a distance behind the dense, swirling dust cloud on a single sway-backed horse.

The wagon hesitated on the other side as the driver noticed and pointed at the sign. Then he heard a woman's loud curse, and the team of horses lurched forward onto the decking. "Clop, Clop, Clip, Clop", the sounds of hooves echoed from the wooden boards as they crossed.

Magnus waited, hidden beneath the bush, tightly gripping the axe handle. Just as the horse's hooves struck the dusty bank, Magnus straightened onto his knees and brought the axe down. Thwack! The ropes snaked through the dried grass like whips. The two logs swung down like a huge double pendulum and struck the piers simultaneously with a loud "Crack." Magnus looked up and saw the front wheels of the wagon rolling onto solid ground. The bridge timbers started emitting loud squeals and pops, as they began a slow shift to one side. Anut must have sensed the motion and urged the animals to leap forward, pulling the wagon fully onto the road just as the loosened sections of the bridge pulled free of the support pillars and splintered into the abyss.

The two men following on the single horse jumped off and ran to the crevasse. They stood cursing as a churning yellow cloud of dust swirled up from the debris and enveloped them. Behind him, Magnus heard the farm woman, and her two sons gasp aloud at the sight.

Anut pulled hard on the reins and stopped his horses at a right angle to the wagon, with the double tree straining between them. "What have you done?" he shouted at Magnus as he stood up.

Sephia said nothing but roughly pushed her husband out of the wagon. He tumbled awkwardly down and fell heavily onto his right arm. "Ow, you broke my arm. What are you doing, woman?" Anut screamed at Sephia.

Sephia, on the other hand, was coolly eyeing Magnus. "So, you know what I have planned for you. Where is my dear niece?"

"You have no niece, you cold bitch. How could you have offered her to that animal?" Magnus shot back and gestured toward the figures standing on the other bank.

Sephia's face registered surprise at that statement, but she shook it off quickly. "Oh, I wouldn't have let him hurt her badly, but I needed to keep him excited about the chase!" Smiling, she eased herself down from the wagon and stood with her feet spread, brandishing a sword that she withdrew from an ornate sheath hanging at her waist. "The bishop has offered a grand reward for your letter from Martin, and I intend to collect it."

"I've never raised a hand against a woman, but I will defend myself," Magnus stated unsteadily.

Sephia threw her head back and laughed maniacally until

she seemed to gasp for breath.   "In our culture young man, both women and men are raised as warriors from birth, and you'll die on my blade today if you don't hand over that scroll right now!" Sephia sprang towards Magnus, and he retreated around the bushes, back to the wagon, still holding the axe.

She thrust forward, and he darted aside to the rear of the wagon as the tip of her sword splintered the wood where he had been standing. Next, she attacked with an overhead blow, and he brought the axe up, blocking her strike with the handle. The blade bit deeply into the hard oak handle and stuck. As she struggled to free it, he wrenched the sword out of her hands using the additional leverage of the long axe handle and threw the weapons over the edge into the chasm. Instantly, she was raining hard blows and kicks at his mid-section. Something made him smile. *She didn't hit like a girl.*

She saw his grin and hesitated momentarily as he watched blind fury engulf her. Spinning backward, she grabbed a fence post from a pile and advanced on him again. The post flew by, just missing his ear, and crashed onto the wagon bed. Magnus noticed that the horses were beyond excited. They were terrified, dancing in place while tethered to the tongue, prancing at a right angle to the wagon. He dove down, rolling beneath the wagon, and jumped up on the other side. He glanced toward Anut, who was still steadily cursing his deranged wife.

Stars swam in his eyes, as he realized she had thrown something that had connected with his skull. He reached out and felt the splintered beam of the fence that ran along the edge of the chasm. Pulling himself up, the world slowly came into focus, and he realized that he must have been knocked cold for a few seconds.

Sephia was stepping behind the horses, ignoring Magnus, as she held a hedge post over her head to swing at her husband. Anut was on the ground beside the agitated horses, cradling his injured arm and pleading for mercy. Magnus just had time to grab a fist-sized rock from beside his feet and throw it at the farthest animal's backside. It struck the right horse just below the tail. In an instant, two lethal hooves cocked and fired into Sephia's midsection. The woman was caught entirely off-guard, thrown violently backward, and tumbled over the railing beside Magnus. As she toppled, she somehow grabbed onto his right hand. He was spun a hundred and eighty degrees until all he saw was the rage-filled eyes of Cynde's aunt and beyond her, the rocky bottom of the abyss. She dangled at the end of his arm, clawing desperately for a better purchase. Clutching the rail with his left hand, he barely avoided following her over the fence and coldly considered the situation. The dried fence rail was bending and cracking as her weight threatened to pull him over the edge. *This traitorous woman was going to get him killed.* Carefully bracing himself, he roughly shook her deathly grip loose. Her nails bit deeply into his skin as she finally slid free, and screams pierced the air for a long moment. He watched with an uncomfortable, twisted satisfaction as her body came to its final rest below. *You won't practice betrayal in this world again!*

"Is she?" Anut sobbed behind him.

"Yes, I couldn't save her," Magnus replied, idly trying to staunch the blood streaming from his arm while still looking at the crumpled form lying amid the rocks. Feeling guilty, he reasoned with himself, *It's justified. I really couldn't save her. She was a sordid soul who would have continued to hurt or kill anyone who opposed her.* But additionally, he knew he should continue to struggle to try to see Sephia as God's child, which Cynde once loved.

Hearing a loud splintering noise, Magnus turned to see the wagon tongue wrench itself in two as the horses continued twisting in a circle. He lunged forward and grabbed the reins just as they began to break stride for a gallop. "Ho! Ho!" he chided gently as they dragged him down the dusty road. Slowly they returned to a walking gait and stopped.

The monk and the barbarian left standing on the other side of the ruined bridge were still yelling expletives, but Magnus ignored them. Turning, he helped the tinker to his feet, and together they led the horses a short distance down the road and away from the cliff face.

The farm woman ran up with the boys on her heels and

angrily confronted the two of them about the damaged bridge. Magnus assured her that the Bishop of Seaford Downs would be happy to pay for the needed repairs, while giving her another handful of coins. That stopped the discussion.

Anut loudly protested the idea of leaving his ruined wagon behind, but Magnus convinced him that repairing it would take far too long. He rushed to gather his sword and belongings from the farmhouse along with some blankets and other odds and ends that the tinker requested from the broken wagon. After tying them to one of the horse's harnesses, the two continued leading the animals toward the shade of a small, wooded area in the distance.

Chapter 25

Anut's Confession

"You'll have to set this." Anut finally said with an awkward scowl as they moved along the cart path winding through dense trees.

Magnus had never set a broken bone before, but he knew it needed to be done. It hadn't yet broken through the skin, although he saw something was protruding at an alarming angle. Searching through the smaller trees next to the path, Magnus found what he wanted. A gnarled tree with a stout trunk had a fork that started just below the height of Anut's armpit. "Over here!" he commanded, tying the horses off.

Anut stumbled through a jumble of twisted vines and roots to the opposite side of the trunk. Meanwhile, Magnus had unsheathed his sword and hacked a limb off that was about the thickness of his thumb. He shortened it and handed the branch to Anut. "Bite on this," he said.

Anut took it obediently and inserted it between his teeth with his good hand. Magnus could feel the man's anxiety. Slowly reaching through the fork, he grasped Anut's wrist and began to elevate it as gently as possible. The older man's knees buckled, and he let out a whimper of pain but remained standing as he leaned hard into the rough bark of the trunk.

"This is going to hurt!" Magnus heard himself say and then grimaced at the ridiculous statement. Taking a few moments to clarify his thoughts, he tried to understand that nothing could be ajar or separate from good in reality. He pulled rapidly and smoothly as he prayed. Anut cried out through his clenched stick, but Magnus pulled until he felt the bones align. As Anut sagged on the other side of the tree, Magnus carefully wrapped the arm with strips of rags and used several branches as crude splints. When he was satisfied, he carefully guided Anut's arm back through the fork as the tinker sank to the ground.

"Thank you, son. I owe you much." the man croaked, still spitting out pieces of bark.

"You owe me nothing, and it is Cynde, and I who will be indebted to you for your assistance in gaining our freedom from this land," Magnus smiled warmly. "We'll spend the night here and travel tomorrow when you've rested."

"What about those heathens who pursue us?" Anut asked.

"It will take them some time to traverse that big gully, but I'm hoping they'll give up the chase and return to the bishop for instructions," Magnus replied.

The tinker replied, "I don't think they will yield that easily. The monk is a zealot, and the barbarian is akin to a beast. I feel we need to keep moving,"

"All right. Can you ride one of the horses?" Magnus asked.

"If you give me a boost." the man said, struggling to his feet.

It wasn't a pretty mounting, but with a fair amount of effort, Magnus finally had the stout tinker astride one of the horses. Winding the reins around his hands, Magnus began leading the way north to what he hoped would be a safe haven.

"Where are we headed?" Anut asked after several hours, comfortably perched atop the horse.

"Riedrag," Magnus replied, inadvertently lying for no perceptible reason. "Cynde is supposed to meet us at your brother's shop."

"Wonderful. I haven't seen him in ages." Anut said, slapping his leg with his good hand, in evident enthusiasm. "Hey, look there. Is that a church?"

They were coming to the edge of the woods, and the trees were thinning. Magnus searched the horizon and saw a pale cross atop a small building in a village. "Or a shrine. It's too small to be a church, I think."

"Why that must be Glastonbury! Osric used to tell me stories about it. How a Joseph of Arimathea gave up his sepulcher to bury Jesus in it, and eventually made his way to these Isles as a missionary. He built the first church here, and you see that thorn tree in the yard?" as he pointed to a brushy sapling.

"Yes," Magnus said, captivated by the story.

"It sprouted from the man's staff overnight when he stuck it in the ground! It supposedly blooms in the winter."

"That is a wonderful tale," the boy agreed.

"And all true if Osric was correct. Not only that, but this Joseph is said to have hidden the Holy Grail from the last supper in a place called the Chalice Well." Anut continued. "That was one of Osric's favorite stories."

"We are all the grail if we carry Christ within us," Magnus said matter-of-factly.

"What is the Christ that Osric spoke of?"

"That is a deep question, but for me, it is the truth that comes as a divine demonstration of God to destroy all errors opposed to the qualities of God. Osric probably told you that Jesus expressed the Christ consistently in his healings and miracles, like when he healed the young boy. **And one of the multitude answered and said, Master, I have brought unto thee my son, which hath a dumb spirit; And wheresoever he taketh him, he teareth him: and he foameth, and gnasheth with his teeth, and pineth away: and I spake to thy disciples that they should cast him out; and they could not. He answereth him, and saith, O faithless generation, how long shall I be with you? how long shall I suffer you? bring him unto me. And they brought him unto him: and when he saw him, straightway the spirit tare him; and he fell on the ground, and wallowed foaming. And he asked his father, How long is**

it ago since this came unto him? And he said, Of a child. And ofttimes it hath cast him into the fire, and into the waters, to destroy him: but if thou canst do any thing, have compassion on us, and help us. Jesus said unto him, If thou canst believe, all things _are_ possible to him that believeth. And straightway the father of the child cried out, and said with tears, Lord, I believe; help thou mine unbelief. When Jesus saw that the people came running together, he rebuked the foul spirit, saying unto him, Thou dumb and deaf spirit, I charge thee, come out of him, and enter no more into him. And the spirit cried, and rent him sore, and came out of him: and he was as one dead; insomuch that many said, He is dead. But Jesus took him by the hand, and lifted him up; and he arose. And when he was come into the house, his disciples asked him privately, Why could not we cast him out? And he said unto them, This kind can come forth by nothing, but by prayer and fasting."48

Anut had a wistful expression as he replied. "I do remember that story from Osric too. Lord, I miss his booming laugh." Anut smiled.

"I do too. He had a marvelous voice," Magnus said with a sigh as they drew close to the village.

"Mind if I stop in on the way by?" The tinker asked. "I've been meaning to pay my respects to Brother Osric. He always tried to get me to pray or visit a church with him, but I never did. I have regretted that ever since I heard of his death."

Magnus gently pulled the horses to a halt outside the small building. A priest was tending a large garden behind the building. Pulling at his robe, he hurried inside through a back door. _So, it was a church, after all._ Magnus helped Anut slide to the ground and walked the horses over to the shade of a small tree while the seemingly converted druid waddled inside on stiff legs.

In a few minutes, the older man returned. "I feel much better now, thank you," Anut said as he stretched his good arm out and grabbed the top of the harness. He also lifted his left leg up, and Magnus dutifully bent over, cupping his hands under the man's foot, and lifting him onto the horse.

Magnus grabbed the horses' reins and glanced back at the little church. The priest's long face instantly melted back into the darkened shadows of the doorway. *That's odd,* he thought to himself but soon forgot about it.

The sun was sinking low on the horizon behind them when a sudden storm materialized. Magnus and Anut urged their horses forward at a gallop toward the only shelter visible, a rocky bluff in a wooded area above a narrow stream. Small hail began to pelt them just as they reached its base and searched desperately for an overhang to escape the coming deluge. Dropping to the ground, they grabbed their belongings from the horses, crawled behind several large boulders, and wedged themselves prone under a small rock ledge.

The wind was howling now as a driving rain drenched them. Thunder and lightning thrashed throughout the skies as a low rumble began and quickly grew into a crescendo that caused the ground to shake. Magnus was afraid the rocky bluff might collapse upon them as he felt a massive swirl of air try to dislodge him. "Hold on, Anut!"

Anut was already bracing himself with his good arm and legs splayed against what footholds he could find. "I am," he yelled back.

The downpour quieted to a soft drizzle in a little while as the sounds of thunder and wind retreated into the distance. Magnus raised his head and looked around. Periodically, a flash of lightning illuminated the area, and he could see that the once beautiful trees were destroyed, stripped of leaves and limbs. "What was that?" he asked.

"The wrath of a displeased god!" Anut said matter of factly. "You never know when one of them will be furious with us, or maybe they do it for entertainment."

Magnus stood and shook his head sadly. He knew he couldn't explain a spiritual God who didn't create earthly havoc to Anut, so he put the idea out of his mind. "Well, the horses ran off, so we might as well make ourselves comfortable for tonight."

"No comfort tonight." Anut grunted and laid back down in the wet grass.

The morning sun revealed the full devastation. Twisted stumps and branches littered the area. Climbing through the maze of wrecked foliage, they finally reached an open meadow on the backside of the bluff, where they were amazed and grateful to find the two horses unhurt and grazing quietly. Anut walked ahead, talking softly to the animals, and slowly grasped each of their reins, handing a set to Magnus. They mounted the horses and rode along the edges of the field until they found a deer trail wide enough to follow. The sun warmed and dried them quickly as they trotted along. Magnus was surprised to see that the destruction seemed to follow a path, and yet some trees and bushes looked utterly unharmed. About midday, they saw a steep side footpath that led up toward a hillfort village. Even from a distance, Magnus could see ruined buildings. "Let's see if we can help those people."

Anut just grumbled something unintelligible and lumbered along behind him.

As they drew nearer, they could hear cries of anguish and shouting. Magnus dismounted suddenly and started running up the steep incline. "I'll go ahead. You stay and tend to the horses."

As he sprinted up the steep incline, some of the inhabitants noticed him and raised an alarm. He slowed his pace a bit and raised both arms to show he meant no harm. A small group of people crowded together at the entrance of the wooden ramparts surrounding the community while cries of distress continued from somewhere inside. "We came to help," Magnus exclaimed.

"Go away, we will take care of our own!" A woman yelled as she shook her fist in the air. A young boy stepped out from behind her, brandishing a sharpened hoe, and advanced towards Magnus as the others egged him on.

Magnus stood aghast for a long moment and then turned and retraced his steps down the hill to where Anut was waiting.

A small cheer went up from the group as the boy returned to them.

"Guess you just can't help some people," Anut said, grinning as Magnus re-mounted his horse. They began riding in a wide arc around the hillside, below the loud jeers and cries of the residents.

Chapter 26

Riedrag

The rest of the trip was blessedly uneventful. Although they passed through several villages, no one seemed to pay close attention to them. Magnus used the last of his coins to buy bread and dried meat, along with an earthen jug that was continuously refilled in the streams that they crossed. Anut said that he had given all his money to his wife for safekeeping. They had nothing left to buy lodging, so the nights were spent shivering under thin blankets with no fire to warm them since the light might invite thieves to their campsite.

On one of the evenings, Anut asked Magnus, "How did you heal Bynelld?"

Grateful for the man's inquiry, he answered, "It wasn't me, always it is God who heals."

"But what did you do to help him? I have practiced medicinal lore for decades, and I don't think my skills would have allowed the man to survive. My patients usually only have at the most a fifty/fifty chance," he added with a tired smile.

"Did Osric ever teach you anything about spiritual healings in the Bible?"

"He told us stories about the man Jesus healing a multitude of maladies, and some about his followers healing too. They were good stories, but I didn't learn any real healing methods from them." Anut said.

Magnus continued: "Most people struggle to understand

the Bible from a material standpoint, instead of listening to the spiritual messages. Most people would rather drink a potion or cover themselves with a poultice than relinquish their treasured belief in a material body. Turn your concept of healing upside down… Rather than trying to understand why a person is sick, or which root to eat to make them well – you need to try understanding why they are unfallen from God's perfect image."

"Ha, ha." Anut roared with laughter. "Do you mean Varnos was unfallen, maybe the salt of the earth when he nearly took your head off? Ha, ha," he finished laughing with a prolonged, racking cough.

"Were there other stories that you enjoyed?" Magnus queried with a serious expression.

"Yeah, my favorite was about a woman fighting a dragon from something called Revelation, **'And there appeared a great wonder in heaven; a woman clothed with the sun, and the moon under her feet, and upon her head a crown of twelve stars: And she being with child cried, travailing in birth, and pained to be delivered. And there appeared another wonder in heaven; and behold a great red dragon, having seven heads and ten horns, and seven crowns upon his heads. And his tail drew the third part of the stars of heaven, and did cast them to the earth: and the dragon stood before the woman which was ready to be delivered, for to devour her child as soon as it was born. And she brought forth a man child, who was to rule all nations with a rod of iron: and her child was caught up unto God, and to his throne.'**[49] I always wondered what that old dragon's seven heads represented."

"I'd say they were the opposite ideas of what God is," replied Magnus. "Things like sin, ignorance, mortality, evil, lies, hate, and death!"

"Hey, that's seven synonyms for the devil!" Anut countered.

"A collection of terms for the greatest lie of all. Did Osric ever tell you what Jesus said about the devil?"

"Just that he was a bad man with a pitchfork that stole men's souls!" the tinker replied grinning.

"The master told a group of unbelievers, **'Ye are of your father the devil, and the lusts of your father yc will do. He was a murderer from the beginning, and abode not in the truth because there is no truth in him. When he speaketh a lie, he speaketh of his own: for he is a liar, and the father of it.'**[50] The devil is the concept that has inhibited the spiritual growth of mankind for centuries," Magnus finished seriously.

"Oh, but you have to love his pitchfork!" Anut replied, laughing.

"Goodnight," Magnus said dryly.

In the morning, they quietly resumed their journey. Magnus wondered when the druid would continue his questions, but he never did.

When the shadows lengthened, they looked for unoccupied groves of trees, away from the main roads and houses, and would eat and drink in them as twilight settled. They had muted, short conversations, always afraid of being overheard. Magnus never felt warmth expressed by Anut as they shared their ideas anyway. He accepted the coldness as a result of the stress of the trip and the shock of his wife's death. At night, Magnus slept fitfully and was often awakened by the sounds of the hobbled horses grazing close by in the darkness. He felt tired and listless during the days as they traveled together for more than a week.

On the eleventh day, they topped a large hill and were greeted with a view of a grassy valley with a rural community nestled in the center of it. "Riedrag," Anut exclaimed and urged the horse forward with his knees.

"Whoa. Let's not be in too big of a hurry," Magnus cautioned and held his horse's head down. They rode into the town and down a dusty street to a large hovel where smoke was rising from a fire pit. A skinny boy was pulling on a long stick attached to a bellows that fanned the flames.

"Faster boy, faster, your sister could do better, and she's younger," a man chided as he worked long tongs in the fire.

Then the man glanced up and squinted at the two travelers. "Anut, is that you?" He asked, spreading his arms wide and running over to embrace the man on the horse without waiting for a response.

"Yes, little brother, it's me," the tinker replied, allowing himself to be lowered to the ground by the much larger blacksmith. "And this is my friend, Magnus." he continued.

Magnus felt his hand swallowed in the massive grip of the blacksmith. "Nice to meet you, sir," he said with a wince.

"Come in, come in and tell us about your journeys," the large man said, motioning to the boy to stop pumping the bellows. "It's been how long, ten years?" he queried.

"Eleven winters!" Anut replied, settling himself on a bench, while Magnus dropped onto a pile of straw near the door. "Where's my niece?" he continued.

"Niece?" the man questioned as his wife handed the two travelers bowls of cold stew and apples.

"Yes, Sephia's brother's daughter. She is supposed to be here by now." Anut's voice cracked slightly as he mentioned his wife.

"We haven't seen her." his brother answered forthrightly.

"I'll bet she stopped at the nunnery in Walesford," Magnus said quickly. "She said she knew a girl from there."

Anut's eyebrows arched and then narrowed at this new revelation.

Magnus saw the man's reaction but had decided that it was prudent to wait in this sleepy village a few days before continuing to where Cynde was really hiding. He didn't know why he was strongly resisting the urge to run to her as he ardently listened to God for instructions. In the morning, he awoke early. The household was silent as he slipped out the door, wondering what Cynde was doing.

Chapter 27

Cynde's Journey

At that moment, standing in the bare woods where most of the trees had dropped their leaves for the coming winter, Cynde could see faint outlines of buildings in a large valley, a layer of dense morning mist hid much of the landscape. She had slogged in a northerly direction through the swamp for one whole day and spent the rest of the time traipsing through the rough countryside, avoiding the main roads where most of the travelers and villages would be. She was young and strong and had successfully avoided any contact with people for almost two full weeks. Still, despite scrounging for anything edible in the countryside during her travels, she was now entirely out of food. *I need to verify that I'm headed in the right direction anyway,* she thought, as she tightly held onto the hilt of her dagger and walked down the hillside.

Creeping closer through the sparse trunks and twigs, she tried to be silent by avoiding the colorful mats of dried fall leaves as well as she could. Soon she reached the rough timber exterior of a ramshackle conical dwelling. A group of chickens scratched in the thatch nearby for anything edible, clucking indifferently. Peering around the wall, she saw an older woman repeatedly striking a flint over a pile of dried leaves and kindling with no success. Hiding her knife and smoothing her matted hair as best she could, she stepped forward and asked lyrically: "Can I help you with that?"

The woman started but didn't cry out as she tried to remember if she knew this young girl. Just the reaction Cynde had hoped for. She quickly knelt beside the lady and vigorously struck the flint against the piece of iron until she was rewarded with a wisp of smoke. Seconds later, a flame crawled upwards, and Cynde introduced herself.

The older woman smiled widely, revealing brownish stubs of teeth. "I'm Laga, thank you, thank you," she muttered.

"What's the name of your village?" Cynde asked.

"Oxnard." the woman replied as she grabbed Cynde's shoulder with a boney hand and slowly stood upright.

"How far is it to Kilpatrick?" Cynde asked, still kneeling in the dust.

"Long way Nord." the woman said.

"Then how far is it to Hadrian's Wall?"

"One und half day Nord." the lady said, indicating the direction with a nod. "You hungry, child? Help me cook." and she waddled into the decaying structure with Cynde close behind.

"How many people live in your village?"

The old woman shuffled over to a small basket filled with dried vegetables and answered as she pawed through it searching for stew ingredients. "Not know, child. My family mostly."

Cynde kneeled next to her and extended her hands. "Let me carry those for you."

"Thank ye. You are kind to an old woman," she sobbed as she handed over a heaping handful of dried beans and peas, with tears filling her eyes.

Confused, Cynde dropped the legumes in her lap and instinctively reached out to hug Laga. She waited until the woman's shoulders stopped shaking, and asked, "What's wrong?"

Laga dabbed at her eyes with a dirty sleeve but couldn't answer and just shook her head.

"Doesn't your family help you?" Cynde urged.

The old woman paused and sat quietly. "They don't need

me, and I don't need them," she answered in a hard voice as she struggled to her feet. "Let's make stew."

Cynde walked steadily down a winding, well-worn path until late afternoon the next day. Laga had fed her very well, allowed her to sleep in her rickety roundhouse, and had given her some additional food for her trip, including some boiled eggs and flat bread. To repay her generosity, Cynde had gathered a large pile of firewood for her hostess in the morning that should keep the elderly woman warm for a month. She felt pangs of regret as she parted with the old woman, and prayed that others in her community would help care for her.

As she walked, anxiety about meeting Calphurnius and the Conchessa of Kilpatrick filled her mind. Plenty of time to worry about meeting them later, she knew, since they lived at least four days away to the Northeast. She illogically hoped that Magnus had somehow gotten ahead of her and would be waiting expectantly for her. As she walked, the country lane gradually widened as additional side trails intersected at odd angles. More travelers and farms appeared also.

She didn't want to be seen or stopped. Several times she had to duck quickly into the thick, waist-high grass that rimmed the road as other travelers approached in the distance, concealing herself until they had passed.

Cynde spotted Hadrian's Wall as she crested a low hill on the second day. She noticed it was in dreadful disrepair but thought it looked magnificent as it stretched in a curving white line across the horizon. She saw a stone structure built into the wall and headed toward it. As she approached, she saw that many of the stones, iron hardware, and usable wood had been removed from the building. However, she still admired the design and effort that had been poured into its construction. She decided to spend the night within its relative safety and fell asleep lying with her back against one of the rock walls.

She was in a boat. She could feel it rocking and swaying in gentle waves. Her hands gripped the dry, splintered wood of old gunwales as she searched frantically for something in the bluish-green water. There, a flash of color, and she saw him. Magnus's face came into focus, as he gazed at her lovingly from beneath the ocean. She tried to call to him, but her breath caught as she choked on the words. His hand moved, and he blew her a kiss as he faded into the depths. "No!" she cried as she suddenly reached out toward the water and struck a hard object.

"Ouch," she said, waking up and finding that she had punched the rock floor with her hand. She shuddered, wondering why she had such an awful dream! Raising herself up, she tried desperately to push it out of her mind. In the dim light of early morning, she decided not to go back to sleep and walked through the vacant gateway. She emerged into a great meadow and narrowly escaped tumbling into a deep, brush-covered pit where she could see a veil of weeds covering sharpened lethal posts jutting up on either side of the narrow earthen path. *I guess that helped keep the Picts away,* she realized. Walking more carefully, she eventually found a main roadway and continued north.

Early in the evening of the third day, she saw another group of travelers approaching. She quickly scurried off into the tall grasses edging the gravel road. While trying to remain hidden, she heard the group of men snickering and making vile comments as they began to walk into the field. Somehow, they had seen her! Making a quick decision, she jumped up and ran as hard as she could up a hillside toward a nearby tree line. She could hear their yells of triumph as they rallied and closed in on her, thinking she was easy prey, but she didn't falter. Cynde sprinted through the trees, hurdled fallen logs, and ducked beneath low-hanging limbs. She heard loud curses as the men ran into branches and thorns in the gathering gloom. When she couldn't hear their cries anymore, she dove headlong into a thick group of pine trees and curled up beneath their shadows. Fighting to control her breathing, she forced herself to calm down. Listening intently, she could hear voices arguing, but finally, they were moving away, back towards the road. Grateful, she lay in the nest of soft pine needles as quiet returned to the forest, and after a long while, she fell asleep.

After that experience, she took longer, more circuitous

routes around any fabricated structures she saw, staying well off the heavily traveled roads. Coming to a large creek in the afternoon, she was unable to find a bridge nearby and decided to ford it. She carefully stepped into the icy spring water and patiently searched for solid footholds with each step. Cynde had almost made it across when she slipped on a mossy stone and completely submerged. Coughing up water, she crawled out on all fours. *I'm glad no one saw that!* Shaking herself dry like a dog, she shivered uncontrollably. She forced herself to move, stood up, and walked, quivering in the light breeze as her clothes slowly dried. That night, as she lay in a thick nest of fallen leaves, her head felt like it would explode amid a series of sneezing and racking coughs. Rubbing her finger against her forehead was excruciating. *I can't be sick. I need to reach Kilpatrick,* she thought in desperation. What would Magnus do? She decided to try prayer. Magnus had taught her the Lord's Prayer at the beginning of their journey. Cynde knew that she would have to understand that she lived in God's universe, utterly separate from the mortal trials she was experiencing. Despite feeling that she lacked cohesive reasoning because of the illness's symptoms, she recited it repeatedly while trying to comprehend what each portion meant. **"Our Father which art in heaven, Hallowed be thy name. Thy kingdom come. Thy will be done in earth, as it is in heaven. Give us this day our daily bread. And forgive us our debts, as we forgive our debtors. And lead us not into temptation, but deliver us from evil: For thine is the kingdom, and the power, and the glory, for ever."**[51] She also struggled to understand that if she was completely spiritual, as Magnus had said everything was, there could be no physical pain in Spirit. She knew she was expressing Love to the best of her ability to complete this treacherous journey. She spent hours praying in agony as she patiently waited for some relief from the physical pain. At some point, she fell asleep.

When she awoke in the morning, she found herself completely free of all the cold symptoms and felt well rested, despite the lack of a full night's slumber. *Magnus must really know some hidden secrets to Life,* she gladly decided.

Her gratitude was unbridled as she resumed her journey in perfect health. Three days later she was rewarded, seeing an odd grass and brush-covered barrier that stretched across the hills in the distance. Finally, there was the Antonine wall.

Late in the day, as she drew closer, she frowned, noticing broken remains of buildings and remains of an old Roman road on the Southside of the wall. Most of the structures had been burned, leaving blackened stone carcasses that trees and other vegetation were slowly entwining. The top of the wall was covered with trees and bushes; in some areas, it had collapsed across the old road, leaving a sloping gash up to the top. Realizing that the only continuous cover in this hilly country was the wall itself, Cynde wrestled to scramble up the closest gap. Once on top, she felt safer, as she could observe the countryside around her while somewhat concealed by the dense shrubbery. With a tired sigh, she began fighting her way through the scrub growth toward the setting sun.

Chapter 28

Expedition

Swaingraf was a bored bodyguard as he leaned against the wall, trying not to listen in on the dull discourse between the two holy men.

It was mid-morning when the bishop finally uttered: "Thank you my son. You have proven your loyalty to the church, and you will be richly rewarded both here and, in the hereafter." Handing the man, a heaping fistful of coins.

"You're very welcome, your Holiness. Please remember our humble parish in your prayers."

"I will, I will… and make sure you send me a flowered branch of your Holy Thorn tree when it blooms for Christmas!" The little man beamed.

"I will your Holiness, certainly it will be an honor."

"Brother Leo come in here," the bishop yelled.

Both guards grasped the heavy latches and pulled simultaneously as the priest's long face retreated quickly through the heavy doors of the bishop's office, and Leo entered.

"Chief Swaingraf, assemble your men. We will be traveling north. Have them secure provisions for a twenty-day campaign."

"Vhat for?" the chief asked.

"It has been revealed to me. I know where the scoundrel is hiding. The one that so easily evaded capture by you both."

he goaded. "Leo, make ready a cart and pack it with enough provisions for a three-week trip. Bring along half a dozen reliable monks too. Arm the monks with the weapons we took from Joedel's soldiers, under their robes of course. Issue habits for the chief's warriors too. Have someone announce to the locals that we are embarking on a mission to destroy a dangerous heretic and reclaim a holy relic of Bishop Martin!" the wizened man said jubilantly as he idly played with a silver dagger.

"Yes, your Holiness, might I inquire as to our destination?"

"We will be traveling north to Riedrag, where we will finally put an end to that boy's devilish works." the bishop said as he plunged the knife deep into his desktop.

Leo's eyes widened as he suddenly opened his mouth, and then wisely closed it.

"Don't dawdle, get to it, brother! Send Brother Kent to me and prepare King Joedel's horse for me," the man said as an afterthought.

"Yes your Holiness, immediately," Leo replied as he turned and hurried out of the office.

"This will be a great event chief," the little man said proudly. "Everyone will see me departing the village on a momentous, holy quest for the scroll of Martin." Brother Kent appeared in a few minutes. "Pack my requirements for several weeks of traveling, but first help me pick out an outfit for my departure."

Gathering up the abbot's finest vestments, the monk hurriedly laid them out in matching outfits. Grabbing his chin, the little man paced and debated long and hard about what he would wear as Brother Kent began dragging a large trunk into the center of the room.

Chief Swaingraf straightened and marched out of the room hiding a smile.

He saw Leo hurrying back toward the dormitory and followed him.

Leo noticed an older friar sweeping out the hallway, "You,

brother Farber, run into the town and proclaim to everyone that the bishop is leaving on a mission to destroy a dangerous heretic and reclaim a holy scroll! Quickly now, don't dawdle." The man looked up in surprise, dropped the broom, and hurried out the nearest doorway.

"Who should I enlist to go along?" Leo earnestly asked the chief.

Swaingraf knew that most monks were now occupied with the harvest, especially the strongest ones. The older friars could not survive such an arduous journey. "Vhy not use de stable hands?"

Leo looked thoughtful. "Good idea, they aren't the smartest monks, but they are hearty," he said as he hurried off toward the animal pens.

Chief Swaingraf rallied his men, and they stood in a loose line with armor and swords presenting protruding bulges beneath the coarse monk robes. The stable workers arrived too, pulling, and prodding some of the horses that had just returned from working the fields. Two oxen were still yoked to a cart, and soon it was filled with provisions, the trunk packed with the bishop's extra clothing, blankets, and many soft cushions.

An hour later, the Holy Father swaggered out of his chambers wearing a heavy golden cape and a tall gold hat trimmed with red plumes. With the help of two monks, he crawled atop the magnificent white horse that had belonged to the recently departed King Joedel.

The chief grinned widely when he saw fear in the little man's eyes as several monks lifted him up to mount the animal. Unfortunately, the horse sensed his trepidation, and if two other monks had not fiercely held onto the reins, the holy man would have tumbled off the back of his steed immediately. The animal was high-spirited, and the two monks continued to struggle to control the animal. Finally, they began leading the horse out of the compound. The bishop sat grinning widely and waving to his public atop the beast's broad back, as the chief snickered. He knew the crowd of peasants' smiles hid derision as the little man was led through the town atop the stallion. *He looked like a child on his first pony ride.*

Chapter 29

Magic?

On the fourth morning, Magnus awoke feeling wonderful. It had been another good night's sleep after one of the best meals of his life. Word had spread that the blacksmith's brother was in town, and the whole community had instantly responded. All of the inhabitants brought a myriad of food and spirits to the blacksmith's home and left them as welcoming gifts for the visitors the past few days. As he wandered the narrow streets in the town in the crisp morning sunshine, he found that nearly everyone greeted him by name. *Maybe Cynde and he could settle here. It certainly is a friendly place, but is it far enough away from the bishop?*

As Magnus walked past one of the small houses, he saw a girl being assailed by a woman shaking a limp kitten in her face.

"You careless, clumsy clod, look at what you've done!" she shrieked, and the girl looked mortified.

"Please, good woman, let me have that," he asked.

She looked perplexed but handed over the tiny yellow corpse with a sneer, "Playing with these kittens, and she sat on the little bugger, she can't control her huge ass."

Armed with his most recent healing with Bynelld, Magnus immediately turned away from the pitiful apparition in his hands. *Father,* he thought, *let me see reality. Let me see this kitten as possessing its true qualities of life, joy, curiosity, and strength.*

Concentrating was difficult while the lady screamed at the

devastated girl. He saw tears streaming down her young face as she gathered up three other tiny kittens, turned and ran behind the house. The lady was still ranting, but she seemed far away as he cradled the little body and focused on asking God what he needed to know. *The girl doesn't deserve the guilt, Father. I know that nothing can stop the flow of your harmonious ideas without exception and that accidents are unknown to you. This tiny ball of fur must now express life because you are everlasting life!* He began to think again of all the spiritual qualities the kitten had as an idea of God: *strength, curiosity, courage, joy, energy, love, health…*

After a few more minutes of silent prayer, he heard the little animal sneeze and begin meowing. Looking down, he saw blood still oozing from its nose and mouth. He held it up with a grateful smile.

"It'll die soon enough, you'll see," the woman snorted and walked away between the huts.

Why can't people ever hope for good results? Magnus mused and returned to his silent prayers.

The girl sheepishly returned and was amazed to find the disheveled kitten alive. He could see the gratitude in her eyes as she asked, "Did you use magic?"

"I suppose it might seem like magic, but it is only changing a belief in matter – into concepts of God," but the girl didn't seem to listen, as she cuddled and cooed to the kitten.

Together they placed it in a basket with its mother and siblings and watched as it screamed and struggled to find an empty nipple. As soon it was eating and quiet, the girl confided to Magnus that she had felt all of its bones break when she sat on it. She motioned for him to follow her into the house, where she sat the basket down carefully. Then she whispered, "Are you an Angel?"

Magnus was surprised that this girl had even heard of angels, and he didn't know how to respond. Stumbling for an explanation, he told the girl that angels were actually God's thoughts being perceived by mankind. "I'm not an angel, but the ideas that I try to express are, and I know that God is the source of Love. You, everyone, and everything are included in his universal embrace, including your kitten!"

He noticed her nose scrunch up, as though she was thinking deeply about what he had said. However, in a few moments, she was again caressing the balls of fur and singing to them with her wavering little voice. Magnus smiled and said goodbye, promising to return soon to visit. In the background, the mother continued to loudly demand, "It'll surely die!" but as he left the tiny, thatched home, he held on firmly to the knowledge that God's ideas never die.

Chapter 30

Kilpatrick

Twilight was turning the hills to deep shades of grey as Cynde traipsed atop the remaining sod ramparts of the Antonine wall and, finally, saw a collection of rooftops spread out in a valley before her. It was a town much larger than Seaford Downs. A wide river ran through it, and she could see a church steeple in the distance. *How am I ever going to find their home?* she wondered, praying that her long, perilous journey was almost over.

She struggled through the rough brush that enveloped the old fortifications for another two hours before reaching the city's outskirts. Seeing the old Roman road that led into the city, she left the relative safety of the wall and slid down to its gravel surface. *Might as well be fearless,* she thought.

Vendors were selling a variety of masks, costumes, and noisemakers in the waning daylight as she passed through the narrow streets. *That's right, Samhain starts tomorrow!* Wishing she could share the festivities with Magnus, she continued through throngs of shoppers. Approaching the center of the settlement, she saw a church spire towering above the other buildings. *Well, the priest should know them,* Cynde hoped as she walked towards it. The church was impressive, solidly built of large carved stones. She found him behind the structure, stacking firewood against an outside wall. "Father, could I have a word with you?"

He straightened painfully and looked grateful for the

interruption. "Yes, young lady, how can I be of service?"

"I am looking for Calphurnius and Conchessa of Kilpatrick." She stated flatly. "Do they live near here?"

"Why yes, they are prominent citizens of our parish. How do you know them? Are you related, perchance?"

"Yes, distantly," she lied.

"Let me put on my wrap to insulate myself from this chill fall air, and I'll walk you to their domicile," he said, retreating into the rear of the stone church. He emerged a minute later, draping a heavy cloak around himself. "This way, young lady, by the way, what is your name?"

"Cynde of Hastell Cenllys," she replied, smiling. "What's yours?"

"Father Amos, my dear. Pleased to meet you."

They traveled down several alleys toward the eastern side of the community and then turned south. Cynde could barely see what looked like an orchard in the gathering darkness as the buildings grew farther apart. Father Amos chatted incessantly as they walked, and Cynde was grateful when they finally arrived at a large stone villa.

The priest rapped heavily on the oak doors until a menacing male voice from within asked, "Who's there?"

"Father Amos and I have a young visitor."

Locking bolts rattled as they were rapidly released, and one of the large double doors began to scrape open. Smiles from a refined couple greeted them as they were welcomed inside.

"Good evening, good evening. This is Cynde of Hastell Cenllys. I believe she is related to you," the priest announced.

"Well, not exactly related yet…" Cynde stammered. "I am betrothed to someone you know, Magnus of Rau. He was a student of Martin, your cousin," she curtsied awkwardly and addressed Conchessa but wondered silently if she should have mentioned Bishop Martin in front of the priest.

The priest had an awkward visage of revulsion at the news that this heathen girl had lied to him, but relaxed to his jovial persona as soon as the Conchessa replied: "Magnus, the dear boy, how is he, is he with you?"

They all chatted amicably for a few minutes more. Still, now both Calpurnius and Conchessa seemed anxious to bid goodnight to the priest. After several futile efforts to extend the conversation, the priest bade them all a good evening, with a hearty admonition that they bring Cynde to his next church service and left.

As soon as the man's footsteps had faded on the flagstones, Calphurnius sternly demanded: "Now tell us the truth."

Cynde's thoughts were jumbled, standing, and staring at more elegance than she had ever experienced. Instead of answering directly, she fumbled with her clothing, withdrawing the worn leather roll containing the scroll from Martin, and handed it to him. Both of their mouths fell open as they quickly recognized the document. Then Cynde found her voice again. "I've been traveling for three weeks through swamps, hills, and forests to get here. Magnus is in trouble. The Bishop at Seaford Downs wants to kill him. He was supposed to meet me here. Is he here?" she asked in obvious distress.

"Not yet child." the Conchessa said, wrapping a steadying arm around the girl's shoulders. "But I'm sure he will be. Come along, we'll get you some food and a nice bed," as she led Cynde through the house to the kitchen.

Cynde was seated at a table eating fruit when Calphurnius strode in. "Does anyone else know you were coming here?" he asked sternly.

"No, we changed our plans in a swamp north of Seaford Downs," Cynde replied and then related the whole story of how she met Magnus, his efforts that had saved the villagers' lives, his incarceration by the bishop, and his subsequent escape, their travels together, and her solo journey from the swamp.

"Do you know we lost our son and daughter to Hibernian marauders? I'm glad he saved your villagers from those mercenaries." the woman said.

"I'm sorry, Magnus told me of your son. His name was

Maewyn Succat, wasn't it?" Cynde questioned.

"Yes, and we persistently pray for his and his sister's deliverance from those heathens," Calphurnius replied with a voice choked with emotion. Conchessa came over and wrapped a caring arm around her husband.

Cynde sat silently for a long moment, remembering the pain she had felt when her mother passed on shortly after Dwig's birth. "How long ago did it happen?" she finally asked.

"It was… years ago," Conchessa answered for her husband. "They burned our village to the ground and took everything from us. Martin's scroll was destroyed in the fire too." Her eyes suddenly filled with tears.

Calphurnius suddenly cut in, "We were at a state function at the Principia in Boltun. We didn't return until two days later…" his voice trailed off.

Feeling the unease, suddenly Cynde spouted out: "I'm sure Magnus's God is with them!" She didn't know where the words came from, shocking herself more than her hosts.

Their countenances instantly softened at her words of hope, and they both smiled. "Thank you, dear," they said in surprised unison and then smiled quietly.

"We will continue to pray for their safe return," said Conchessa.

"But we know that God is caring for them, and they are in their right place even now. They both must be learning quite a lesson about life," her husband added.

Cynde stifled a yawn, and Conchessa gripped her hand. "That's enough for tonight. Let us continue our discussion after you've rested." The lady led her through a well-maintained inner courtyard, toward the rear of the house. "Here is your room, sleep well." Then she added, as she closed the door, "I will include your young friend Magnus in my prayers for his quick and safe arrival."

Cynde looked around the room. It was nothing like her father's rough country inn. There were tables, oil lamps, a small hearth with a few coals glowing in it, and a stack of firewood nearby. She shoved several small sticks down into the ashes and stacked some larger pieces on top. *That will keep me warm,* she thought as she yawned widely, not bothering to cover her mouth, and then she saw it. In the far corner of the room was an actual bed. She had heard her aunt Sephia describe one before with her usual disdain for the indulgent extravagances of the Romans. She shivered at the mere remembrance of the vile woman. *Well, if she didn't like it, it must be incredible.* Minutes after she lay down on the fluffy feather mattress, she was asleep.

Cynde awoke and shivered in the cool early morning air. She hopped out of bed and scurried quickly over to the gray pile of ash in the fireplace. Grabbing a medium-sized stick, she dragged it deeply, back and forth, through the ash pile. After several strokes, reddish-orange coals emerged, glowing in the darkened room. Carefully she stacked kindling on top of the embers, and in a short time, flames flickered up the edges of the wood, gradually warming the room. After stacking several larger logs on top, she wrapped herself in a woolen cloak and laid back on the bed in a fetal position. *Magnus, where are you?* she wondered until she fell asleep again.

Light knocks at the door awakened her. "Yes!" she answered.

"Breakfast is being served, milady," the voice of a servant girl called.

"I'll be right there," Cynde said, thinking that she had never been called a "lady" before.

Conchessa and Calpurnius welcomed her to the table, and she sat down across from them. They shared a breakfast of dried fruit and flatbread and chatted with small talk until Conchessa asked how she had slept.

"Well, except that I am desperate to know where Magnus is," she confessed.

"I will send out some discrete inquiries with some trusted acquaintances. Until we receive news, consider yourself a guest of this house for as long as it takes," Calpurnius announced.

"Thank you, but I'm not used to being a guest. I will want to contribute in any way that I can. Cooking, cleaning, gathering firewood, anything," she added.

"Thank you, I'm sure you will be a welcome addition to our household, but for now, can you tell us anything more about the bishop and Martin's message? Are we in mortal danger?" Conchessa asked with determination.

Cynde bit her lip and considered the question seriously before she replied. "Maybe. My aunt was awfully interested in that letter, and they would have killed Magnus for it, I know! Would your local priest report to the bishop?"

"I don't think they are in communication since we are so far north of Seaford Downs, but we can't take any chances. I'll have Sypher, our gardener, keep an eye on the good father. He spends a lot of time at the church, tending to the garden, and does some handyman work too. Meanwhile, we need to hide your scroll," Calpurnius said.

"Where? We certainly don't want to put it where we hid ours before. Someone might set a fire and destroy it too!" said Conchessa.

They were all silent until Cynde suddenly giggled nervously. "I know one place the bishop would never look. The church!"

"You're right," Calpurnius exclaimed. "You have a marvelously devious mind for such a young girl. They would never suspect it was hidden in our church, but where could we hide it?"

Conchessa asked, "Calpurnius, do you remember the baptismal basin we donated to the church for holy water? Didn't the stonemason carve the base hollow?"

"Yes, to save weight on the church floor. That is perfect, my dear! It still would take at least eight men to carry it." Her husband answered.

"You shouldn't try before the Samhain celebration ends, there will be too many souls roaming the streets," stated Conchessa.

"Yes, we will have to wait until the third day. It should be a perfect Hallows Eve tonight. The moon will be full and cast sharp, bright shadows, and the air will be crisp, but not frigid.

Do you have any disguise our young guest can wear tonight?"

"I'm sure that I do," Conchessa answered as she hurried toward a large chest.

"If the basin is so heavy, how will we lift it in secret?" Cynde asked, ignoring the banter about the festival.

"We Romans are all engineers," Calpurnius said proudly. "Have you ever heard of leverage?"

Chapter 31

Charlatan

The next days passed pleasantly enough. Magnus was able to participate in the villagers' Samhain celebration with wonderful foods, drinks, and costumes. He hoped Cynde was experiencing similar festivities, even while he missed her terribly. Magnus even helped with some of the residents' preparations and clean-up after the revelries. Everyone seemed to be enjoying themselves with the notable exception of Anut, who seemed to grow more sullen daily.

Magnus had checked on the kitten every morning, and it was happily playing with its siblings, much to the chagrin of the girl's mother. He was afraid that the villagers might accuse him of witchcraft, but so far, everyone had been cordial to him. Anut was the only one acting oddly. The man had asked him with escalating frequency about Cynde's friend at the convent and her exact travel plans. The tinker appeared agitated by Magnus's casual but increasingly complex fibs. He wondered how long he could continue without trapping himself with one lie too many. If Anut would stop asking about Cynde, Magnus reasoned that they could be on their way to meet her tomorrow. *Or maybe I should just go now, by myself.* The idea surprised him. It was a quiet thought that he felt he probably should listen to. In the past, he realized that he usually had problems when he didn't listen to tiny inspirations.

He was still considering it when Anut walked up behind

him early in the afternoon. "What are you doing? I've been looking all over for you?" the man demanded, obviously irritated.

"I'm just contemplating this peaceful village life. I want to live in a place like this someday. Everyone is so friendly," Magnus stated, wanting to lighten the mood.

Anut averted his eyes. "Well, now my brother wants us to gather some wood to repay their kindness. Let's go."

Magnus followed Anut down the road to where the horses had been hobbled. Releasing one, they tied an axe to the harness, and Anut led it out of town with his good arm toward a large forest in the distance. "Why so far from town?" he asked.

"That's where they told me to go. Just follow, will you?" Anut grunted aggressively, ending the conversation. Magnus wondered who *"they"* were but followed along silently.

Anut stopped the horse on the outskirts of the tree line, and together they built a two-pole sling for the horse to drag, tying a long branch to either side of the harness, and tying some smaller spreader poles to lay the firewood on. The tinker then led the horse deep into the woods, away from the smaller trees on the edges. Here were old-growth trees. Oaks with trunks larger than two men could reach around. The tinker walked on until he paused in a small clearing.

"Is this a Druid place of worship?" Magnus finally asked when he could contain himself no longer.

"Yes," Anut replied in a hostile, gravelly voice.

Magnus gasped involuntarily as the man turned towards him. Anut's face was a mask of rage. "What's your problem?" he heard himself say with false bravado.

"You are the problem," the man said, shaking the beefy fist of his good arm at him. "You and your loathsome ideas, the poisonous thoughts you have spread to my people and throughout this land. I had to kill Varnos because of you. Because of you, my best friend Osric is dead. Because of you, my niece is in danger and separated from her family. Because of you, my wagon and money are gone…. My wife is dead."

Tears flowed from the man's eyes, and he was choking on the words now. Finally, with a great show of effort, he spit on the confused young man.

Magnus couldn't believe it. Anut was blaming him for everything, and someone was clapping? He looked behind himself, and the wizened little bishop stepped from behind one of the largest trees and walked forward, clapping slowly. Immediately, other men in monk's robes stepped out from hiding, and surrounded Magnus.

"Anut. That was an admirable recitation of this young man's crimes. I doubt that I could do better myself. Your wife is surely looking down on us from heaven and is so proud of you today. I'm sure she is extremely relieved that you have now brought her killer to justice," the little man purred, drawing closer to Magnus. "Unfortunately, after hearing these persuasive arguments, I must sentence this young man to death for heresy and high crimes against the church and the public in general. Pay the informer!" He announced loudly, careful to remain beyond Magnus's reach. A monk appeared from behind another tree, carrying a large leather bag that jingled as he walked, and dropped it at the tinker's feet. "I'll expect part of that back in tithes when I see you at church!" the bishop said with a wink in Anut's direction. The tinker replied to the man with a wane smile and a shrug.

Magnus's head was spinning. He felt weak and nauseous. *What had happened?* He remembered Jesus's words. **"Now the brother shall betray the brother to death, and the father the son; and children shall rise up against their parents; and shall cause them to be put to death. And ye shall be hated of all men for my name's sake: but he that shall endure unto the end, the same will be saved."**52

Anut must have sent a message to the despot at that little church in Glastonbury! He had planned to deliver me to these goons all along. He did it for the money! he realized. Shocked as he watched the tinker pick up the heavy bag of coins with his good arm, sling it onto his back, and begin walking away toward the horse without a backward glance.

"That was quite a performance. You should have been a thespian rather than a tinker! What about Cynde?" Magnus yelled on shaky knees.

Anut didn't break stride as he made an obscene hand gesture and replied loudly, "She's no blood kin to me." He tied the bag of gold onto the travois, and began to lead the horse away

Sensing Magnus's weakness, the little man almost touched noses with him. "I don't expect you to surrender Martin's document, so we'll search you in a moment," the little abbot was actually laughing now. "Let me introduce you to a dear old friend of yours," he said.

Magnus turned and saw a colossal warrior entering the clearing. He did not recognize the man until the light filtering through the trees revealed a jagged scar running from the man's ear to his mouth.

He managed to say, "You're a Pict!" Then a huge, callused fist slammed into his temple, and a kaleidoscope of colors erupted in his mind just before the world swirled into darkness.

Magnus was awakened by a feeling of Deja' Vu. The sun was shining, and he stood up, staring at a vision he had seen before, except it was now exquisite! Marble pillars stood like rows of glistening sentinels. The pools were filled with clear, azure water, and he could see large, brilliantly colored fish swimming lazily about. Bushes, trees, and flowers were growing in abundance, but it was obvious that they were being well maintained.

Glancing around, he noticed a well-dressed gentleman sweeping rose petals from a tiled walkway. Addressing him, Magnus asked, "Excuse me, sir, but... what is this place?"

The man did not answer audibly, but he smiled graciously and motioned to a point behind Magnus. Turning around, Magnus looked at another image he recognized, the massive tree! Even from a distance, he could see sunlight dancing off the leaves and birds flitting in and out of the branches. It was magnificent! It was if the whole garden had been reborn!

Magnus began walking toward the tree. He could see that it grew from both sides of a large river, bridging both banks. Just like the revelator

described he thought: joining all nations under the one true God! **"And he shewed me a pure river of water of life, clear as crystal, proceeding out of the throne of God and of the Lamb. In the midst of the street of it, and on either side of the river, was there the tree of life, which bare twelve manner of fruits, and yielded her fruit every month: and the leaves of the tree were for the healing of the nations. And there shall be no more curse: but the throne of God and of the Lamb shall be in it; and his servants shall serve him: And they shall see his face; and his name shall be in their foreheads. And there shall be no night there; and they need no candle, neither light of the sun; for the God giveth them light: and they shall reign for ever and ever."**[53]

The view was beautiful, but he was more aware of visions suddenly filling his head with limitless ideas. God, incorporated and reflected in all the vast aspects of the universe! As he neared the tree, the concepts of harmony, health, and intelligence became more substantial to him than the polished stones he was treading on. The physical image of the tree rapidly faded, replaced by a concept of one and only one source of everything. As temporal limits fell away, he saw that Spirit was the fabric of the universe. The world shimmered in dancing light. His mind's eye watched objects being formed as spiritual ideas before being perceived materially. He felt he could comprehend the basics of reality, harmony, infinite Life, Love…, God.

Magnus awoke in the late afternoon. He was kneeling on the forest floor, blindfolded, with his hands bound behind his back, and his torso resting on a rough, hewn stump. Realizing that his head wasn't throbbing from the chief's blow, he desperately fought to hang on to the fragments of his ethereal experience in the garden.

He could hear curious onlookers gathered in a circle around him, breaking his concentration. Someone approached and shoved a knife blade under the blindfold, cutting it free along with a portion of Magnus's left ear. *I probably won't be needing my ears much longer anyway;* he thought as he gritted his teeth in pain. Glancing up he saw the Saxon chief sliding his dagger into its sheath. "You looked much better in blue," Magnus muttered.

The man's huge broadsword hung by his side. As he patted it affectionately, he grunted in an unfamiliar accent, "For you."

Stepping back, he made room for the little Abbot-Bishop to hurry into Magnus's view and announce, "I'm sorry you two didn't have more time to chat earlier, but the chief here is a man of few words anyway."

"Why was he painted and masquerading like a Pict? Why did he raid the village? What are you doing to these people?" Magnus's questions came in a torrent.

"Easy, my young friend, I have time now to reveal all to you. First, you have one final chance at a full life. Let me know where Martin's letter is in your next utterance, or you won't be leaving this glade!" the man replied with a cynical air.

Magnus swallowed hard but kept his composure. "It is not yours," Magnus said.

The little bishop seemed to be more amused than annoyed. "That isn't an inspired statement, young man. Too bad you've taken a dead-end path for your life, so much promise wasted...tsk, tsk. Now in your final minutes, lying to a man of the cloth." Leaning closer, he growled. "Every holy artifact on this wretched island belongs to me. I just don't understand this younger generation," he announced, throwing up his arms and turning around to smile at the group of monks and warriors surrounding him. Laughs and guffaws punctuated his statements. Turning back, he added. "I know that you gave it to your little girlfriend! We will find her, with or without your help," he paused to give weight to his words.

Magnus stoically peered at him, hiding his rampaging emotions, and remained silent for a moment. He had learned not to smile at the small man. "Even if you and your hired band of mercenaries find it, you won't be able to understand it because it's written in the language of God!"

The man turned purple in an instant. "I am the holy leader of this region, you worthless piece of dung. I alone am worthy of deciphering the words of Martin!" he fumed. "You are deplorable!" he roared and slapped Magnus hard across the face.

His cheek stung, as Magnus managed to say, "I must Love all who hate me. I'm sure the chief priests said the same about Jesus – and you know he was innocent."

The little abbot sneered and fumed for a few more seconds as he turned and stomped back and forth. He then seemed to regain some of his composure and changed the discussion. "Allow me to explain Chief Swaingraf and his men's purpose," the bishop continued. "As the spiritual guide of this province, I decided that it would be prudent to invite him and his men to both pretend to be savages from the north, and at the same time, to be our new protectors."

"How could you destroy those people's lives?" Magnus choked, looking around and seeing only the monks and barbarians surrounding him. There were no locals here.

"For the greater good, of course. You see, my young idealist, I am bound by a sacred covenant, not only to protect the Lord's church, but to swiftly advance his teachings among the heathen Celts. Those savages see me as a hero. Even though Claudius and his fellow soldiers returned to Rome, we will still maintain an orderly society in our region."

"You twist the Truth of God, and your grateful subjects will fill your collection plates." Magnus frowned.

"To over-flowing!" The abbot smiled and clapped his hands gleefully.

Magnus enunciated his next words slowly: "The root of all evil. You worship at the Altar of mortality." He noticed a small movement in the trees beyond the man and realized he needed to keep the conversation going as long as possible.

A cloud of unease descended over the little man's happy visage. "Any last words?" The small man asked with another sneer.

"Yes," Magnus answered, smiling as warmly as possible while looking directly into his eyes. "I had a dream after the chief here rocked me to sleep. That ethereal vision answered my questions about the future of this world. Ever since Bishop Martin left us, I've been afraid that the teachings of Jesus are being lost, that the science of Christian healing will be lost. This very day I dreamed that I walked in the Garden of Eden restored by true Christians, whose motives are love and charity, instead of hate and avarice. That dream showed me that good, the reality of mankind, cannot be destroyed! As Pontius Pilate heard, your limited mortal thoughts and actions have no lasting power. **'Then saith Pilate unto him, Speakest thou not unto me? knowest thou not that I have power to crucify thee, and have power to release thee? Jesus answered, Thou couldest have no power at all against me, except it were given thee from above: therefore he that delivered me unto thee hath the greater sin.'**54 I know now that others will follow me with even purer motives even as you reject me, like it says, **'Jesus saith unto them, Did ye never read in the scriptures, The stone which the builders rejected, the same is become the head of the corner: this is the Lord's doing, and it is marvellous in our eyes? Therefore say I unto you, The kingdom of God shall be taken from you, and given to a nation bringing forth the fruits thereof. And whosoever shall fall on this stone shall be broken: but on whomsoever it shall fall, it will grind him to powder.'**55 The stone which the builders rejected will become the cornerstone of the real church, not yours that is built on sand – like the account in Matthew, **'Therefore whosoever heareth these sayings of mine, and doeth them, I will liken him unto a wise man, which built his house upon a rock: And the rain descended, and the floods came, and the winds blew, and beat upon that house; and it fell not: for it was founded upon a rock. And everyone that heareth these sayings of mine, and doeth them not, shall be likened unto a foolish man, which built his house upon the sand: And the rain descended, and the floods came, and the winds blew, and beat upon that house; and it fell: and great was the fall of it.'**56 Think about it!" Straining against the ropes, he glanced around at the uneasy audience and added: "Christianity is supposed to be a religion of thinkers... not just followers. God will not always be ignored. The darkness of mortality will lift from your eyes, bishop, and you, too, will find atonement with the one true God in this life or one of your next ones!" Briefly, he noticed another flash of bright blue in the foliage beyond the monks.

"Your dreams mean nothing now. I am pronouncing judgment on you for high crimes against the church! The penalty is death, and I sentence you to an eternity in hell!" bellowed the holy man.

Magnus almost smiled, thinking. **"Whither shall I go from thy spirit? or whither shall I flee from thy presence? If I ascend up into heaven, thou art there: if I make my bed in hell, behold, thou art there. If I take the wings of the morning, and dwell in the uttermost parts of the sea; Even there shall thy hand lead me, and thy right hand shall hold me."**57 He wasn't worried about ever being separated from God. "God still Loves you, and why can't you forgive me like our Master forgave the adulterous woman?" he said with a steady gaze into the man's murderous eyes while retelling the story of the adulterous woman. **"Jesus went unto the mount of Olives. And early in the morning he came again into the temple, and all the people came unto him; and he sat down, and taught them. And the scribes and Pharisees brought unto him a woman taken in adultery; and when they had set her in the midst, They say unto him, Master, this woman was taken in adultery, in the very act. Now Moses in the law commanded us, that such should be stoned: but what sayest thou? This they said, tempting him, that they might have to accuse him. But Jesus stooped down, and with his finger wrote on the ground, as though he heard them not. So when they continued asking him, he lifted up himself, and said unto them, He that is without sin among you, let him first cast a stone at her. And again he stooped down, and wrote on the ground. And they which heard it, being convicted by their own conscience, went out one by one, beginning at**

the eldest, even unto the last: and Jesus was left alone, and the woman standing in the midst. When Jesus had lifted up himself, and saw none but the woman, he said unto her, Woman, where are those thine accusers? hath no man condemned thee? She said, No man, Lord. And Jesus said unto her, Neither do I condemn thee: go, and sin no more."[58]

"Silence the blasphemy!" the bishop hissed. "Kill him, kill him now!"

The Saxon chief raised his broadsword. Magnus thought he heard him grunt. "I'm sorry." There was no way to escape, not even time to pray when a sudden vicious cry erupted from all around them. Then screams punctuated the cacophony of sounds as several monks fell, mortally wounded by Pict spears. Magnus watched as Leo's face contorted in pain. A gleaming silver tip exploded from his chest, twisted rapidly ninety degrees, and withdrew itself before the monk had time to utter a sound or even fall to the ground. His body collapsed in a heap, with sightless eyes wide open.

Magnus did not hesitate. He sprang forward and ran as though pursued by the devil himself. Several of the garish, blue-tattooed warriors glanced at him but, noticing his tied wrists, kept their attentions turned to the rest of the survivors who had assembled themselves into a loose defensive ring around the shrieking little bishop. The Saxons were inflicting casualties on the intruders now but could only glare as Magnus sprinted into the depths of the forest.

Chapter 32

Concealment

The night was dark and silent as Cynde and Calpurnius huddled in the shadows of one of the large stone buttresses that lined the outside of the church. He carried a long chunk of a wagon tongue, a rope, and assorted wooden blocks in a sack. Absent-mindedly, she touched the spot where the leather pouch with Martin's letter was hidden in her bodice. Calpurnius had covered the leather with a thick coating of wax to seal the document from moisture. Above them, a tiny glint of starlight was magnified through a stained-glass window that Calpurnius's gardener, Sypher, had secretly unlatched earlier that day.

Calpurnius pressed the end of the wagon tongue firmly into the ground with his heel. Then they wedged it against the buttress at an angle. He then wrapped several loops of rope around the tongue, tied it, and steadied Cynde as she began creeping up the narrow, angled ramp. At the top, she reached for the window frame and started to swing it outward. A loud screech shattered the silence, and she stopped immediately. Sypher should have oiled the hinges.

"Slowly," Calpurnius whispered.

She started pulling again, no more than a quarter of an inch at a time. It produced a series of small pops but was much quieter than her first pull. Warm air escaped from the interior and warmed her face as she finally managed to drag it fully open. She grabbed both sides of the window frame and heaved herself up and through it into the darkened interior. Still clinging to the frame, she lowered herself quietly to the wooden floor.

Calpurnius followed quickly, scaling the wagon tongue, and propping himself on the window ledge so that he could pull it up with the rope. Then he fed it through the window and down to Cynde, who silently laid it on the floor. Dropping down next to her he whispered, "Follow me." Carrying the tongue between them, they wound their way through the pews to the church's main entrance. Calpurnius stopped just inside the large double doors. "There it is," he whispered as he pointed.

In the dim light, Cynde could barely see a large stone structure setting in a small alcove.

Calpurnius dug into the sack that he had carried on his back and pulled out a series of small wooden blocks, along with one very large one. Getting down on his knees, he felt along the lower lip of the basin for a spot where the mason had left extra material over a large notch in the carving. Satisfied, he slid the large block within a foot of the basin. Taking the wagon tongue from Cynde, he whispered, "When I lift it, stack the smaller blocks evenly underneath the gap on either side of the lever."

Cynde nodded in agreement and knelt down while he slid the tongue over the fulcrum and under the lip. Grasping the very end of the lever with both hands, he pulled down gradually. With a grinding sound, the heavy basin released its grip on the floor and tilted up. Cynde stacked the wooden blocks in place by touch alone since she couldn't see anything in the darker floor shadows. "Ready?" he asked.

"Uh huh," she replied.

Releasing his pressure, the basin tipped forward slightly. Small cracking sounds came from the wooden blocks as the stone rim impressed deeply into them. Without a word, Cynde pulled the leather pouch from her bodice and laid prone on the floor. Crawling forward, she pushed the pouch up inside the hollow base as far as possible and then backed out.

Calpurnius again strained to pull down on the lever when she was clear. Cynde quickly gathered the small blocks back into the bag. He then lowered the basin and stooped to help her put the large oak fulcrum into the sack. Cynde took a few moments to sweep her hand around the base to eliminate any evidence that it had been tampered with. Together they exited the church the same way that they had entered, but in quiet triumph.

Just to be sure, Calpurnius crept around to the rear of the church, and peered through the small window at the still form of the priest, who was snoring loudly. "Sleep peacefully, father," he whispered as he turned and headed for home with Cynde on his heels.

Chapter 33

Desperate Flight

Magnus didn't think as he ran through thickets and branches. They tore at his clothes and flesh as he ran, but he did not care as long as he was still alive. With his arms bound behind him, he knew that he was lucky not to have stumbled yet. He gasped for every precious breath. Fears of horrible unseen pursuers drove him as he bounded through the forest. Blood pounded in his ears, and Magnus could not hear water rushing ahead. Without slowing his pace, he burst through some tall bushes and fell face-first into a turbid rocky stream. *Great, I escaped beheading, only to drown myself in this torrent,* he thought sourly as his body tumbled, rolled, and slammed into large limestone boulders strewn across the bottom. Then he recalled his favorite story about floating in the bible. **"So he went with them. And when they came to Jordan, they cut down wood. But as one was felling a beam, the axe head fell into the water: and he cried; alas master! For it was borrowed. And the man of God said, Where fell it? And he shewed him the place. And he cut down a stick, and cast it in thither; and the iron did swim. Therefore said he, Take it up to thee. And he put out his hand, and took it."**[59]

I certainly should float better than an axe head! Magnus thought, as he felt himself losing consciousness rapidly, his legs still strove weakly for purchase in the rushing water. Suddenly he felt his heels wedge against a large rock. He kicked upward as hard as he could and was rewarded with a lungful of fresh air as his head broke the surface. He continued being swept down the creek until he collided heavily with the trunk of a large tree that had fallen into the water. Steadying himself against its bulk, he struggled, wading toward the rocky bank. Exhausted, he fell to the ground and suddenly realized that he had made a big mistake. Pain racked his body from the broken ribs and collarbone he sustained in his collisions with the rocks and tree trunk. He kicked and rolled, desperate to get back on his feet. The water had loosened the heavy hemp rope binding his wrists, and he finally wrested them free and was able to push himself up and stand. He felt the broken pieces of bone moving in his side as he breathed shallowly, trying to clear his head. There was a narrow deer path up the embankment, and he set off slowly in that direction before slowly returning to the bank and painfully bending down to retrieve the loose coil of rope. *Better not leave any evidence for them to track me,* he realized. Finding a small tree limb, he began sweeping away his footprints as he backed up the narrow path. He dropped the branch at the top of the hill and staggered off through the trees, trying to put as much distance as possible between him and any pursuers.

Two hours later, his throat felt parched in the unseasonably warm temperatures, and he wished that he had swallowed more water in the stream. At least his clothes had mostly dried. Slowly, he wandered through the twilight. Clouds gathered quickly, obscuring the moon, and he was grateful despite the possibility of rain. *If anyone is tracking me, they won't be able to follow my trail in the darkness.*

He experimented with his body in different positions as he rested periodically in his trek. He finally found a knurled oak tree that he could lean against and rest his left arm on a shoulder-level branch as he sat on a large rock. He found more relief from pain in that contortion than any other. As he rested throughout that long evening, he repeated the Lord's Prayer in an endless murmured strain.

The first streaks of morning sunlight stained the dark sky

as Magnus tore himself away from his rooted crutch and meandered through the early morning chill. He fashioned a loop from the length of rope that he had saved. Draping it over his neck, he grabbed it with his right hand to help hold his other arm level with his shoulder as he walked. Discomfort dogged his every step over the uneven ground. He used the position of the sun to guide himself ever Northward. Early in the morning, he saw the path becoming rocky where erosion had uncovered shallow rocky shale on the hills. Then, at the top of one of the hills, the path split into three different directions. He prayed for clear guidance, and the words from Isaiah came to him, **"And thine ears shall hear a word behind thee, saying, This is the way, walk ye in it, when ye turn to the right hand, and when ye turn to the left."** 60 He chose the right path, hoping it would be right, and continued on his way.

He thought constantly about Cynde and hoped that she was faring far better than he was with his pursuers, but then he would arrest his dark notions and try to count his blessings as he realized he could be missing his head. He often stopped to rest and drink from the small creeks that he encountered periodically. Magnus found no food other than a small cache of walnuts that he gathered into his shirt. By the end of the day, he could see a slight serpentine line of bright white over and through distant hills. "Hadrian's wall." he moaned hoarsely and smiled.

The clouds persisted throughout the day and made the night grow dark quickly. He was exhausted, having fought against both the pain and the long walk throughout the day. He spent the night in a jumble of large stones beneath a large rocky ledge. He carefully selected a spot where he could sit and yet support his left arm at shoulder level. Using his right hand, he smashed the walnuts with a rock and greedily ate even the smallest pieces. After finishing, he was extremely thirsty but knew a drink would have to wait until he found another stream. Fatigue overwhelmed him, and he fell fast asleep. He only napped for a short period, before having to move and relieve the unceasing, stabbing pains. Later, he thought he noticed a faint smell of smoke and realized that someone could be trailing him. Summoning all his resilience, he stood up. The moon had risen, and the clouds had dissipated somewhat. He could faintly see whitish stones in the path reflecting moonbeams. With a sigh of resignation, he forced himself to trudge off towards the wall.

By early afternoon, he could feel a major change in the air. Soon, the wind picked up, and the low clouds darkened considerably. He had reached the stonewall, but needed to find a decent shelter soon or he knew he could easily die of exposure. Large raindrops hit his face as he noticed a boxy abutment poking from the wall in the distance. Magnus hurried through the waist-deep grass that edged the crumbling fortification, trying not to stumble. Sheets of rain were falling now. Someone could be living in the old rampart, but he didn't care as he rushed to escape the deluge of rain that was now pelting him.

His clothes were sodden as he stumbled through the remains of a wooden doorway into an open courtyard. To his right were two openings in a low building. This must have been a Milecastle. One was built every Roman mile in the wall. The first doorway opened into an empty room with large wooden pegs driven into the plastered walls every few feet. *Probably an armory,* he imagined. The next room had been the sleeping area for the soldiers. Wooden bunks ran around the walls like a series of large shelves. A broken table lay upended on the floor. Thankfully, most of the tiles were still in place on the beams supporting the aging roof. Suddenly, a passage from the bible popped into his mind. **"In my Father's house are many mansions: if it were not so, I would have told you. I go to prepare a place for you. And if I go and prepare a place for you, I will come again, and receive you unto myself; that where I am, there ye may be also."**61

Safe from the wind and most of the rain in this prepared place, he felt blessed as he listened to the water gushing off the roof. *This is a real gully washer,* he thought with gratitude. He was pleased that it would completely erase his tracks. Easing himself into a sitting position against one of the lower bunks that looked fairly sturdy, he placed his arm on the upper berth and promptly fell asleep.

Chapter 34

Pursuit

The chief was breathing heavily as he struggled to withdraw his sword from the tattooed body lying at grotesque angles beneath him. Gradually it came free as flesh and bowels still clung to the blade. *A few more of these blue-tinted devils, and we would have lost,* he considered grimly. Wiping the back of a gritty, blood-smeared hand over the sweat on his brow, he turned and faced the bishop. The little man cowered at his visage covered in gore, and the chief could not suppress a smile as he said, "It be safe now."

The small man emerged slowly from a cleft in a hollow tree, visibly shaken with an ashen white face. Silently, he stared at the heaps of bodies strewn around the clearing. "Why has God done this? Why? Why?" he asked in a perplexed voice. "I had him. I had him right here!" he said as he marched over and slapped the tree stump where the boy had almost been beheaded. Color rose rapidly in his face as terror was replaced with righteous indignation. "I had him until you devilish bastards showed up and ruined everything!" he screamed as he picked up a large rock and smashed it down on the face of a lifeless Pict warrior. "Why? Why? Why?" he continued as he straddled the body and beat it with his tiny fists.

Turning his attention back to Swaingraf, he said, "You have to find him. Search for him, go now!"

"But vat about dis?" The chief pointed at the dead monks,

Picts, and a couple of his own warriors.

"They are dead!" the bishop announced with sarcasm and then screamed, "Forget them, catch that heretic!" adding, "I'll take care of these poor souls." Swaingraf watched with disgust as the little man's shoulders sagged, and ignoring the dead, turned for the long walk back to the town. "Why?" the bishop suddenly blurted out loudly. "Why did you help him, Beelzebub?" as he staggered on through the woods.

Shaking his head, the chief scowled as he turned and motioned to his remaining men to follow him in the direction that Magnus had fled. One lone monk had survived the onslaught and stood rooted, unsure of what to do.

"Go with them, you idiot, and be a liaison between them and the peasants. Tell the chief I will await news at the church in Riedrag," the bishop yelled, and the monk scurried after the group.

This is ridiculous, ruminated Swaingraf as he led his men through the forest. They were searching for the slightest signs of Magnus's footfalls. He should have beheaded the little tyrant instead, but then he might never get paid. *Still, it might be worth it*, as he fantasized and smiled. *He'd do it by golly as soon as he and his men were paid!* He didn't trust the devious little man, and he'd be sure to avoid King Joedel's ignominious fate. The late afternoon shadows were rapidly growing longer as they neared the stream and found the spot where Magnus had plunged through the bushes into the surging waters. *He must be dead*, he decided remembering that the boy's hands had been tied behind him.

"Ve need to find da body. Split in two groups. Scour da banks for any sign uf him," the chief growled, as he pointed to three of the men, and then at the opposite bank. Grumbling under their breath, the three waded into the icy cold water and made their way to the opposite side.

Slowly walking down the stream, both groups examined the ground intently. On approaching the downed tree, one of the warriors knelt and examined the grasses closely. "Here's something," he yelled, holding up a single strand of hemp.

Cursing, the chief waded into the waist-deep water and across to the other bank. Grabbing the hemp from the man, he studied it. "Could be, but where did he go?" he asked. In the fading light he knew that any evidence would be trampled by his men, so he ordered them all back across the creek to camp for the night.

At first light in the morning, they filed back into the cold water. They spent a several hours methodically working back and forth on the wide grassy bank, looking for anything out of the ordinary. Finding nothing, the chief turned his attention to the thin dirt pathway leading over the hill.

"I've checked. There are no footprints at all," One of his men said, seeing him study it.

"Vould you say dis is a deer path?"

"You know it is," said the warrior with a confident smile.

"Den maybe you can tell me where de hoof prints of de deer are, moron! Follow me!" The chief roared to the others and trotted up the path. Stopping at the top, he carefully scanned the ground and found the sweeping stick and Magnus's faded footprints. "He survived," he announced loudly and began running through the forest.

The group trotted along the path until nearly noon and stopped when they found the rock-studded trail branch in three different directions. They had no way of knowing that Magnus had stood on this same spot only hours before.

"Which way?" one of his men asked.

Swaingraf was trying in vain to pick out any disruption in the rocky surface caused by a footprint. Finally, he decided, "He vas trying to go to sea and escape to Hibernia before. Ve vill take de western path. Hope he not changed his mind."

Hours later, they still had not seen any definitive proof that Magnus had taken the trail before them. The chief finally reversed his decision, and the group of mercenaries headed back toward the fork.

They had just reached it when the storm overtook them. Hurriedly they tried to construct rudimentary shelters from any tree branches and sodden leaves they could find.

Eventually, they gave up and squatted on the ground in misery as they waited for the downpour to stop.

"Why are de Gods against us?" the chief pondered out loud, shivering as icy rain washed over his body.

Chapter 35

Deception

Magnus slept a little better inside the protective walls, and only stirred a few times during the night. Sunlight streamed through the open doorway when he awoke the next morning. Standing, he reached up to grab the loop of rope around his neck and felt his right shoulder slip back into its socket. *Wow, I didn't know that was out!* Amazed, he slowly rotated his arm back and forth. *That really feels close to my body. What a healing!* he realized as his elbow brushed against his side. He paused to give thanks, before stepping through the doorway. There he noticed large puddles formed in the courtyard flagstones. He slowly knelt and drank for several minutes with a cupped hand. Next, he headed outside the walls and noticed some yellowed stalks of volunteer corn in a field of tall grass a short distance away. *The soldiers must have had a lovely garden here.* He poked around in the heavy weeds and gathered all the scrawny ears of corn he could find. He also noticed where wild animals had unearthed and chewed on several small potatoes. Digging into the soft earth with his good hand, he found several more. He felt much better after chewing the hardened grains off most of the ears and eating a some of the raw potatoes. It was his first large meal in three days. He filled his shirt with anything remotely edible that he could find and headed back to the Milecastle for a long brunch. With his stomach full, he retired to the bunkhouse and took another nap.

There she is again! He saw the woman materialize gradually as the leafy surroundings came into view. The lady whose white dress he had ruined on one of his previous visits was walking toward him along a stone path with another man in white robes. Magnus was sitting with his back firmly against a large wooden building. Looking up, he realized it was not a building at all, but a massive tree trunk. Branches entwined everywhere and stretched to the horizon. In the distance, he saw a thin white line that must have been the stone trellis wall he had crashed through, when pursued by angry serpents. The Tree of Life. I'm sitting beneath the Tree of Life!

Standing up, he rapidly looked around, trying to drink in every aspect of the view. To his right was a wide, placid river with all manner of waterfowl. Ducks, geese, cranes, and swans were all cavorting, swimming, and flying harmoniously. On the other bank of the river was another gigantic tree trunk. Above him, birds flitted through the masses of conjoined branches, chirping and singing in a profusion of sounds.

Magnus heard a noise behind him and turned just as a huge lion emerged from a row of bushes. Frozen in terror, he stood motionless as the big beast padded past him, just inches away. Magnus smelled the pungent aroma of the big jungle cat. He watched, mesmerized, as it continued down to the edge of the river and began lapping up water next to a herd of fluffy sheep that were also drinking. His head was spinning. He had seen illustrations of fearsome lions and tigers but had never smelled one. It's all one big concord, he thought, looking at the various animals meandering beneath the tree. Across the river, he saw herds of deer and cattle and groups of people in the distance, gathered around the other massive trunk of the conjoined tree.

"Hello, young man!" The words startled him as he spun toward their source. "Thank you for your efforts on our behalf," the woman in white continued. Magnus stared, his mouth agape, as he suddenly could not fail to recognize the stately being standing aside her. With a slight swoon, he immediately fell on his face in full supplication.

"My Lord!" he uttered as he shook involuntarily.

"Rise Magnus." The voice was strong and commanding, yet soft with massive amounts of compassion. He felt waves of strength flow through his body and flung himself upright from a completely prone position. "How did I do that? Oh yeah, it's a dream," he remembered.

"No, my earnest disciple, it isn't... It's the reality of all things continuing to enter your consciousness," Jesus replied with a bemused expression on his face.

Magnus stood with his mouth open as a multitude of questions jogged for position in his thoughts. Jesus said, "Come, walk with us, my son." Taking the boy's elbow, he guided Magnus down a wide stone pathway toward the river. "I know you, my Lord, but who are you?" Magnus asked the woman after finding his voice a moment later.

"I am a seeker of truth, like yourself," she replied sweetly.

"But he was crucified four hundred years ago and ascended and..." his voice trailed off as he lost his train of thought.

"And you want to know where you are, why he is here, and what these dreams have been showing you... right?" she asked with a wink in the direction of Jesus.

"I can see that you already know what this place is, and since my Father is everywhere, so am I... including here," the Lord added.

"You're a spirit?" Magnus asked.

"No, not a spirit, spiritual. I, we all, reflect the one Father/Mother God and all his attributes. You are an infinite being, and so is everyone else."

"I am infinite?" Magnus tried to imagine but couldn't conceive how he could be considered infinite.

"Your thoughts are limitless, and you will gain other aspects of it soon," the woman said.

They all stopped at the river's edge and sat down on some finely crafted stone benches.

Magnus gazed at the shimmering river. He had never seen water so clear and pure. Multitudes of fish were visible, swimming more than a stone's throw away. "So, what are these dreams showing me?"

"Not dreams, spiritual concepts. They show progress and the sure conclusion to your efforts," the lady said. "Your perception of the world is changing as this garden did, from the dark and sinister place as it appeared on your first visit to a harmonious, vibrant oasis in a disbelieving earth. Ultimately the whole earth will be transformed, with an understanding of the one true God on everyone's lips."

"Your efforts in the cause of righteousness are never unnoticed. Be in the world, but not of the world," Jesus added.

"But what if I die before I finish like my friend Osric did? How is my job going to get done?" he asked.

"Did you not understand my demonstration?" The Lord replied with such force that Magnus shrank backward. "I proved that death is unreal. This is reality," he said, pointing his fingers in a wide arc around the garden. "Life doesn't stop. Osric is still expressing good and reflecting God's attributes. Nothing stops or starts in infinity. God is expressed everywhere! God is the only action, and in reality, we reflect what he is." Then he added: "These material forms that you see are not real and will fade as you learn more, but the harmony, love, and perfection are real and will be continually expressed."

"Nothing starts or stops in infinity," Magnus repeated to himself. "I'll be doing God's work before and after the seeming change called death. If I'm not afraid of death anymore, I'll be a better healer."

"You are right, my friend. Always strive to bring the Kingdom of God to whatever plane of existence you are on, but don't be afraid to leave that plane for another if you are forced to because God is always with you!" the Lord replied.

Magnus immediately thought, **"Jesus saith unto him, I am the way, the truth, and the life: no man cometh unto the Father, but by me."**[62] Then he said: "Because I am infinite?"

"Yes, you are because God is," his two companions chimed together. The three of them sat in quiet harmony, drinking in the views of the garden while lost in contemplation, and feeling peaceful, until Magnus finally asked, "How did you walk on water?"

"I told you; Spirit is the fabric of the universe. I might have just as easily walked on air," Jesus said with a serene smile as he and the woman arose, stepped lightly upon the water in the stream for a few steps, and then strode upward quickly in a widening arc through the thin, gilded air.

Magnus watched as they rounded some branches and were lost from sight. Looking down, he could still see faint ripples from their footsteps in the water...

He awoke in a lazy haze, realizing he had slept until almost noon. He took a quiet minute to memorize the incredible dream, if it was a dream. Then he shook the cobwebs from his head and immediately started gathering a meager stash of provisions into his tunic. Running outside, he stepped into the largest puddle he could find and furiously stomped back and forth until his sandals were covered with a thick layer of oozing brown mud. Then he entered the Milecastle and climbed to the top of the crumbling stone wall. Magnus walked toward the late afternoon sun, stopping periodically to check his tracks. After a few hundred feet, his feet had dried to the point that they were dropping only a few crumbs of hardened dirt at each step. He sat down with his legs hanging over the wall and rubbed vigorously on each foot until they were fairly clean. Then he retraced his path atop the fortification, being careful not to disturb any of his artfully crafted footsteps, as he watched the hills in the distance for any sign of his pursuers. *Just in case my visitors show up, I hope they enjoy a trip to the seaside.* He chuckled as he hurried atop the wall in the opposite direction. He kept walking until he reached the third Milecastle, then he raced down the steps and crawled through an opening in the rotting boards of the sagging gate that led to the Northside of the wall. Struggling through waist-high grass, he headed north toward the Antonine wall.

Chapter 36

Accident

In the morning, Swaingraf sent scouts down each of the two remaining paths and waited for their return.

You've got to admire this boy's pluck. He just doesn't stop, thought the chief, as he sat alone by a small fire, trying to get warm.

"I found a bit of the shale broken in a few places and also a possible soft imprint made by a man's sandal-clad foot," the first man to return said to the chief breathlessly.

"Show us," Swaingraf commanded, and the group set off on the path to the right after leaving a marker for the other scout to follow them.

One day later, the small band of sodden Saxons and one priest staggered into the Milecastle, where Magnus had found shelter. Walking in wet clothes after their night spent exposed to the storm, they were chafed and miserable. With a loud sneeze and rattling breath, the priest weakly announced that he could travel no farther and collapsed, shivering, into a corner of the building.

"Look, he's been here." one of the other men announced, pointing at the half-dried footprints leading up the steps to the wall.

With a cry of victory echoing in the late afternoon, the men's wet leather-clad feet splattered on the rocks as the group ran to the top of the wall and turned to follow Magnus's trail.

"Stay to da center." the chief commanded. "Dere are

loose stones along da edges."

They were making good progress in the gathering darkness, and Magnus's tracks had long since disappeared.

Curious, wondered Swaingraf, *why would the boy have had that much mud on his feet?* He had been pondering that fact repeatedly for hours when he suddenly stopped. "Ve are going da wrong way!" he bellowed. "Dat bastard has tricked us again!" Swinging around in a fury, he accidentally knocked one of his own men off the wall. The man screamed for a second and then was suddenly silent, as he lay splayed across large rocks that had fallen from the wall. His body lay twitching as life ebbed away.

"Damn," he finally said in a defeated voice when the corpse showed no signs of life. "Ve go back and follow dat Devil's trail."

"But we need to provide him a funeral!" his second in command stated flatly. The men had been unhappy when they could not stay and dispose of their dead properly after the Pict raid.

"Yes, yes, ve should be close to another Milecastle. Ve'll descend and give him proper send-off. Be quick about it," he suddenly realizing he shouldn't have said, Be quick about it. He could feel the resentment boil around him.

They silently trudged onward in the moonlight and finally descended the steps to the small courtyard. The chief gave out orders in a reticent tone, sending one group for firewood, while others went off to retrieve the body. He then directed the building of a bier and finally, set a torch to it.

Typically, the Viking funeral was a celebration, but there was no celebration tonight. The men stood seething and lost in their own thoughts as flames consumed the last embers. Wordlessly, they divided up in the sleeping area and settled down for the night. Swaingraf felt that none of his men would dare confront him directly, but he also knew they had lost much of their confidence in him as a leader – which could be dangerous. *Why had he turned so abruptly? Killing a man in a fair fight was one thing, but causing death through a reckless accident was a bad omen. He would need to find a way to cheer his men up quickly. Maybe there would be a town or village where he could buy them some ale, and they could chase the local wenches around...* Let them vent a little while, and things will be right again, he hoped, but another idea nagged at him. *How many more might die on this quest for one scrawny boy? Oh well, that's the way mad obsessions work.* Overly exhausted from the mental frustration, along with the day's physical efforts, he couldn't force himself to fall asleep and awaited dawn with reddened eyes.

Chapter 37

Antonine Wall

Magnus had traveled steadily since leaving his false trail and only stopped to slake his thirst in the small pools of water left over by the recent rain. He loathed walking in the heavy grasses and weeds of the open landscape. His path through the sweeping grassland would be clearly evident to any experienced tracker. When he could, he walked on rocks, logs, sometimes even an old stone Roman road, anything he could find to obscure his trail from the Saxons. He knew they would probably chase him down eventually, but he wasn't going to make it easy for them.

By the morning of the third day, he could see an earthen embankment in the distance with the remains of a Roman road beside it. He smelled smoke about midday and soon reached a gap in the wall. He noticed that a long section of paving stones had been removed from the roadbed beside the wall and used to construct a small village. Magnus carefully approached the closest building.

He was almost to it when a cluster of villagers suddenly appeared, glaring menacingly at the interloper.

Magnus swallowed hard and raised his right hand in a universal greeting. An older man clutching a scythe stepped away from the group and advanced toward him. "Wot do ye here?" the man asked.

Magnus stammered, staring at the long-bladed farming

implement. "I, I'm a, traveling to…"

"Why you no raise bot arm?" the man said, eyeing the rope sling knotted around the young man's neck.

"Bandits!" Magnus blurted out. "Broke bones, but I escaped."

Satisfied, the man called out in a rapid-fire language that Magnus could not understand. Several women surrounded him, tugging on his clothes. He followed willingly. They sat him down next to a steaming pot of vegetable soup and coaxed him to eat several bowls of it, as the men crowded around in a circle eyeing him with unrestrained curiosity. Conversations erupted throughout the group sporadically, but the older man quieted them all with abrupt hand signals.

"Bandits, dey follow here?" the older man asked emphatically when Magnus had finished.

"Maybe, but I tried to give them a false trail to follow."

"You go!" the older gentleman shouted and turned, issuing orders to the citizens. They started to scatter in small groups. Magnus wondered if they were taking up defensive positions.

"You must tell me which way is Kilpatrick?" Magnus pleaded repeatedly. He only received a vague pointing of the old man's finger in a Westerly direction. Realizing he was being shunned, Magnus turned and walked away under the noon sun. He was grateful for the villager's victuals, though, and felt strengthened. He noticed that his arm felt better too. Gingerly raising it over his head, the bones didn't grind together as they had before. Giving thanks to God that they had quickly knitted, he suddenly remembered the words: **"Heal me, O Lord, and I shall be healed; save me, and I shall be saved; for thou art my praise."**63 Then he scaled the embankment at the West side of the cleft and walked along the crumbling wooden ramparts through the lengthening shadows of the afternoon.

Chapter 38

An Apparition

Cynde sat alone on one of the small hills surrounding the large village. The sun was setting behind her, and shadows were growing longer. She sat and watched the town's occupants scurry around in their end-of-day routines. She wondered where Magnus was. It had been almost two weeks since she and Calpurnius had secreted Martin's scroll under the baptismal fount in the church. *He should be here by now!* she thought, feeling like there was an empty hole in her stomach. She ached for his touch.

The Conchessa had been the first to recognize her constant pain. "He must be someone really special!" she had said.

"Is it that obvious?" Cynde had replied, knowing that it was. Her love for him had been growing despite the unbearable separation that she was enduring. She had tried to explain it to the Conchessa but couldn't. There was love in her heart, and there was heartache, but there was also something darker, a foreboding that gnawed at her subconscious thoughts.

She enjoyed the villagers here. She had made friends with many of them, especially the children. Sometimes though, she had to just get away and face her fears alone. Sitting in the cool fall breeze, she reminisced about her father and Dwig and missed them terribly, but she needed Magnus. He was a part of her that had been missing throughout her life. She suddenly realized that she felt complete with him. "There was a hole in my soul that knowing you filled," she said quietly to herself.

Turning her attention back to the scene below, she noticed a lone figure striding atop the remnants of the Antonine wall on the other side of the village. Watching intently, she recognized something in the man's gait. Suddenly, she threw herself forward, running down the hillside, trailing tears of joy!

~

Magnus had walked through the night and well into the next day. Numb with exhaustion, he moved mechanically through the maze of shrubbery atop the weathered earthen embankments. Seeing a large village in the distance, he was determined to reach it before he stopped for the evening. The sun sank quickly, but he had reached the outskirts well before twilight. Seeing a breach in the earthen wall at the center of the village, he willed himself to continue walking. Once there, he carefully crawled over the exposed jumble of rotting wooden retaining timbers and slid down the turf ramp on his back. Pushing himself upright, he slowly stood in the soft thatch. It had been a long trek, and he straightened himself slowly, as an old man would. He hoped this hamlet would be Kilpatrick because he was so tired. Every joint ached, but he was grateful since his broken bones seemed knitted together again in the short time following his collision with the tree in the river. "Thank you, God!" he mouthed as he scanned the small city and headed towards an open market at the center of the town.

"What town is this?" he gasped at the first vendor's table he came to. The rough benches held an assortment of pottery items.

"Kilpatrick!" the grubby man answered indifferently, noting Magnus's horrendous appearance, and straightening up slightly as local customers approached.

"And where might I find Calphurnius of this village?"

The fellow's eyes narrowed for a moment before he pointed a dirty finger down the street. "Straight out, on the southeast edge of town."

"Thank you, kind sir!" Magnus replied, but he was already

being ignored. He shrugged and trudged on through the boisterous groups of late-in-the-day shoppers. Goats, pigs, chickens, and geese flopped, fluttered, bleated, and cawed, adding to the discordant sounds of the marketplace. Magnus watched his steps carefully through reddened eyes as he threaded his way through the crowd, and up the road. If he had turned around, he would have seen the old man ardently staring at him, to the dismay of his regular customers.

~

Cynde almost missed seeing him as she scurried through throngs of people in the street, until catching sight of his wild, filthy hair. She pressed and elbowed through a grumpy group of matronly women until she could throw her arms around him. Caught unaware, he stiffened in her grasp until he heard her voice, turned around, and melted into her arms.

With his hand firmly clenched in hers, she led him to a nearby alley. Propping him up against a wall, she stepped back and took stock of her man. She decided he looked haunted, hunted, ill, and ready to perish - much worse than when she had seen him the first time. "Come along, baby, let's get you mended!" He didn't resist as she continued to drag him through side streets for the next half hour. Finally, they emerged at the Eastern edge of town, onto a grassy hillside, with a Roman-style villa perched atop it. Cynde was quiet but continued pulling him along after her until they finally entered Calphurnius's house.

"I presume this is your Magnus?" asked Conchessa.

"This is he, but in a dreadful condition," Cynde added.

"My boy, let's get you into a bed this instant." Conchessa said, quickly appraising him. She led him to an anteroom, where he immediately collapsed onto the blankets and passed out.

"He looks half dead! Did you see his ear?" Cynde whined to Conchessa in a hushed tone as they left the bedroom.

"He has had an awful trial, that's apparent," replied the Conchessa, "But give him a little time, and he'll bounce right back. It's obvious that God is with him," she promised, and followed it with a reassuring hug.

Dinner that night was filled with speculation about what challenges Magnus had faced on his quest to find them. Cynde kept checking on him throughout the meal. Afterward, Conchessa met her in the hallway with a thick woolen cloak. "Here my dear. I know you won't be able to sleep in your room tonight," she said with a wink and strode off.

Cynde crept soundlessly into his room. He still lay in the same position that he had fallen asleep in. Magnus was dirty, smelly, and snoring, but Cynde did not care. She arranged the heavy cloak over them both and spent hours holding him until she fell asleep too.

Chapter 39

Sanctuary

Magnus awoke mid-morning to find an array of breakfast food and juice beside his bed. He drank some of the juice but realized that he needed to wash before he would have much of an appetite. He walked out of the small room into an open atrium surrounded by a columned porch on all four sides. *I wonder if they put me in the garden because of my foul odor?* Finding a large door in one wall, he entered the main house.

Cynde had been sitting with Conchessa, but immediately jumped off the couch and ran to embrace him. She tried to look overjoyed, but a wrinkled nose betrayed her, and she reluctantly released her grasp.

"I know. I can't stand myself either," he said with a weak smile.

Conchessa just pointed to Sypher, whom Magnus followed into a small room furnished with a shining copper tub. Quickly stripping out of his grime-stiffened garments, Magnus gratefully sank into the warm water and began building a froth all over his body with a cake of lye soap. Sypher said nothing but gathered up the foul-smelling clothing and quietly left the room.

An hour later, Magnus exited the room sheepishly, wearing a robe and slippers that were far too large for him. "Do you think I'll grow into this if I eat all the food, you left me for breakfast?"

Cynde and Conchessa laughed, and Conchessa said, "We will feed you so well that you'll need to dress with a tent soon," and laughed some more.

Cynde ran to him and sniffed the air approvingly before kissing him. "What happened to your ear?"

"One of the Bishop's mercenaries played barber and shaved me a little close. I'm lucky that's all he cut off!" Magnus replied. "Do you still have Martin's letter?"

"No, we hid it in the local church, beneath the baptismal fount," Cydne said.

"Good girl. That should be safe for centuries! I need to make a copy of Martin's scroll, but I think I can do it from memory. Do you have a quill and parchment I can borrow?" he asked Conchessa.

"Yes, but you had better eat first. You must be weak from your journey," she said, gently guiding him back to the bedroom.

He was nearly done eating when Sypher returned with his clothes, freshly washed, and mended. Ignoring the dampness, he slipped them on in a side room.

When he returned, Conchessa had a quill and ink well, along with a small roll of parchment, waiting for him. He immediately sat down with Cynde by his side. He spent the next hours composing and forging a manuscript similar to Martin's. Finishing, he tried to remember how the holy man had signed his name. Finally, he gave up and signed Martin's name in his own scribble. "There, hopefully that will pass for the original. Now we need to decide on a plan of action…"

Conchessa interrupted. "Let's wait until Calpurnius returns home this evening. Then you can tell us all about your journeys and challenges and formulate a strategy. Now, I think you need to relax, decompress, and spend some quality time with Cynde."

Draping his arms around Cynde, he said, "I'm sorry, I'm so wrapped up and lost in this struggle…," and she kissed him.

Later in the afternoon, Calpurnius returned, and they all gathered around the dinner table, even Sypher, eager to hear of Magnus's exploits in the past weeks.

He explained it all with as much detail as he could remember. Cynde was visibly shaken by the recitation of her uncle's betrayal, but remained composed as Magnus finished his harrowing story of escape. "Unfortunately, I am sure they are still searching for me. I hope to bring no violence upon your household, so I need to leave soon," he added at the end.

"We need to leave soon," Cynde corrected him.

"I doubt whether this crazed bishop would be brave enough to attack Roman citizens, but in this cruel and greedy world, we need to take precautions. I am sure some of our less reputable villagers took notice of your arrival yesterday, and gossip spreads quickly," Calpurnius said. "Sypher, load the chariot with food, blankets, and spare clothing, I will take this young couple to my hunting cabin in Oakshire tonight." Sypher immediately left the table to rummage for the required items as Calpurnius continued. "Magnus, I have a leather case for your scroll here, it should help to convince the bishop that it is a genuine article," he said as he handed him a shabby but ornately tooled cylinder with brass accents.

"Thank you sir - that will be perfect," Magnus smiled as he rolled the delicate parchment up and slipped it inside.

"Now, Cynde and you need to get dressed in warm clothes. We will leave in about an hour, and it is a brisk evening tonight," he stated as he stood and offered his hand to his wife.

It was a moonless night as Magnus and Cynde crawled atop the pile of bundles in Calpurnius's chariot. "It is old but well built," he beamed as he climbed in behind them. Conchessa waved from the doorway as the reins flicked across the broad backs of the horses, and they were off!

A cold wind bit at their exposed faces and hands as a sliver of the moon lit the heavily rutted cart path. Calpurnius seemed oblivious to the chill as he stood upright and urged the horses on with a non-stop oration. Sporadically they would see a flickering light from a fire inside a home, along their route. Still, they met no other travelers on the road.

Cynde and Magnus cuddled together, trying to duck from

the icy wind but enjoying every second of the ride as their driver dutifully averted his eyes from his young passengers. Ruts, rocks, and tree limbs punctuated the journey with large jolts at irregular intervals. Several times they nearly tumbled out, only to be gripped and pulled back by Calpurnius's strong right arm. After a couple of hours and countless turns on side paths through a darkened forest, they felt the old carriage begin to slow.

"Are we there?" Cynde asked.

"Yes, we are!" Calpurnius answered triumphantly. "Help me carry those bundles to the cabin."

Carefully sliding out of the chariot after being cramped for the duration, Cynde and Magnus took a few moments to rub and test their legs. Then they each grabbed armloads of wrapped parcels and followed Calpurnius into a small cabin.

"These are simple accommodations, but you should be safe," the man said as he began unrolling blankets and separating the food and clothing. Cynde hastened to hang the food from the ceiling, out of reach of vermin, while Magnus gathered the clothing and folded the blankets into neat piles.

"Tomorrow, I will endeavor to investigate whether you two are still being pursued." He strode over to the fireplace, taking an iron striker, flax, a flint stone, and some fine wood shavings out of a leather bag. Working quickly, he started a fire, to which he added larger dry kindling from a nearby pile until he had a roaring blaze in the hearth. "There, you two should be snug from now on. This cabin is remote, but don't venture too far from it. There is a water spring behind the house and plenty of firewood around outside," he added, motioning toward an axe in the corner.

"Thank you sir, we can never repay...,"

"You safely delivered Martin's document, which is more than enough recompense. Just be safe and quiet until my return," he cautioned as he closed the door.

In a minute, they heard the horses snort, and the sound of the chariot rolling through some dried twigs as it turned and headed back towards Kilpatrick.

"I thought he'd never leave," grinned Magnus as he spread his arms wide.

Chapter 40

Brutes Arrive

Descending the Antonine wall to the gravel covered street, the chief and his men entered the city. Villagers scattered as the intimidating group of mercenaries glowered at them.

Confronting a small man in a narrow doorway, Swaingraf asked in a hoarse growl, "Vat village es dis!"

"It is Kilpatrick," the man volunteered squeakily as he seemed to shrink into the woodwork.

"Und ware es da inn?"

"Straight down this street, several of them," the man said as he cowered.

Swaingraf turned his back to the man with a loud guffaw. "Ve vill have fun tonight mit da bishop's gold!" he announced loudly as his men grunted their approval in unison. *Then we see the local priest tomorrow, and he can contact the little despot about where the boy's trail leads,* Swaingraf thought to himself. With a satisfied grin, he turned and trudged toward the center of town, with the others following.

They had checked on the sick monk as they passed the Milecastle, where Magnus had left the false trail, but he had been so weak and feverish that they decided to just leave him to die there. The rest of the journey had been an easy one for the hardened men as they marched eastward atop the crumbling stone ramparts until they spotted a faint track of flattened grasses at the third Milecastle and began to trail the boy to the northwest. In three days, the group reached the outskirts of a decrepit village next to the remains of the Antonine wall. The small village had been curiously deserted when they arrived, but they quickly found Magnus's tracks where he had crawled atop the deteriorating embankment and headed west. This Village of Kilpatrick was the largest town they had seen in many days, a perfect size for his men to have some sport with the locals.

The roadway widened slightly, and from the shouts and singing flowing from open doorways, they knew they had found the main thoroughfare with the alehouses.

"Stay together, ve stay in a group!" the chief ordered. With a muttering of consent, the men reluctantly complied. "Right den, now ve have fun!" Moving into the first establishment, they surrounded the nearest table of local patrons. The residents quickly shared anxious looks among themselves, and hasty excuses for leaving flowed freely until the table was completely emptied. "Bring drink!" they shouted in unison, following it with raucous laughter.

A harried proprietor hurried over to the table with his arms wrapped around eight mugs. "I'll bring a jug too," he said quickly.

"Und food!" replied the Swaingraf loudly. "Minstrel, play…" and a man hesitantly began to sing as he plucked at the strings of a homemade instrument.

Seeing that the interlopers were staying only to enjoy themselves, easy conversations swiftly resumed among the remaining customers.

In a short while, platters of steaming venison and pork were brought to the mercenaries' table, along with apples, bread, beans, and porridge. The news of strangers in town spread quickly. A group of local women arrived and promptly introduced themselves to the men, thereby obtaining free meals and drinks with displays and promises of affection.

An untidy group of rough men entered the building at one point during the evening, but noticing the physical size of the strangers and the polished weaponry brandished by them, hurriedly left again. *They didn't even buy a drink,* Swaingraf noticed.

Later, the chief spoke to the owner and obtained lodging for the night after dropping the proper quantity of gleaming coins into the man's sweaty hands. As each of his men approached a drunken stupor, he guided them in turn to the sleeping area. With the last of them bedded down, he ran the remaining wanton women off with verbal threats until they darted out into the street. Then he chose a soft spot to settle down and sit to keep watch throughout the night. He knew his men had needed this diversion to move past the many disappointments of this fruitless chase, now they should be loyal once more.

No more than an hour later, he heard someone bump into a table and curse quietly. The inn was completely dark. Ashes had covered the glowing red coals of the fire until they smoldered, only emitting a thin wisp of smoke. Soundlessly, he drew his sword from its scabbard and crept over to the doorway. A dark shape filled the void as he heard a muffled step. He aimed at the center and drove the sword forward. Two cries of pain erupted in the night as the chief struggled to free his weapon. Other sounds of men falling over furniture and scurrying away quickly followed.

When quiet returned, Swaingraf shuffled carefully over to the pile of coals and stirred them with the tip of his sword. A flame flared up quickly, and he threw some more sticks on top. With the light from the fire, he could see two carcasses lying where he had struck them down with one powerful thrust. He recognized the bodies from the group of ruffians that had briefly stopped by earlier.

With a sigh, he wandered back to the sleeping area where his men were still snoring soundly. He was confident that the other rogues would not be returning. He laid down on some soft hides and promptly fell asleep.

The chief awoke before first light and began to harass his men to wake them up. They stood up groggily and, one by one, filed outside to relieve themselves. Returning, they donned their weapons slowly. *At least they can stand up*, he thought with a grin. Then he heard the innkeeper complaining loudly in the next room as the man came into the dining area and saw the overturned and broken furniture.

"What have you done?" cried the innkeeper as he entered and saw the two dead men lying in a large pool of partially dried blood.

"Dey come in a group and tried ta murder us in da night," the chief answered evenly. "Vhy, you vant to join dem?"

"Ahhh… No!" the man answered abruptly. "Those local scumbags, you had to do it. They got what they deserved. I'll have them hauled off right away."

"Fine, und bring breakfast first."

"I…, I…, I will…, right now, sir," the man said as he turned and hurried away.

Swaingraf smiled. *This man was not going to be a threat.* Swaingraf lifted his leg and nonchalantly stepped over the corpses. Several of his men followed and knelt, searching the cadavers for any valuables. They found only a couple of coarse knives and continued on into the eating area.

The proprietor was now busily stacking vittles atop a bench that had not been damaged. "Help yourselves, gentlemen," he proffered.

The men quickly grabbed armloads of food and sat on remnants of furniture as they ate quietly.

"Vhere ist your local priest?" the chief asked as he finished eating.

"Oh, just take a left outside my door, follow the road for four more blocks, and the church will be off to the left."

Dropping a few more coins onto a bench, Swaingraf waited patiently until his men finished their breakfast. Without another word, they filed out of the lodgings into a chilly early morning fog.

Chapter 41

Premonition

In the morning, Magnus awoke to the smell of eggs and bread cooked in the hearth. Cynde looked at him and said, "My, but you are a sound sleeper. I had to tend the fire all night, bring in water and cook while you slumbered on."

"I'm sorry…," was all he could think to say before she handed him a steaming plate, while he sat in the bed.

"Right then. You get to wash the dishes," she said with a wink.

I am so lucky. He happily devoured the food as he watched her tidy up the cabin. *I wish life could stay like this...* Suddenly a cold chill ran violently up his backbone, eliciting a moan.

"What's wrong?" Cynde exclaimed.

"I don't know, I was feeling really grateful for you, and everything – then suddenly, I felt icy fingers gripping my back."

"Witchcraft!" Cynde cried definitively. "Someone is attacking you!"

Holding up his hand for quiet, Magnus was silent and praying to know that he was doing what was right, that it would bless others – and also that God was a constant protection to Cynde, himself, and everyone. In a few moments, he spoke. "I don't fear what men might do to me. Life is eternal. If we can't escape together, I want you to live and be happy in this world until we can reunite in the next one."

"No, we have to be together. I need you!" she insisted,

recalling the dream she had about the rowboat.

"We are together, and we will always be together. Even if worlds separate us for a time, I will always be in love with you," he said with a wane smile. "Always."

"Why are you saying these things? Did you have a vision?"

"No, I don't know why. Just a feeling. I just want to know that if, for some reason…, if we are separated…, you will live life, love again, uh…, and protect the secret of Martin's scroll, and share it with others if it seems right."

Gathering her composure, she said, "You know I will. Now no more foolish talk, I need firewood, and you had better wash those dishes this morning, or you won't be having lunch."

With a groan, Magnus quickly finished eating and crawled out of bed. *That may be the quality that I admire the most, her forceful tenacity!* He dressed quickly and grabbed the heavy axe.

"Make sure they aren't too big for the fireplace, and I need kindling too!" she demanded.

"Yes ma'am," he said, kissing her quickly and trying to ignore the unease in her eyes as he headed out the door into a cloud-covered morning.

Magnus finished cutting and stacking the wood in a couple hours. Then he obediently washed the dirty dishes while Cynde prepared lunch. They ate quietly, each apparently lost in their own thoughts and concerns. When they finished eating, the clouds had dissipated, and Magnus suggested, "Let's take a walk in this bright fall sunshine."

The brilliant light of midday lifted his spirits, and he quickly forgot about the random chill as they frolicked through the gently rolling hills. Slowing periodically, they both scanned the countryside to see any sign of neighbors or travelers but saw no one. Around one o'clock, the sky darkened dramatically as menacing clouds began to gather again. They quickly began a return trip to the tiny cabin, with Magnus anticipating a peaceful evening together. He was hoping to soon be cuddled and snug before a roaring fire, gently holding Cynde in his arms. Suddenly, they heard the faint hoof falls and snorts of horses approaching in the distance.

Chapter 42

Alert!

The chief noticed a boy sweeping the sidewalk outside the church. Sypher noticed the group of warriors approaching, dropped the broom and quickly darted inside. A moment later a priest hurried out to meet them.

"Are you da priest here?" the hulking chief inquired.

"Yes…, yes my ah…, son, I am Father Amos, what can I do for you?" as the priest craned his head back to gaze into the chief's steel blue eyes.

"Haf you seen a stranger boy here?" he grumbled as he motioned to the town.

"No, no…, I mean yes, I might have. Whom do ye seek?" Amos replied as a bead of sweat appeared on his brow.

"A boy, name uf Magnus uf Rau."

"Yes, I mean no, I haven't seen him myself. Obe, one of my parishioners said he saw a young man who walked into town on the remnants of the Antonine Wall. That was a few days ago."

"Vhere ist he?" the chief roared.

"I, I, don't quite know. Wait, let me think. There was a pretty girl who said she was betrothed to a Magnus, yes, from close to Seaford Downs! I sent a dispatch to the bishop there, asking about her."

"Vhere are dey?"

"I don't know if it's the same boy, but the girl was visiting

Calpurnius and his wife. They live at the edge of town, right down this road to the southeast."

"Did you hear from de bishop?"

"No, but I sent him my message, ah let's see, nearly two weeks ago." he paused as a robust cart, pulled by two stout oxen, rolled to a stop next to the church. The monk driving the cart leaped to the ground, pulled off a ladder that was hanging on the side, and hurried to assist a small man clambering down from atop a cushioning pile of blankets and soft bundles — while another friar began to unload the cart.

"Take those things inside the rectory. I will stay here. Where is the priest of this parish?" the small man questioned as he stood and stretched his back.

"I am sir, and you are…?"

"Bishop Corizone, you may call me Excellency. The Lord's hand brought your messenger to Riedrag as I sojourned there. Luckily, he also had a letter for the local priest, and thus I received your dispatch."

The chief smiled but said nothing. He had noticed the outlines of swords and daggers hidden beneath the monk's robes. Un-trained and un-proven, these guards would provide little security for their holy leader if they were ever in a true fight.

"And you, Chief Swaingraf, you should have run our young scoundrel to ground a week ago!" the self-righteous bishop announced flatly, but quickly changed the subject when he noticed the man's smile abruptly morph into to menacing scowl. "So, he is staying in this village, priest?"

"Yes, that is, I think he might be…, at the home of Calpurnius. He is one of our leading citizens. A town father, your Excellency."

"Why did he come all this way to the home of this…, Calpurnius? Do you know?"

"There is a girl. She said she was engaged to the young man. I took her to their house, and I have seen her in church, and several times in the village since then. She is a beautiful girl…"

"Enough! I have heard enough. Chief, give me an hour or two to freshen up, imbibe some vittles, and we will pay those fine citizens a visit," the bishop said, suddenly turning and striding towards the church. The priest hurriedly rushed forward to open the door for him. "Put my things back into the cart." the bishop said over his shoulder as he entered the church.

The chief watched as the boy he saw earlier exited through a small side door at the back of one of the transepts and crouched below a low stone garden fence. Then the lad scurried behind the next row of buildings until he was out of sight of the church. *Quite odd. It looks like he could be running off to warn someone.*

"Chief come in here now!" the bishop yelled.

Pompous idiot, Swaingraf thought as he turned and headed to the church.

Chapter 43

Sound the Alarm

Calpurnius had returned home to sleep around three in the morning and had just finished a late breakfast when Sypher flung the door open with a loud bang! "Sypher, what is wrong?"

Quickly Sypher recounted what he had seen in a voice punctuated by gasps for air.

"Then we must act quickly. Hitch the team again now! Conchessa!" he yelled.

"What is the matter?" she shouted from the atrium.

Instead of answering, he ran to her, grabbed her hand, and drew her into one of the side rooms. She smiled until she saw the stern demeanor etched on his face.

Speaking quietly, he said, "The pursuers are at the church. I have Sypher getting the chariot ready. Gather your valuables and meet me at the barn. Send the other servants away."

Her eyes drew wide, but without a word, she hugged and kissed him and left to discharge the two maids.

Calpurnius turned and entered his bedchamber. Placing both hands on a large wooden chest, he slid it to one side and stuck his dagger into a small crack beside a large flagstone in the floor. He pried the stone up far enough to get his fingers under it and lifted up, tipping it against the outside wall. Reaching in, he unpacked various items from his hidden armory. He drew out a large crossbow with two quivers of bolts, a gleaming sword and scabbard, breast and backplate, and a helmet. Without hesitation, he donned the armor. Wrestling with the straps on the breastplate, he noticed it seemed a trifle small. He finally attached it by boring a couple extra holes in the leather strips with his dagger. Finished, he wrapped his heaviest cloak around his shoulders and strode out, looking every inch, a military man.

Sypher was finishing harnessing the horses when Calpurnius appeared with his weaponry. "Almost ready sir! Just a few more minutes and I'll have everything prepared."

"How long before they said they would come to this house?" the Roman asked again.

"The little man said it would be an hour or two."

"It's been nearly an hour now. Where is Conchessa?" he said, gazing intently towards the church steeple for any signs of movement. He thought he saw a small group of men milling around the cemetery behind the church but could not be sure. *Luckily, the morning sun will be shining in their eyes all the way here if they come.* He also noticed the lack of wind, although to the west, there were dark clouds.

Conchessa appeared, her face flushed with exertion. "I'm ready," she said, climbing aboard the chariot with a blanket wrapped around her most cherished possessions.

Sypher had finished hitching the horses and took a few steps backward. Calpurnius jumped aboard and raised the reins, then he stopped with his head cocked as if listening. "Sypher, an idea just came to me. You come with us. We may need you." Absently realizing that he had once again listened to the still small voice of God. **"And he said, go forth, and stand upon the mount before the Lord. And behold, the Lord passed by, and a great and strong wind rent the mountains, and brake in pieces the rocks before the Lord; but the Lord was not in the wind: and after the wind an earthquake; but the Lord was not in the earthquake: And after the earthquake a fire; but the Lord was not in the fire: and after the fire a still small voice."**64

Without the slightest hesitation, Sypher grabbed the side

rail and vaulted up beside him.

Calpurnius raised the reins again and snapped them down on the horse's broad backs. "Heeyaw!" and they were off! Calpurnius first drove the chariot to the east, hoping that the aggressors would see his rising trail of dust in the still air and be lured in that direction. Then, as he passed behind a low hill, he turned south. Conchessa and Sypher both clung to the handrails as the chariot bumped and jumped violently beneath them. Calpurnius seemed to be in perfect control, standing upright, absorbing the impacts as though he were standing on the deck of a boat in heavy seas.

They finally arrived at a well-worn cart path and turned westward toward the cabin. The ride was much smoother now, as the two passengers shared grateful glances of relief.

"I hope they will follow our dust cloud toward the sun. That should buy us another hour or so," Calpurnius shouted.

"I only saw an ox cart, but the mercenaries were all on foot," Sypher yelled back.

"That will help delay them a little longer. Now we all need to pray for a plan to provide Magnus and Cynde an escape from this bishop," Calpurnius cried above the sounds of the galloping horses.

Chapter 44

Getaway

Ascending to the top of the nearest hill, Magnus and Cynde carefully peered at the small dust trail rising in the distance.

"Is it Calphurnius?" Cynde asked, squinting.

"I'm sure it is, there are not many chariots in this part of the country, and it's moving too fast to be a farmer's cart. Something must be wrong." *Why would he be returning so soon?* Magnus wondered. "Let's be careful and stay hidden in case it isn't, though. There are plenty of thick bushes and rocks on the hill above the cabin. Hurry, we can hide there."

Together they dashed through the thick grasses, staying low. Finding a large boulder enshrouded by shrubbery, they crouched behind it. They could see down to the bungalow and the approach roads. A couple large rain drops fell as the air cooled, and thunder rolled in the distance. A minute later, the chariot came into view. Magnus put his hand on Cynde's arm to prevent her from standing and giving away their position, but as she recognized the occupants, she tore away from him and began running down the hill.

"Hello," she shouted as she waved excitedly, with Magnus following close behind.

The small party waved back as they stiffly exited the chariot and tested their travel numbed limbs.

"What happened?" Magnus blurted as he rushed towards the group.

"Your tormentor has arrived with a small army of mercenaries," Calpurnius said arching his back. "Sypher, tie the horses. It will be raining soon. They won't be here for several hours, but we had best not take any chances. Grab what you need, and we all will head south towards Craig Intahl on the coast. I know a man near there who should have a boat available."

Without a word, Cynde and Magnus turned in unison and headed toward the cabin to gather their food and possessions. Once the bundles were loaded onto the chariot, Sypher worked a few more minutes to erase evidence of the cabin's recent use.

Pointing to the blackened skies, Calpurnius said, "Those rain clouds should help disguise our tracks. It will take a couple of days to reach Craig Intahl, but I know of some pagan ruins on the way where we can stay tonight. The girls will ride in the chariot. Sypher you, and Magnus mount the horses."

Magnus walked toward the closest horse, whose back was coated in a white froth where the leather harness had rubbed against him on the journey. The smell in the air was a heady horse odor. With a sigh of resignation, Magnus ran forward and dove onto the steed's back – sliding forward on his stomach while grabbing the harness straps. The horse had barely moved, and when he finally pulled himself up into a sitting position on the animal's broad back, his belly was soaked with horse sweat. He blushed at the clapping and cries of "Well done!" from the others.

Calpurnius lightly flicked the reins, and they started forward, rolling slowly across the trackless grassy hillsides. Within minutes, a light rain began to fall, and Magnus had to close his eyes against the stinging drops. *At least it's not a torrent.* After a couple of hours of repetitive bouncing, Magnus began to wonder if he should have walked instead. Thankfully, the rain tapered off after an hour and finally quit. The wet leather harness slipping back and forth was rubbing the insides of his legs raw. At last, they slowed as some cylindrical stacks of stone came into view perched on the steep and stony hillsides of a small canyon. The sounds of rushing water echoed loudly off the high rock walls.

"There is a small corral for the horses at the center of these ruins. Beyond that, there is a wooden bridge to the other side of a river," Calpurnius declared as they approached the first stone building. "Sypher and I will tend to the horses. Please prepare the bedding and some food. Unfortunately, whatever we eat will have to be cold. We do not want the smell of smoke leading them to us."

Magnus gratefully slid off the horse and painfully hobbled back to the carriage, as he gingerly rubbed the insides of his soaked pant legs. "Did you enjoy the trip?" Cynde asked with a tired smile.

"Well, at least I had a better view than you did since you only saw the horse's rumps!" he replied with his own weak smile. Then he wandered off to see what the rest of this odd, deserted village looked like. Every deteriorating building he entered had piles of flat stones scattered in disorganized piles. "These may come in handy," he declared to himself.

Cynde quietly helped Conchessa arrange the bedding and laid out small piles of apples, bread, and dried deer jerky on a clean rock ledge. A jug of mead rounded out the dinner offering.

Magnus meandered around various rocky outcroppings, overgrown with thick blankets of vines. Eventually, he saw the other two men rubbing down the horses and feeding them grain in a small, stone-fenced corral. Passing other buildings, he saw a torrent of water roaring through the narrow walls of the channel and a small wooden bridge perched precariously above it. *It is in worse shape than the one I destroyed by Clataguay.* Looking up, he noticed forlorn trees overhanging the canyon with thick vines draping down the canyon walls on the other side. *I wonder if those are strong enough?*

He returned to the others and the group ate and drank mostly in silence or with muted voices. Finally, Calpurnius whispered that he would take the first watch, followed by Magnus and then Sypher.

With that, everyone else retired to the bedding piled atop

the rocky surfaces and tried to make themselves comfortable.

A few hours later, Magnus felt a foot prod his side. He started, trying to drive the cobwebs of sleep from his mind as he struggled to unwind his arms from Cynde.

Standing up, he beckoned to Calphurnius and quietly said, "I've been praying for a solution. I think I should meet the little abbott. I need to try to give him this forged parchment – and perhaps end his foolish chase!"

"How could you confront him when he is surrounded by those trained murderers?"

"I don't know. I'm still working on that part. If you have any ideas, let me know, please?"

"I will. You are a brave lad, but I've been wondering, if things go bad, how many men have you killed?"

"One, by accident," Magnus said truthfully.

Fastening his eyes on him in the moonlight, Calpurnius asked. "Can I depend on your sword in a fight?"

"Yes sir!" Magnus answered emphatically. "Understand that I hate no man, but I will kill to protect the innocents that villains may harm next. It was a struggle for me since Jesus allowed himself to be killed, but he did not stand between his sheep and the wolves. They only wanted to kill him. **"And while he yet spake, behold a multitude, and he that was called Judas, one of the twelve, went before them and drew near unto Jesus to kiss him. But Jesus said unto him, Judas, betrayest thou the Son of man with a kiss? When they which were about him saw what would follow, they said unto him, Lord, shall we smite with the sword? And one of them smote the servant of the high priest, and cut off his right ear. And Jesus answered and said, Suffer ye thus far. And he touched his ear, and healed him. Then Jesus said unto the chief priests, and captains of the temple, and the elders, which were come to him, Be ye come out, as against a thief, with swords and staves? When I was daily with you in the temple, ye stretched forth no hands against me: but this is your hour, and the power of darkness."**65 If it comes to a fight, I will love the evil ones to death!" he said with a slight waver in his voice.

The Roman smiled widely, "I know you will, son, I know you will," as he turned and headed over to a vacant bed roll.

Magnus scaled the rock wall in the moonlight and sat praying and watching for any appearances of movement in the darkened hills. Hours later, he heard rocks clatter below and saw Sypher picking his way up in the dark.

"Thanks for coming, but I doubt if I can sleep anyway," he said.

"It is my turn sir. I must do my duty," Sypher replied.

"Speaking of duty, I need you to promise me that you will do anything to keep Cynde safe and beyond the reach of that crazed bishop."

"I will sir, but why do you ask that of me?"

"If anything happens to me, I need to know that she will be well out of harm's way and stop calling me, sir. We're about the same age. Call me Magnus."

"Thank you si…, Magnus."

"That's better Sypher. How did you become a servant to Calpurnius?"

"The last of my family died three winters ago. After that, I suffered horribly from depression. My life, I felt, had no meaning. I had been helping Calpurnius with small chores. He understood my struggle to find purpose, and they took me in. They treat me as one of their own. Maybe it's because their son and daughter are lost to them. They are teaching me how to be selfless, giving, nurturing, and that is helping to rid myself of fear, self-centeredness, and self-loathing," his voice trailed off as he looked somewhat embarrassed.

"It is evident that you are devoted to them. I pray that they are also reunited soon with their children. I have a feeling that they will be," Magnus said, quickly changing the subject.

"Do you think something is going to happen to you?" Sypher asked.

Magnus hesitated, "I hope not, but I can't rule it out. I've given up on finding a safe space in this life. I find myself retreating to spiritual space more and more, which leaves the demons of this life without power. Prayer is the only reason I've made it this far. I decided that I am going to try to meet the bishop a final time and see if I can surrender my forged letter in exchange for our lives. I've been working on a plan while sitting here. If Calpurnius thinks it has a chance, I'll do it."

"How?"

"Still working on it, I'll let everyone know in the morning," he said as he began his descent.

Magnus was near the river, dragging wood and vines onto separate piles when he saw Cynde approaching in the dim light of dawn.

"What are you doing?" she called out.

"I'm trying to save our lives. I've decided to meet with the man and pass off my fake scroll to his holiness."

It took her a moment to process what he had said. It sounded like a bad idea to her, but he looked so earnest that she just asked, "What can I do?"

"I need these green vines woven together into a rope long enough to stretch from here to that tree on the other side," he said, pointing at a pitiful oak clinging to the edge of the stone bluff.

Without another word, she pulled a number of the vines toward a lone sapling, tied them to it, and began threading them back and forth over each other – while she worried about what he had in mind. In a little while, Sypher showed up and started helping her.

As the sun began to rise over the horizon, Calpurnius walked up to Magnus. "I left Conchessa on watch. What's your plan?"

Chapter 45

Duped

"Where are they?" The bishop growled, "How did they escape us again?"

The chief watched with a bemused expression as the little man struggled to tip over a counter filled with pottery. With a loud crash, its contents spilled across the floor. They had spent nearly an hour searching and ravaging the villa on the bishop's stern orders. He had hoped to find a secret room where Magnus was hiding.

"He ist a smart one," the chief grunted. "Dey head east dis morning."

"What! How do you know that?" the man inquired.

"Do you not see da dust cloud?" Swaingraf answered with his eyes twinkling.

"No, I didn't see a dust cloud," the small man shrieked, "Why did you not you tell me?"

"You order us to search, dat's vat ve did," the big man grinned unapologetically.

Fuming, the little man turned and strode out of the house with a reddened face, spurting out. "Track them!"

"Not yet!" Swaingraf replied. "Don't you smell dat?"

"I don't smell anything, you big oaf. What are you babbling about?"

"Big storm. Ve vait," said the chief as a crack of thunder punctuated his statement.

The bishop didn't argue after glancing at the growing tumult outside, but diligently searched the villa for the best bed. He stretched out in comfort and waited impatiently for the storm to pass.

In an hour, the storm was over, and the air smelled sweeter.

Swaingraf didn't hesitate and let out a long whistle. Immediately his men began to appear around him. "Ve trail dem now," he pronounced as they filed out into the sunshine and began trotting beside the faint indentions made by the chariot wheels in the roadway before the rain.

The chief heard the bishop yell at his two monks, and they helped him crawl atop the cushions in the cart. Then they quickly scrambled aboard, and the driver snapped the reins, following the procession of mercenaries.

As the day's shadows grew long, the little man loudly demanded that the mercenaries continue tracking the apostates and instructed his monks to stop, feed, and erect a shelter for him.

The warriors began to grumble, but to their amazement, the chief acquiesced quickly. As they walked on, Swaingraf silenced their chatter with a hand motion until they had rounded a small hill. "Ve vill track dose renegades for da bishop all night, or til we make dose trees dere," he said, pointing toward a small grove just ahead. His men suddenly laughed loudly and increased their pace.

After a quiet night spent among the trees, the mercenaries grudgingly resumed tracking. Where the chariot left the pathway, it was easy to spot the tracks impressed into the tall waves of wet grass by the team of horses. They were keeping up a good walking pace when the chief smelled smoke. Searching the horizon, he noticed a thin wisp rising several miles ahead and broke into a run.

Late in the afternoon, the group of armed men reached the derelict stone structures and crept through the ruined village with their weapons ready - until they came upon the burnt shell of the bridge. The decking was gone. Only a few smoldering twigs still held it together above the churning water. On the other bank, the chariot ruts were easy to see leading westward.

"Enough for today." Swaingraf proclaimed, as he stretched out on a broad, flat rock and motioned for the others to do likewise. As he lay on his back, he looked up at the scrub trees, rocks, ruined buildings, and vines. He saw a thick group of vines hanging down the bluff on the other side of the river. *Strange how vines grew and twisted around themselves,* he thought, and then he snored.

They heard the rumbling ox cart enter the deteriorating village an hour later. "What are you doing?" the bishop squealed.

Doing nothing to stifle a large yawn, Swaingraf rose slowly. "Vhat do it look like? Ve rest," he said, stretching his back.

"Where are they? Why did you stop chasing them?" the little man bellowed as he tried to crawl out of the cart.

"Dey burn da bridge," Swaingraf said evenly.

"Well, forge the river, and be after them!" the man exclaimed, with his tiny chest puffed out.

"Maybe ve trow you in river. If you make it, ve follow you?" the chief asked quizzically.

Gazing at the surging rapids, the man's demeanor suddenly changed. "Is there another bridge or crossing nearby?"

"Do not know," the large man shrugged.

"Chief Swaingraf, please have your men split up and scout up and downstream for a crossing that won't endanger our lives," the bishop said tersely.

Wearing a broad smile, the chief motioned to his men, and they immediately split into two groups. "If ve find nothing by dark, ve return here," he announced, and the two groups started walking in opposite directions.

Chapter 46

Proposal

"Make up my bed and dinner," the diminutive man shouted at the two monks as they hurriedly unpacked the cart. The bishop stood and muttered "What a God-forsaken place," as he surveyed the ruins.

Magnus had heard and seen everything, peering through cracks between the stones of one of the buildings close to the river. Inside, he had hastily constructed a separate rock wall to shield him from sight if someone happened to enter the dilapidated hut. Now he waited for near darkness to make his next move.

The bishop decided to stay in one of the buildings on the other side of the corral. He quickly retired after his meal, ordering the two monks to stand guard outside the entrance.

In the twilight, Magnus crawled through a small hole he made by pulling loose stones out of a wall facing the river. Digging in the soft mud by the rushing water, he found a single vine that was buried in the sand and wrapped around a tree root. Tugging on it slowly, he pulled it out of the water. In the dim light, he could see a thick cluster of vines move closer to the river. Soon it was in his hand, and he began to scale the rocky wall of the canyon. The cooking fire had dwindled to coals by the time he reached the crest of the bluff. One of the monks was just throwing a pile of sticks on it when Magnus yelled. "Bishop, I have something for you."

Awakened from a deep sleep, the little man stumbled out of the doorway. "Where is he? Kill him!" He slurred at his monks, who stood frozen, trying to locate the voice amongst the echoes of the canyon.

"They need not consider killing me. I come as a friend to bargain," Magnus shouted.

"I make no bargains with heretics!" the wizened man shot back, locating the voice, and pointing at the top of the rock wall.

"I give you Martin's letter. You stop chasing us. It is a simple deal."

The man paused to consider the offer. "And you will stop preaching your lies?"

"You have my word on that. I will leave. You will never hear of me again," Magnus promised.

"Let me see the letter!" the man demanded.

"Here," Magnus said, tossing the ornate tube. It landed at the man's feet.

He quickly scooped it up, opened it, and began reading. "You are right. It is his proclamation. You have fulfilled your part of the bargain! Unfortunately, I do not honor pledges with heretics, take him," he cried,

The guards sprinted forward, clumsily drawing swords from beneath their habits. At the same time, Magnus heard the first group of mercenaries returning from their search upstream.

"You are not a man of God. You are dishonest!" he yelled at the little man as he tightened his grip on the vines. The guards were halfway up the hill when Magnus launched himself into the air. He heard the vines stretch and snap as he hurtled across the frothing water and leaped free, hitting the ground, and rolling as the vines swung on. Jumping up, he drew his sword and cut the vines as they swung back so no one could follow him. Turning, he waved at the small figure on the other bank, jumping up and down in a blind fury. Then he started jogging along the chariot tracks as the moon rose into a clear night sky.

~

The chief heard the bishop shouting as he and his party returned from their trek south. Grinning, he refused to increase his pace, and the others dutifully fell in step behind him.

As they approached the wrecked bridge, he saw the holy man sitting with his head in his hands while the others encircled him. Swaingraf couldn't resist saying with a straight face, "I heard de celebration. Good news?"

The man on the ground stared up at him with reddened eyes and an impossibly red face. Obviously, rage made it impossible for the bishop to talk. He drew himself up slowly and walked back to his bed. Others begin to explain what had happened, followed by snickering and muted giggles which grew into raucous laughter.

Somehow, the chief knew that the holy man was desperately praying for Magnus to die!

Chapter 47

Frustration

"How did you fare?" Clapurnius asked as Magnus walked into the camp an hour later.

"I didn't. That is the most hard-headed man I've ever met." He knew that only an idea of the bishop as God's child might help heal the animosity he felt toward the man, but he was too tired to put forth the effort.

"I suppose we need to discuss your escape plan from this island then," the Roman said.

"Can it wait? I'm exhausted," Magnus said as he leaned hard against a tree.

"No, I'm afraid not. Conchessa and I will leave you tomorrow and return to our villa."

"Why?" Magnus asked, astounded.

"Because that will give them a false trail of chariot tracks to follow on our circuitous route back to Kilpatrick. It should give you a couple more days of safety. Once there, I will raise a small army among the townspeople, and annihilate those villains if they ever dare to return. Here, I have written a letter of introduction for you to give my old friend at Craig Intahl. He will arrange passage for you, and give him this." he said, handing over a leather sack of coins along with the parchment. "His name is Pontius. You can't miss his villa. It overlooks the sea from a rocky ledge. Now get some sleep. We will start early."

Magnus almost replied that it was already early but instead stumbled over and snuggled up to Cynde, still wearing his sword. In moments, he fell asleep.

The bishop and his hired mercenaries were pursuing Magnus through a maze of rock-ribbed canyons. He heard them close behind him as he stumbled and crawled forward over boulders on the canyon floor. There, he heard water flowing, if he could just make it to the water, he might have a chance of escape.

Gritting his teeth against the pain of exertion, he pushed forward and finally saw the foaming river ahead. He held up his staff at the edge of the roaring river, and the water thrashed back and forth until a walkway appeared between tall walls of liquid.

Quickly, he slipped off the bank and staggered across the wet, mossy rocks, smelling the mud, decaying plants, and fish in the thick, humid air. Crawling up the opposite bank, he turned and saw that the small man was just descending into the riverbed, with the warriors close behind.

With an air of superiority, he raised his staff and waved it over the stream bed, but nothing happened. Again, he waved it back and forth more vehemently, but still nothing. He tried it again with more vigor, grabbing the end of the staff and swinging it over his head - still, the walls of water stood motionless as his foes drew closer. They were going to catch him! Turning to flee, he ran face-first into a rock wall that wasn't there before. What was going on?

"Wake up. You're going to bruise me with that sword," Cynde said, swinging a boney elbow into his ribs.

"Ow, I'm sorry, but I was just running away from the bishop and his goons. I didn't know what I was doing."

"Wow, I knew it must have been a bad dream, but I didn't imagine it was that bad," she said, re-positioning herself to sleep.

And why didn't waving my staff work like Moses's hand did. He wondered as he dozed off. **"And Moses stretched out his hand over the sea; and the Lord caused the sea to go back by a strong east wind all that night, and made the sea dry land, and the waters were divided. And the children of Israel went into the midst of the sea upon the dry ground: and the waters were a wall unto them on their** right hand, and on their left. And the Egyptians pursued, and went in after them to the midst of the sea, even all Pharaoh's horses, his chariots, and his horsemen. And Moses stretched forth his hand over the sea, and the sea returned to his strength when the morning appeared; and the Egyptians fled against it; and the Lord overthrew the Egyptians in the midst of the sea. And the waters returned, and covered the chariots, and the horsemen, and all the host of Pharaoh that came into the sea after them; there remained not so much as one of them."[66]

At first light, Calpurnius roused them all. Sypher unhobbled the horses and harnessed them to the chariot while the others quickly loaded it. Then Sypher and Magnus reluctantly mounted the two animals again.

Calpurnius began driving at a trot, and Magnus bounced so hard that he feared his teeth might fall out. "Ccccoouuld yyoouu pleaaase gaaalllop?" Magnus finally spouted.

Laughing, Calpurnius said, "Just making sure that you two were awake!" as he eased the reins and coaxed the animals into a smoother gait.

They journeyed southwest for several hours until Calpurnius pulled the team to a gentle stop where a small foot trail led off southward. "Here we must part, my friends. Take that path. You are a good six or seven hours away from the village. Sypher, you go with them. Return to us when they are safe." Sypher looked up quickly, surprised at the command, but accepted without comment.

Once again, Magnus gingerly slid off the horse's back and stood rubbing the soreness from his legs. Then he shuffled over to help Cynde and Sypher wrap food and other items in cloths for their journey.

"I had hoped to take you all to the sea, but this should better conceal your escape," Calpurnius said as he buried Magnus in a bear hug. Conchessa hugged him next with tears in her eyes, saying that she would pray for them all, along with pleas to try to find her son Maewyn Succat and daughter in Hibernia. After their goodbyes, the three stood and watched the old chariot rumble away.

"Well, let's be off," said Sypher as he turned decisively toward the pathway.

"Wait!" Magnus commanded. "Don't walk directly to the trail. There are already old footprints there. Let's leave them undisturbed, so it looks like no one has traveled here in several days. Walk over on that downed tree," he said, pointing at a fallen oak whose trunk intersected the path. The others quickly climbed through the thick nest of dead branches while Magnus picked up a broken limb and brushed away their fresh footprints.

"That should conceal our route," he said as he threaded his way through the tree branches and dropped onto the trail behind them. Then the little group fell into a fast trot down the winding path.

~

"I hate leaving them," Conchessa said, clutching her husband's waist as they traveled a short distance away. "I fear Magnus is the last young man that truly understands Martin's words."

"We must protect Martin's treatise for future pioneers in Spirit!" Calpurnius replied with determination, feeling the weight of responsibility. "Others will read and understand his scroll. The ideas will not die with the boy, and I have a feeling we will see them all again."

Conchessa offered a resigned smile as she hugged her husband even tighter.

Chapter 48

The Chase Resumed

In the morning, the mercenaries trotted north to where one group had found a low water crossing the day before. There the river widened, and the flow was noticeably slower. The chief and his men slogged through the icy water and crawled up the other bank while the bishop silently rode atop his ox cart with his white knuckles holding tight to the wooden slats.

Once safe on the other side, the little man announced, "Men, I have decided to give an additional bounty of five gold pieces to every man here as soon as that heretic is killed!" There was a slight murmur of affirmation in the group but no exuberance.

The chief grimaced. *Maybe he should have told us that before we forded an icy river.*

Turning south with their clothes sopping wet, they hurried back toward the ruined town and followed the chariot tracks to the southwest. It was late in the afternoon when the chief held up his fist.

"Why are you stopping?" demanded the bishop. "Follow the tracks."

"Dey stop here," Swaingraf growled.

"Why should they have stopped here? A potty break?" yelled the man angrily.

"No, but dey did stop," the chief murmured. "Wheels rolled back und forward. Da horses stomped hooves here more times!"

The bishop descended from the cart, crouched, and squinted at the tracks. "Could be," he said.

"Spreadt out und check fur tracks!" the chief commanded.

A minute later, one of his men responded, when he found the spot where the three had jumped from the tree trunk.

"My cart can't navigate that narrow trail!" the small man moaned as the chief and his men began to give chase.

"Den run like us!" Swaingraf yelled as his legs pumped harder. *He probably wants to kill me after that remark, like he dispatched King Joedel.* The chief thought smiling, as he watched the little man bounce and curse in the distance.

"Light a signal fire each night so we can find you!" screamed the bishop as his driver futilely tried to find a smooth path through the rough countryside covered with rocks and dead tree branches.

~

Magnus, Cynde, and Sypher had stopped several times to rest as they threaded their way toward the coast. They thought their pursuers would follow the chariot tracks, and that they would be safe in their travels now. Shadows were long, and they were close enough to smell the ocean when Magnus noticed a small flash in the hills a distance away. "Look! Is that our friend the chief and his men?" he asked, pointing. Cynde and Sypher both stared, and each could see brief flashes of polished metal in the waning sunshine.

"How did they track us?" Cynde wailed.

"I don't know, but we have to move and keep moving until we find Pontius and shelter for the night," said Magnus. "It looks like they are still about two hours behind us, and darkness should stop them in the next half hour."

Running forward, they noticed thin trails of smoke rising from a coastal village ahead of them. "That has to be Craig Intahl!" Magnus wheezed. "Look for a home on a rock ledge."

"There's one." Cynde puffed, pointing off to the right as she charged ahead. The others followed her quickly through the gathering twilight.

~

The chief motioned to stop and sniffed at the freshening air carrying the smell of the sea. He had seen movement far ahead, but it could have just been a couple of deer. The last rays of the sun were blinding, and the spot where he had seen movement was just deepening shadows now. Turning around, he saw the ox cart slowly traversing a rough hillside in the distance. "Ve camp," he growled to his men. "Make a fire for de bishop ta see."

An hour later the bishop's ox cart finally arrived. The chief noticed that his excellency was in a dreadful state after bouncing all day atop the cart. He had thrown up repeatedly on the journey, and vomit stains ran down his once-grand vestments. However, he had doggedly urged his men to continue the chase. Weak and weary, his monks had to lift him out of the cart and lower him to the ground. There they had to wash him and change his clothes as they set up camp for the night.

The chief moved closer, enjoying the bishop's discomfort. "Ve be close to catch dem," he announced. which elicited a small smile from the man.

~

After another hour, Magnus's group finally reached the villa and took a long moment to rest and gaze at the moonbeams reflecting off the ocean under a star-speckled sky. Then Magnus strode up to the threshold and knocked on the door of the house.

"Who is there?" a gravelly voice called out.

"Sir, Calpurnius of Kilpatrick sent us to you."

"For what end?" the man replied slowly.

"He said you would help us to escape from our pursuers. I have a letter and some coins for you," he added.

"Who is his wife?" the voice demanded after a long pause.

Now Cynde chimed in, "Conchessa!"

Almost immediately, Magnus heard a locking board being removed, and the door swung open. A paunchy, middle-aged man stared warily at the disheveled travelers standing on his doorstep. His eyes stopped on Cynde, and Magnus sensed his lecherous thoughts. "Here!" Magnus said as he fumbled and quickly offered the leather sack, breaking the man's mesmerism.

Pontius took it with look of doubt, but his eyes softened as he read the note from Calpurnius. "Safe passage to Hibernia?" he finally said. "I think I can arrange that." smiling as he shook the pile of coins into his hand.

"We need it immediately," continued Magnus. "We are being followed by agents of the Bishop of Seaford Downs."

"How close are they?" the man queried.

"I'd say about two hours if the darkness didn't stop them for the night," Magnus said.

"Not much time. You'll need to move quickly." Motioning with his hand for the group to follow, he paused to light a torch from the fireplace and led them through his villa. He finally stopped at a large weaving showing multitudes of gleaming white buildings and towers. "A relic of my time in Rome," he announced proudly.

Cynde stared at the tapestry open-mouthed. Magnus grasped her hand and gently pulled as she stood transfixed.

Gingerly, Pontius drew it to one side, revealing a small opening in the rock wall. "A secret passage," he murmured as if he could be overheard. "This opens to the beach below the hill and saves almost half an hour off the path from the village." He entered, and the others followed close behind.

The rock walls were damp, and the passage smelled musty. Smoke from the torch stung their eyes, and the flickering light danced over rocky outcroppings. Sypher stumbled continuously in the dim light as he followed at the rear of the group. After a long series of steep turns and twists, the passage started to level off. Finally, they could smell fresh sea air and noticed the night sky's faint illumination at the cave's exit.

"Let me see if any of my fishermen friends are still on the beach," Pontius said as he handed the torch to Magnus, walked out of the cave, and disappeared from view. Before Magnus could stop him, Sypher slipped by, muttering, "I don't trust that bloke." He ran through the entrance and dissolved into the darkness beyond.

Cynde reached out and wrapped her arm around Magnus's waist. "He'll be alright," he said reassuringly. Minutes crawled past before they heard a distant cry, and Sypher rushed back into the cave.

"Run!" he stammered as something hit a rock next to his head with a clang. "They are going to kill us!"

Magnus didn't hesitate but quickly began re-tracing their faint footprints up the incline.

Struggling for breath, Sypher rattled out the story in bits and pieces. He had followed Pontius while lurking in the shadows of the bluffs surrounding the beach. The man had walked straight across the sand to a decrepit fishing boat that the mariners had pulled out of the water. Two men were sharing a jug of ale before heading up the path to their cottages. Sypher crept close behind one of the boats and overheard Pontius say, "I'll share these gold coins with ye, but I keep the girl – agreed?"

Magnus gasped as he felt Cynde's grip tighten at those words.

"I started running back, but one of them must have seen me," Sypher continued.

"Good thing you snuck out," Magnus said as he heard a man's loud curse echo throughout the grotto. Then he whispered. "They must be trying to follow us without a light. Let's stay silent until we reach the villa."

They threaded their way through the dank, narrow passages and finally emerged from behind the tapestry. Ripping it down, Magnus cried. "Here, help me throw anything combustible into the entrance." Grabbing chairs, stools, and a pile of firewood, they soon had a waist-high pile. "That's enough," he said as he thrust the torch into the old, tinder-dry fabric. Flames erupted and spread quickly, sealing the exit with clouds of acrid smoke.

"Let's get out of here," Cynde said and took the lead

running through the house.

"Now what?" Sypher asked as they once again stood on the stone patio overlooking the coastline.

"We keep moving west," Magnus replied. "There must be another village where we can borrow a boat."

"Steal one, you mean?" Cynde questioned.

"Only if we have to," he responded as he turned and followed a narrow trail across the cliff under a blanket of stars. Exhausted, they staggered along the jagged edges of the rocky ridge for the next hours, desperately trying to put distance between them and Craig Intahl.

Several times a missed step caused one of them to trip and fall, but they gamely tottered on. Cynde finally proclaimed that she couldn't go any farther, and the group sagged to the ground for some precious hours of rest.

Chapter 49

Closing In

The sun had not risen, but Swaingraf was already rousing his men. "Get up, ready to hunt. We leave now." Without a sound, the men obeyed, quickly gathering their equipment while eating bits of deer jerky and dried fruit. The chief began walking toward the coastline, and his men hurried to follow in single file.

"What is going on?" the bishop yawned loudly as he stumbled forward rubbing his eyes.

"Ve chase de boy," the chief stated flatly, smiling at the puny man.

"Alright, I'm awake, you two help me up," the bishop demanded, and the two monks hurried to assist the bishop on his climb into the ox cart.

Swaingraf watched over his shoulder as the man rolled over the stanchions and fell into the cart. He knew that he couldn't be looking forward to another day of being jostled, but he had to admire him a little for refusing to give up the chase. Turning around, the bishop held onto the cart's rough wood frame and stared toward the distant seacoast.

"Follow my mercenaries," he demanded loudly, and the driver slapped the oxen lightly with his whip.

The chief scanned the horizon as the small column moved forward with the first rays of sunlight behind them. "Dere be houses," he cried as he increased their speed to a fast trot.

Within an hour, they could see a group of villagers gathered at a house perched near a cliff, and they slowed to a walk when they smelled the smoke that still sat heavy in the air around the stone cottage.

"Vat happen here?" The chief demanded as the villagers turned and stared fearfully at the group of armed men approaching.

"They ruined my tapestry! They burnt my furnishings!" a middle-aged man with a red face howled. "They said they needed my help, and this is how I am repaid," he continued angrily.

"A boy und a girl?" Swaingraf inquired.

"No, two boys and a girl. My two friends and I were almost overcome with the smoke, we barely made it out alive," he said as he laid his hand on his forehead for dramatic effect.

"Vich vay did dey go?"

"Is there a reward?" the man asked earnestly.

"Yes, I vill not kill you, now vich vay?" the chief answered, slowly grinding the words through his teeth while placing his hand on the hilt of his sword.

The man blinked dumbly before quickly pointing west.

"Tanks." the chief said, turning as his men rallied toward the top of the bluff. One of them cried, "Footprints here."

"Ve be close, run now," Swaingraf yelled as the group sprinted forward across the rocky ledges.

~

A habitual early riser, Cynde had awakened the others as the first rays of sun lightened the horizon. Slowly they fell into step behind each other across the rock-ribbed landscape. Magnus had been trying to pray and draw closer to God throughout the morning, but he was constantly losing his concentration as Cynde and Sypher chattered constantly throughout the trek. He knew they were talking to fend off the exhaustion enveloping them all. Magnus tried to raise his thinking above the tumultuous ideas constantly oppressing him. Finally, with a loud sigh, he abandoned his prayers and let his mind go blank. *Just one step in front of the other,* he thought. In another hour, they reached a large grassy crest above a hill covered with heavy scrub growth that sloped down to a narrow sandy beach by the sea.

"Look, maybe we can borrow one of those," he said, pointing downward. A village stood high on the opposite hill, but several boats and a few small buildings were on the shoreline below. A handful of men were struggling to launch one of the boats in the early morning sun. One of them cried out as he pointed up at Magnus, and the group of fishermen started running toward the safety of the small village. A narrow pathway ran along the hill's ridge, then diagonally down to the beach. Suddenly, an arrow ricocheted off of a rock by Magnus's foot. "Run!"

Chapter 50

Final Dash

Exhaustion fled from their bodies, replaced by a sudden influx of adrenalin as the three sprinted forward simultaneously. A barrage of arrows suddenly struck the ground where they had been standing seconds before.

They were now below the crest of the hill and out of sight of the mercenaries. Still, Magnus knew that his group would afford easy targets once the archers arrived at the crest. He also knew they would be surrounded if they stayed together. Thinking of some way for Cynde and Sypher to escape capture, he suddenly screamed. "You two, head down to the beach, disable the other boats, and take the last one out."

"I won't leave you!" Cynde cried.

"You have to," replied Magnus. "We need to disable the other boats and launch one. If we keep running as a group, they will stop us – but if I can draw them away, you can get the last boat ready, and I'll run and jump in before they catch me! Now, scatter!" Magnus cried, motioning wildly with his arms."

Cynde opened her mouth, no doubt to refuse, but stayed silent as she realized he was correct. "I love you," she said quickly and headed off the path with Sypher close on her heels.

Surprised that she hadn't objected, Magnus yelled after her: "I love you too, sweetheart!" He scrambled, fleeing through clouds of blowing dust on the ridge ahead of the pursuers. Glancing over his shoulder, he saw men scampering quickly down the trail behind him. Magnus quickly threaded his way through a narrow path of rough brush running parallel to the ocean. Ahead it veered down the hill toward the sea.

His limbs felt heavy and unresponsive. He knew he should pray and that some law of God could deliver him from this torment. Merciless ideas cascaded upon him that he was too drained and depleted to think clearly. He suddenly stumbled on a rock and almost fell as another arrow sliced by his ear. *Thank goodness for that rock!* He continued to zig-zag down the narrow path. Bushes were growing taller on this section of the trail. *I hope they shield me from those archers, at least the arrows stopped for the moment,* he thought gratefully.

Trying not to stumble, he stole furtive glances toward Cynde as he ran. He saw that Cynde and Sypher had reached the beach and were busy gathering the oars from each boat. He also saw several attackers that had abandoned the chase for him, struggling to run straight down through the heavy shrub growth toward the sea. As the warriors drew close to the beach, Cynde and Sypher ran toward the last skiff. *They better hurry,* he prayed. Another series of quick glimpses showed them throwing armfuls of oars into the last boat. Then Cynde was pulling on the bow while Sypher buried his feet into the sand – pushing on the stern. The marauders were just stepping onto the sand, when a large wave hit the beach and traveled up to encompass the vessel. With the added buoyancy, it came free. Magnus watched with relief as Cynde dove in headfirst and wiggled around to get her feet under her. She grabbed two oars, set them into the oarlocks, and began rowing furiously. Sypher dragged himself over the stern and struggled to push and paddle with a single oar. The warriors were standing on the beach now, but the small vessel was beyond their reach as it bobbed gently on the breaking waves.

Magnus could see the small fishing shacks ahead and off to his left as he reached the bottom of the hill. The sand was deep and loose here, and he struggled for every step as he fought his way toward the buildings. Another glance back showed that the warriors were still gaining on him and forced him to redouble his efforts. Sweat flowed into his eyes as he desperately kicked his aching legs forward, even as he felt their movements slowing. He had reached the first shed and was just about to duck behind it when an object struck him in the shoulder. He spun around and fell heavily on his side. Pain seared through him like a hot knife, and he saw the protruding bloodied point of an arrow that had pierced him. He tried to rise, but any movement caused him to nearly black out. He tried to pray, but his mind seemed foggy and distant as he was suddenly overcome with a wave of depression.

Chapter 51

Defeat

Magnus lay motionless and defeated, steps away from the weathered wood building as he watched the horde approach. Swaingraf issued a command to his men, and they immediately ceased the assault. The chief strode forward, dropped to one knee, and said, "Wisht I had a hunert men like you." then he whispered, "I promise da little man follows you soon to da other side." Reaching behind Magnus, he snapped the arrow in two, grabbed the metal tip, and jerked the shaft through as Magnus passed out.

He was kneeling face down, with his face buried in a sea of soft grass. Magnus raised his head a few inches to look around but shut his eyes immediately. The light here was blinding, nearly like what he had experienced on the cliffside road.

He felt weak and tried to organize his thoughts but only succeeded in sitting quietly while a strange clutter of ideas filled his head. Peering carefully, he gazed downward into the shadow cast below his body. He noticed the grass was thick, with a purplish hue. Strange-looking insects crawled through the thatch. In moments, Magnus noticed that he had become somewhat accustomed to the brilliant light so that he could squint at the landscape. Bizarre, colored trees grew at the edges of the meadow he was in, and further on, he saw angular outlines that could be a city in the distance.

Somewhere across the glade, Magnus heard someone calling his name. "Magnus, my friend, I've been waiting for you."

The daylight was still so intense that he could hardly open his eyes. He barely made out a dark shape bounding toward him through the tall grass. "Osric, but you're…"

"Dead on my last plane of existence! You were right. It's all true." he said with a wide grin.

"That's good news because I'm about to lose my head again," Magnus said earnestly while thinking how close he came to decapitation with the chief's sword before the Picts attacked. He reached up and touched his cheeks gingerly with both hands.

"Really, my friend, you know you never had a material body, and you don't have one now!" Osric wriggled a fat finger, admonishing him.

Magnus covered his eyes with his hands and tried to recall the last shreds of what was soon to be his former experience. Would Cynde remember him? Who remained to carry on the message of Christ to that world?

"What is the matter, my friend?" Osric looked perplexed as he stared down.

"I'm not done. I still have so much to do. I love Cynde. I'm not ready for…for…" Magnus's voice fragmented into sobs.

"Don't worry Magnus, God is still here…, and there, and everywhere!" The monk stated gently as he grasped an arm and lifted Magnus to his feet. "The bishop can't destroy us… We are still us!"

Those simple words began lifting the burden of an unresolved life from him immediately. **"Peace I leave with you, my peace I give unto you: not as the world giveth, give I unto you. Let not your heart be troubled, neither let it be afraid."**67

"You're right, absolutely. There is no stopping and starting in infinity!" Magnus replied, wiping his eyes. He was grateful for the spiritual realization that God is limitless, and his work is already complete, as it is written. **"Thou art worthy, O Lord, to receive glory and honour and power: for thou hast created all things, and for thy pleasure they are and were created."**68 *He recalled his dream of speaking with Jesus, "Always strive to bring the Kingdom of God to whatever plane of existence you are on, but don't be afraid to leave that plane for another if you are forced to because God is always with you!" Magnus relaxed as he pondered. God must have a purpose for him in this place too. His eyes were getting accustomed to the harsh*

sunlight, and he could gaze around without blinking now. "Where are we, Osric?"

"I don't know, but I'm sure we are with God." the monk replied, smiling. "Because we can't be anywhere else, right? Don't be too concerned about the world you left. The darkness will lift from their eyes. Since God is All, it has to, and the darkness that clouds mankind's minds is naught."

Magnus smiled.

A bucket of salt water splashed into his face, and he awoke, finding himself bound and kneeling with his head resting on a large driftwood log next to the pounding surf. The sun still rode low in the sky, and he realized that he must have been unconscious for just a little while. He felt extremely weak. A dirty rag had been wrapped around his shoulder, barely staunching the flow of blood. The Saxon warriors stood around him in a loose circle, and he saw an ox cart parked on the ridge above. "Good morning to you, young man." the bishop squeaked in his ear. "You are indeed a worthy adversary."

He squinted, noticing that the little man held his forged copy of Martin's scroll tightly in his hand. "Please, you have what you want. Now I'm leaving this island forever. I beg of you, let me go." Magnus pleaded.

"Afraid that's not good enough, my boy. I will, however, finally destroy this accursed scroll," holding the parchment high. "You had your chance before to surrender it and live, but you have cost me considerable time, effort, and money since that occasion. Today however, I see no Picts hiding on this beach to finagle another one of your miraculous escapes from my hand. Now you shall be leaving this world forever," he said with an easy grin. "Make him die slowly," he chuckled to the chief.

"No! Dat I vile not. He es a varrior vat I respect," replied Swaingraf indignantly.

Looking up at the hostile eyes of the chief and the other warriors surrounding him, the bishop acquiesced quickly. "Fine, just kill him. Do you want to see your woman one last time, boy? She is going to watch your execution," he added. Some of the warriors shuffled aside so that he could see the shoreline.

Magnus strained against the ropes until they cut into the flesh of his wrists and shoulders, and he felt a warm trickle of blood leach from beneath the rough hemp bindings. Then he wrenched his body around until he could look at the ocean, and see the small boat, still bobbing on the waves with Cynde and Sypher looking over the stern at the figures on the beach. *I love you!* He suddenly realized that he had loved her more deeply in the last couple of months than any other man could in a lifetime! *I'm giving up my life, so you can be free.* He suddenly sobbed, remembering a passage about Jesus. **"Greater love hath no man than this, that a man lay down his life for his friends."**69

"Any smart words now, miscreant?" spat the bishop.

Magnus paused to urgently pray before responding, "I wish I was a better disciple of Christ, that I could have healed your resentment - but I'm grateful that my prayers have brought me this far. I wish I could make you understand that Jesus strove to teach and illustrate the power of spiritual Life. We are filled with too much self-centered, material audacity to fully demonstrate his Kingdom on earth, but we should follow his example to Love others and heal them as much as possible!"

Feigning a yawn, the man said, "I know that our Lord Jesus healed the sick and sinful, but Rome has proclaimed that the church needs to educate and consolidate the masses into a cohesive state of subjection. It will be his 'kingdom on earth' once we control all the people."

"Mankind needs spiritual development, not material control. Look away from what appears real toward true grace and humility. Love others as you love yourself." he said, thinking, **"A new commandment I give unto you. That ye love one another; as I have loved you, that ye also love one another. By this shall all men know that ye are my disciples if ye have love one to another."**70

Leaning close and whispering in Magnus's ear, the man said quietly. "Oh, I intend to love them as subjects. They all need to accept me as their undisputed leader. However, it is very difficult for me to love barbarous peasants as much as I do myself." Then he announced loudly. "You are living in the past young man."

Straining at his bonds, Magnus twisted to look at the man and said as lovingly as he could, "The Kingdom of God is still everywhere now! Please study the words on that scroll, don't destroy it. They are a guide to eternal life."

"Oh, I will definitely peruse it while I almost make an exact copy. It will have a few minor changes in the wording that will support our efforts in this land of heathens. That copy will have a prominent place in our church as a holy relic of Martin, and this will be ashes." the man whispered into his ear with a satisfied smile as he stuffed the roll of parchment back into the leather cylinder.

"I know you have a desire to be a follower of God. You would have to if your claim to be an agent of His church is sincere. I bless you and continue to pray for your eyes to be opened. You cannot force people to be a loving church community through violence incited by dogma and fear. The power of Love needs to induce humanity to embrace religion." He finished pondering the statement, **"Ye have heard that it hath been said, Thou shalt love thy neighbour, and hate thine enemy. But I say unto you, Love your enemies, bless them that curse you, do good to them that hate you, and pray for them which despitefully use you, and persecute you;"**71

"You are wrong, my son." the little man laughed. "Even our loving and humble master drove the money changers out of the temple with a whip, remember?" **"And Jesus went into the temple of God, and cast out all them that sold and bought in the temple, and overthrew the tables of the moneychangers, and the seats of them that sold doves,"**72

"You know that was to preserve the temple's sanctity for

God instead of man's avarice." **"And said unto them, It is written, My house shall be called the house of prayer; but ye have made it a den of thieves."**[73]

"Well, I guess I'm not perfect, but I will advance his marvelous teachings among these heathens, even as I profit handsomely by it."

"God will not be mocked!" Magnus replied. **"Be not deceived; God is not mocked: for whatsoever a man soweth, that shall he also reap."**[74] "I'm sure you will reap material riches, but I doubt they will profit you in this or the next life,'" he admonished. **"It is the spirit that quickeneth; the flesh profiteth nothing: the words that I speak unto you, they are spirit, and they are life."**[75]

"You no longer need to be troubled by such trivial thoughts," the man replied with a note of exasperation.

Magnus decided to try a different tactic to diffuse the seemingly hopeless situation, "Can't you find it in your heart to forgive me? I'm no threat now. Please give me a chance to explain the ideas that Martin cherished."

"Young man, the great apostle Saint Paul once said, **'The last enemy that shall be destroyed is death.'**[76], well, if you manage to heal this wound, I will be your most ardent disciple!" the wizened man said sarcastically and quickly nodded to the chief.

Magnus surrendered all to God at that moment, knowing that his fight was lost. The words of Jesus sprang into his mind, **"Father, if thou be willing, remove this cup from me: nevertheless not my will, but thine, be done,"**[77]

Chapter 52

Resurrection

Suddenly a flash of brilliant light blinded everyone! It stopped, but as the men were blinking, it flashed again. "What is that?" the bishop wailed.

Shielding his eyes with his broadsword, the chief squinted toward the ocean. "Dere, da girl." He pointed. Cynde held something over her head that reflected the morning sun's dazzling light.

The bishop strode through the group of men to get a clearer view, and Magnus was momentarily forgotten. "What is that?" he screamed over the sound of the waves breaking.

"Gold," she yelled. "I'll trade you this solid gold torc for Magnus's life."

The bishop suddenly tugged on Swaingraf's arm and whispered, "Chief, that golden relic in the girl's hands is the largest neck ring I have ever seen. It looks to be worth three months of offerings at our church services. I want it. I will be able to wear it as I administer blessings to the poor." The bishop stepped forward quickly and then yelled. "All right, I agree, but you and this heretic must never revisit these shores again, or you know what will happen. Row onto the beach and bring it to me."

"No," Cynde said defiantly. "Let Magnus go first. Put down your weapons and move back off on the beach."

"The boy has had a difficult morning. He is injured and

would need assistance to get to your boat," the bishop cajoled.

"Let the chief help me," Magnus suddenly added weakly, still kneeling with his neck on the log.

The little man quicky considered his options and called the chief over for quiet instructions. "We will draw back to the edge of the beach. You release the boy and help him through the surf and into the boat. Once she gives you the torc, grab the gunwale, and flip the boat over." he snickered.

"But you gaf your word."

"I said they must never return to these shores again under penalty of death. I wouldn't want to break a promise," the little man giggled.

Looking distraught, the big man began removing his helmet and armor.

"What are you doing?" the bishop questioned.

"I not wear metal in zalt water," he answered. Taking his dagger, he made a show of roughly cutting Magnus loose and dragging the boy upright.

Magnus tried to ignore the pain, but a small cry escaped his lips, eliciting a large smile from the bishop. "I trust you have learned not to spread lies about our faith from now on. If you persist, next time, you will not be so lucky," he admonished with a quick nod to the chief.

The warrior shoved Magnus forward so hard that the young man fell to his knees. Brutally, Swaingraf grabbed him under his good shoulder and pulled him upright again, as he motioned for his men to move back, well away from the ocean.

The big man violently dragged him toward the surf. *He must have absolutely no compassion*, Magnus thought. Once in the water, the chief grabbed the neck of his shirt and pulled him backward through the crashing waves.

Now that he was out of the bishop's earshot, the warrior spoke. "Vhen ve get to boat, I vill liff you in. Den grab oar. Vhen de girl give me gold, hit my head with oar good. You know?"

"Yes, sir, thank you," Magnus replied with surprise. He thought the bishop would try one last trick, but this man was standing up for principle in the only way he could. *He was giving them a chance to escape.*

The chief stood chest deep in low waves, and Magnus was coughing up seawater when they drew close to the rowboat.

"Stay back!" Cynde commanded as she brandished an oak oar over her head.

Magnus retched and managed to say, "It's ok Cynde, he's a friend."

Confusion painted her face as she reluctantly lowered the oar and reached out to him.

The chief grabbed Magnus with one hand under his good arm and the other under his buttocks. With a slight groan of effort, he lifted the young man up and over his head into the boat.

For a long moment, they smiled and looked at each other. Magnus hoped that his unbounded gratitude showed through his eyes. As the chief turned to accept the golden torc from Cynde, Magnus struggled to lift a heavy oak oar and swing it. "THWACK!" The sound reverberated across the waves.

Magnus watched as the men on shore strained to see what the sound was. One of the warriors yelled, "He hit the chief!" Sypher was rowing vigorously as Magnus reached out to embrace Cynde with tears of relief in his eyes. They had beaten the bishop. They had escaped!

Suddenly Magnus heard a resonating cheer from the mercenaries, and he wiped at his eyes to clear his vision. A hand had emerged from beneath the waves and held the golden relic aloft. Soon the chief's head bobbed up with his other hand rubbing it gingerly as his men charged across the beach to assist him.

Magnus watched as the little bishop immediately fell to the ground, obviously offering up a loud, reverent prayer to God for deliverance of the precious treasure.

~

When Chief Swaingraf stumbled out of the surf, he immediately went over and donned his helmet. "To protect dis knot on da head." he announced, and his men cheered loudly again. Then he marched over and presented the glittering prize to the bishop with a flourish. "He hit me vhen I grab dis." he said.

"Thank you chief, you have done a great service to the church and to me personally. You and your men will be richly rewarded when we return to Seaford Downs." the man promised as he gently stroked the heavy gold torc. Hot tears of joy welled in his reddened eyes as he began to amble slowly up the hill toward the ox cart.

"Tanks" the chief said as he reached up and adjusted his helmet with a feigned wince.

~

"I am so grateful to the both of you. I knew my life in this world was over, and I'm sorry you lost your beautiful torc." he said to Cynde, "What made you think of offering it?"

"I don't know. I guess maybe it was a "still small voice" of God," she grinned.

Magnus smiled as he slumped down painfully into the stern. Cynde and Sypher both smiled widely at him before Cynde leaned forward to kiss him. Sypher dutifully ignored their embrace as he pulled harder on the squeaking oars.

"I really hope I am worth what you traded for me."

Cynde said, "Shush. The bishop can have the gold. I got the treasure," Then she kissed him again. Reaching beneath her skirt, he watched as she tore several long strips of white cloth off an undergarment to re-bandage his shoulder.

Magnus relaxed as Cynde gently cleaned and dressed his wound. It had opened and was bleeding again after he had swung the heavy oar toward the chief. *I missed his head by only a fraction, so it should have appeared authentic from the shore, and I certainly smacked the gunwale loud enough*, he thought, smiling.

Cynde paused as she finished tying the bandage. "I can't believe that huge beast turned into your friend."

"He never held a personal grudge like the bishop did. He was just doing a job to get paid."

"I guess, but it is still amazing," she whispered.

"Yes, God is," he said as he reached over and pulled her

to his lips. Noticing with a smile that Sypher was still doing his best to keep his eyes averted as he rowed along the coast. Then he thought, **"Love worketh no ill to his neighbour: therefore love is the fulfilling of the law. And that, knowing the time, that now it is high time to awake out of sleep: for now is our salvation nearer than when we believed."**78 *Love triumphed,* Magnus realized as he settled himself in the dingy and watched the sunlight dance on the waves. He was sorry that Cynde had given up her valuable torc to save him, but with Cynde in his arms and his growing knowledge of God, he felt like the wealthiest man in the world.

"Peace I leave with you, my peace I give unto you: not as the world giveth, give I unto you. Let not your heart be troubled, neither let it be afraid."79

To be continued…

Epilogue

The world is experiencing exponential changes in inventions, human rights, and the globalization of ideas. At the forefront of this movement are the increasingly spiritual perceptions of no material limits to mankind as a whole.

Saint Martin of Tours was just one of many people who recognized God as a readily available source of healing. History is filled with others who have expressed the spiritual insight requisite for cures and relief from discordant issues. Many of the unconventional ideas accompanying the healings appear to coincide with, or support, advancing theories in the material scientific world.

Jesus and other prophets left a legacy of dominion over the evils faced by mankind! Hunger, insanity, illness, greed, and even man's greatest nemesis – death, were all shown to be powerless by the humble Nazarene and others. He told his followers, **"Verily, verily, I say unto you, He that believeth on me, the works that I do shall he do also; and greater works than these shall he do; because I go unto my Father."**[80] What could be greater than the miracles of Christ's ministry? How about having them repeated and expanded worldwide? What would the world be like today if Christians practiced Christian healing with the same earnest efforts as Jesus's disciples did?

As Saint Augustine of Hippo, (who lived 354-430 AD), wrote: "Miracles are not contrary to nature, but only contrary to what we know about nature."

Most people worship the material world. Whereas the only way to apprehend the reality of the true Spirit, God, is to see how **unreal** materiality is. "There are none so blind as those who will not see." 1546 (John Heywood)

Jesus said: **"Think not that I am come to send peace on earth: I came not to send peace but a sword."**81 He destroyed the limitations of a mortal existence! For those demonstrations of spiritual power, he was demonized and maligned by a populace fighting to preserve their beliefs in a corporeal God.

Today there are people of all ages and races who rely on spiritual truths – instead of material methods, for healing all manner of life issues. They walk unseen among you. As John stated, **"Behold, what manner of love the Father hath bestowed on us, that we should be called the sons of God: therefore the world knoweth us not, because it knew him not. Beloved, now are we the sons of God, and it doth not yet appear what we shall be: but we know that, when he shall appear, we shall be like him; for we shall see him as he is. And every man that hath this hope in him purifieth himself, even as he is pure."**82

Our material world today is embroiled in challenges. Conflicting perceptions rage between groups and individuals, and yet spiritual healings are occurring today as they have for centuries. Proof that a true concept of God will still the mortal tempest.

"God is our refuge and strength, a very present help in trouble."83

Bible Passages:
1. John 18:36
2. Romans 12:19
3. 2nd Corinthians 10:4
4. John 8:28-29
5. Exodus 4:1,8
6. John 3:13,17
7. Psalms 16:6
8. Acts 17:22-25
9. First John 4:8,16
10. Genesis 1:31
11. Isaiah 11: 1-6
12. Matthew 23:9
13. Matthew 28:6-7
14. John 14:12
15. Mark 3:7-11, 22-26
16. Genesis 1:1
17. Genesis 1:31
18. Matthew 5:38-39 & 18:21-22
19. Isaiah 53:3-5
20. Luke 24:32
21. John 2:1-11
22. Matthew 5:14-16
23. John 14:16,17
24. John 14:26
25. Romans 8:31
26. Luke 12:15-21
27. Matthew 10:8
28. Exodus 33:17-20
29. Acts 26:13-15
30. John 8:15-16
31. Mark 16:17-18
32. Matthew 18:2-5
33. Matthew 15:22-28
34. John 18:36
35. Matthew 23:10-12

36. 2nd Corinthians 10:3-5
37. Acts 16: 25-26
38. Philippians 4:19
39. Romans 8: 38-39
40. John 8:43-45
41. Matthew 12:25-28
42. John 6:16-21
43. Luke 1:76-79
44. Luke 3:4-6
45. Exodus 20:2-4,7,8,12-17
46. Acts 9:1-8
47. Joshua 6:2-5,20
48. Mark 9:18-29
49. Revelation 12: 1-5
50. John 8:44
51. Matthew 6:9-13
52. Mark 13:12-13
53. Revelation 22:1-5
54. John 19:10-11
55. Matthew 21:42-44
56. Matthew 7:24-27
57. Psalms 139:7-10
58. John 8:1-11
59. 2nd Kings 6:4-7
60. Isaiah 30:21
61. John 14:2-3
62. John 14:6
63. Jeremiah 17:14
64. 1st Kings 19:11-12
65. Luke 22:47-53
66. Exodus 14:21- 23, 27-28
67. John 14:27
68. Revelation 4:11
69. John 15:13
70. John 13:34-35
71. Matthew 5:43-44
72. Matthew 21:12

73.	**Matthew 21:13**
74.	**Galatians 6:7**
75.	**John 6:63**
76.	**1ˢᵗ Corinthians 15:26**
77.	**Luke 22:42**
78.	**Romans 12:10-11**
79.	**John 14:27**
80.	**John 14:12**
81.	**Matthew 10:34**
82.	**1ˢᵗ John 3:1-3**
83.	**Psalm 46:1**

ANTOINE WALL
12
13
14
HADRIAN'S WALL
16 15
HIBURNIUM
11
10
9
BRITAIN
8
7
6
5
3
4
2
1
1 SEAFORD DOWNS
2 CASTELL HENLLYS
3 CLITSON
4 RODARIK'S FARM
5 THE GATHERING
6 LEISWISTER
7 CLATAGUAY
8 GLASTONBURY
9 WALESFORD
10 REIDRAG
11 OXNARD
12 KILPATRICK
13 OAKSHIRE
14 RUINS
15 CRAIG INTAHL
16 FISHING VILLAGE

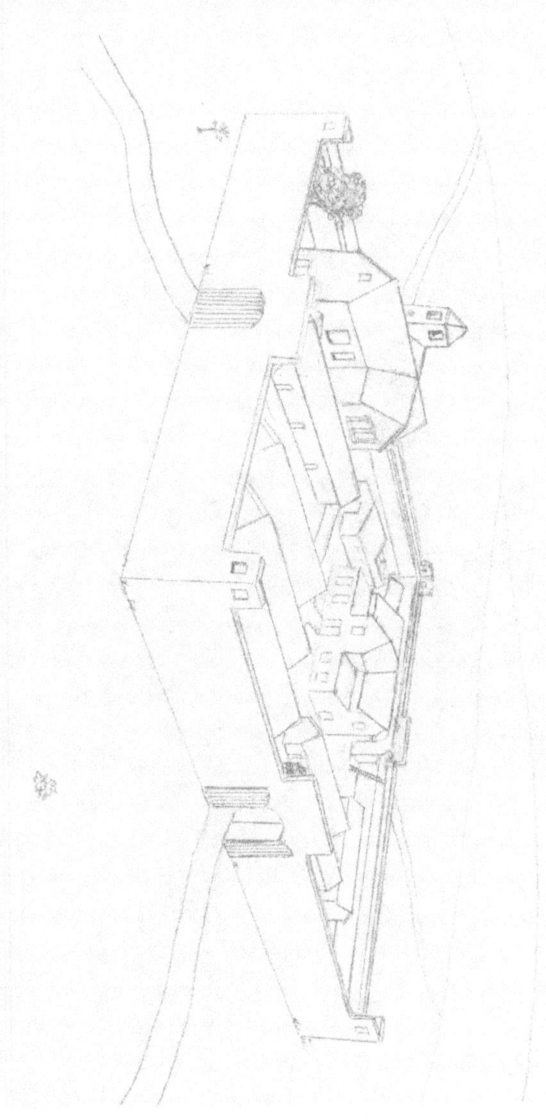